I0668135

Coyote Heart

Second Edition

Paula Margulies

One People Press
San Diego, California

Acknowledgments

I wish to express my sincere thanks to Palomar Community College professor and linguist, Eric Elliott, for his generous time and assistance in reviewing the Luiseno translations that appear in this text. I would also like to thank Elsa Garcia at the Mission San Antonio de Pala for her guidance and support.

I am particularly indebted to my writing friends who have critiqued, proofread, or otherwise helped with this novel, including Dan Beedle, Gerri Brooks, Matt Coyle, Murray Hagen, Dan Jeffries, Bryna Kranzler, Nina Ronstadt, John Van Roekel, Cathy Worthington, and Bonnie Zobell. Many thanks to my editor, Carol Newman Cronin, for her help in polishing my writing and making it shine, and to Bridget Chicoine, for her formatting expertise and publishing guidance. I am also extremely grateful to literary agent, Bob Tabian, for believing in this book in its earliest form.

Finally, much gratitude and love to my husband, Dan, and my children, Max and Sasha, who gave me the space to write on Sundays and never, ever, made me feel guilty.

No $úun lóoviq.

Chapter 1

The coyote was in the yard again. Carolyn watched as it nosed around the flowerbed and the trees by the back fence. It stepped lightly, as if the earth was hot to the touch, its mottled brown fur ruffling in the breeze whenever it lifted its head.

The animal stopped and stared through the kitchen window.

Carolyn thought it made eye contact, but before she could be certain, it darted through the fence. Twice before it had appeared, like a warning sign or a premonition, and both times the creature had vanished into the canyon preserve. She felt as if she'd conjured it, a ghostly figure from her subconscious. After the last sighting, it had lingered in the back of her mind all day. Today, the coyote had seen her, and that bothered Carolyn more than its sudden appearances, leaving her feeling naked and exposed, as if she was being watched.

Carolyn turned and wiped her hands on her apron. At the breakfast table, Everett mopped up the last of his fried eggs with the edge of his toast. When he finished, Carolyn gathered his plate and silverware and then stood, fingering the checkered tablecloth.

"There was a coyote in the yard."

"Oh?" Everett sat back in his wheelchair. He put down his napkin and rolled the chair over to the sliding glass door. "Was it a big one?"

"No, not too big. It's been here before."

"They're getting desperate when they come into the neighborhood in broad daylight."

The peal of the doorbell signaled the arrival of Ben Miller, the sweet-faced college kid who helped Everett take his morning bath.

Although Carolyn was strong for her small frame, the awkwardness of wrapping her arms around her 180-pound husband to lift him over the edge of the tub had become too much. They had hired Ben six months after the accident, and the three of them had settled into a regular morning routine.

Carolyn listened to the rumble of Everett's voice and the gentle laughter of Ben's responses in the bathroom down the hall while she fried eggs for herself and looked through the grocery ads. The two men could be father and son, so easy was the banter between them. When Ben wheeled Everett back to the kitchen, his white hair quickly drying in the early summer heat, Carolyn raised the frying pan in Ben's direction.

"Breakfast?"

"Love to, but I've got a final to study for. Thanks anyway."

Carolyn watched as Ben settled a blanket across Everett's lap. Her gaze lingered on his kind hands, the way his hair flipped into a double cowlick at the back of his head.

Once Ben left, Carolyn did the dishes while Everett read the paper. The silence between them used to be easy, but now, with Everett home all the time, it had grown palpable, like a stranger at the table. Carolyn felt as if her marriage stalked her, the dependencies closing in on her until, at times, she could hardly breathe.

She and Everett had lived in this house on the edge of the Penasquitos canyon preserve their entire twenty-five years together. They could have moved when they got the settlement from the car accident three years ago. Instead, they remodeled the house to make it wheelchair-friendly and bought a dark blue Toyota van with a hand-operated gas pedal and brake.

"What are your plans today?" she asked, running the dishes under lukewarm water. Everett had retired from his engineering job soon after coming home from the hospital.

"Thought I'd try to fix the back gate hinge. Maybe work on the Toyota a bit."

Carolyn knew that Everett would spend most of his time constructing his model airplanes. He had a number of them laid out in various stages of assembly in his study. Some days, he played blackjack at the Indian casino down the road, and occasionally, Carolyn would find him asleep in front of a soap opera when she came home in the afternoon. Other days, she was greeted with the sound of little pops coming from the backyard, where Everett used his rifle to take potshots at the empty soup and juice cans he lined up on the fence.

"Well, don't work too hard." She placed a hand, briefly, on his shoulder.

On the way to the library, where she worked part-time, Carolyn noticed that the shopping center, the fire station, everything she passed was the same as it had been for a decade since the last remodeling phase. So much had changed for her in the past three years, and yet the world remained indifferent to her circumstances and the dull structure of her life.

She didn't see the dog until after she hit it.

Just outside the library entrance, as she turned into the driveway, Carolyn felt a quick thud. The wheel jerked in her hand. Hands shaking, she pulled into the first space and looked back to see a medium-sized dog stretched out on the concrete. She ran to its side. It was a female collie mix, still breathing. The animal raised her head an inch and squinted at Carolyn out of wet, brown eyes. Carolyn felt around the fur on its neck for some sign of ownership.

"Here, let me help you." The tall, dark-skinned man reached down and lifted the dog in his arms. Carolyn hadn't noticed him until he spoke. "If you open my door, I'll take her to the vet in the shopping center."

Carolyn, unable to talk, followed him to a scraped and dented white pickup truck, where she pulled open the driver's side door and pushed the seat forward. The man placed the dog in the section behind the driver's seat on top of a worn gray blanket. As he got behind the wheel, Carolyn walked around the truck and reached for the passenger door handle. Should she let him take the dog alone? It didn't seem right to do so; the responsibility for injuring the dog was hers. She pulled the door open.

"Can I ride with you?"

The man nodded and Carolyn studied him a moment. Was this a safe thing to do? She glanced behind the seat at the dog lying on its side. It lifted its head and whimpered when it caught sight of her. She decided there was no time to waste and climbed inside.

As they slowly drove toward the shopping center, Carolyn removed her phone from her purse and dialed her supervisor's number. After explaining what had happened, she reached behind the seat.

"I'm Carolyn Weedman."

The dog pushed its wet nose into her hand, reassuring her that it was still alive.

"Roy Washburn." He spoke without taking his eyes off the road. "How's she doing?"

"Okay, I think." Carolyn smoothed her hand over the dog's head. "I don't know what happened. I was turning into the library lot and the next thing I knew… "

"Dogs will do that," Roy said. "They're like spirits. Fly right out into the street before you even see them."

Carolyn took a moment to study him as he steered the truck into the shopping center. He had shoulder-length dark hair and skin barely wrinkled by the Southern California sun. His aquiline nose jutted from his face, prominent and full; his lips, by contrast, seemed thin and tight. Carolyn caught a faint leather scent from his rawhide jacket and noticed that his jeans were worn and faded. Without thinking, she pushed her thick curly hair behind her ears and straightened her blouse.

The veterinary office was warm and had the moist, almond smell of vitamins and wet fur. Carolyn talked to the receptionist, a young girl with a nose ring, while Roy took the dog into the trauma room. He and Carolyn sat together in the cramped waiting room while the vet assistant took x-rays. Then the vet, a stooped, gray-haired man with wire-rimmed specs, called them back.

"She's a lucky one. She's got two broken ribs but, otherwise, she'll be fine. We'll keep her overnight to make sure she's stable. That okay with you?" He looked first at Roy and then at Carolyn.

"Oh, she's not ours," Carolyn answered. "I looked for a collar, but she didn't have one."

"Well, she's in good shape. Healthy coat, standard weight. My guess is that someone will be looking for her. We can call the animal shelter tomorrow."

"What happens if no one claims her?" Carolyn asked.

"They'll adopt her out, unless you want to keep her."

"I'll take her." Roy spoke before Carolyn could say anything.

Carolyn paid the bill and they went outside. They stood for a moment, awkward and silent.

"They'll take good care of our dog," Roy said.

"Your dog," Carolyn emphasized. She pulled her purse tighter over her shoulder.

"Right," Roy said. He waved toward the truck. "Ready to head back to the library?"

"I guess I should."

Carolyn climbed into the passenger's seat, then turned to Roy as he revved the engine. "Actually," she said, "can I buy you a cup of coffee? It seems the least I can do."

They went to the Starbucks at the other end of the shopping center. Sitting in the cushioned tub chairs at a table by the window, Carolyn twisted her mocha in front of her. Roy sat quietly, the steam from his tea sending smoke signals in the air between them.

"You seem nervous," he finally said.

"Oh, I'm not, really." Carolyn stopped moving her cup and put her hands in her lap. "I'm just a little thrown by what happened, I guess." She decided to change the subject. "Do you live near here?"

"I live on the Pala Reservation," he replied. "Up off Highway 76." He took a sip of tea. "I teach history at Mira Costa College. You?"

"I work at the library. Just part-time." Carolyn stared down at her coffee. "I used to go to Mira Costa. I wanted to be a teacher, but never finished. When I was twenty, I met my husband and thought being married was more important." She stopped and gazed out the window. "I never went back."

"Marriage always seems important at twenty," Roy said. "I thought it was. My marriage lasted fifteen years. Even though we had no money, those were good years."

"What happened?" Carolyn asked.

"Sonia died of cancer six years ago. Fought it hard, but it finally got her."

"I'm sorry."

On the way back to the library, they sat without speaking. Roy navigated toward the entrance and parked the truck in front of the drop-off box.

"Well, I can't thank you enough," Carolyn began.

Roy raised a hand to stop her. "No thanks necessary." He reached into his back pocket and pulled out a worn leather wallet. "Here's my number at the college. Call me if they can't find the dog's owner."

Carolyn watched as Roy pulled out of the lot. She waved briefly, the white card like a bandage across the palm of her hand.

Everything was simple, really. You just point and shoot. Like the commercials on TV, Everett thought. It didn't matter if it was a camera or a gun, as long as your aim was true. He lifted his rifle, sighted the black and orange Minute Maid can on the back fence and pulled the trigger. The gun's kick was followed by a thunk, the can popping off the fence and spinning in the air before falling to the ground.

Everett rested his rifle on his lap and closed his eyes. He let the sun linger on his face and listened to the sound of the grasses rustling in the summer breeze. The air had the warm, cedar smell of the fresh wood chips that their gardener, Arturo, had laid out yesterday. Everett could detect the slight scent of eucalyptus and bergamot, both abundant in the canyon outside the yard.

When he finally opened his eyes, he noticed that nothing moved in the preserve. It was one o'clock—too hot for most canyon creatures to be out except the rattlesnakes. He surveyed the plants along the fence: the hairy red bottlebrush, the towering purple bougainvillea, the lemon and orange trees Carolyn had planted ten years ago, now lush and green with developing fruit. Everything they had placed along the periphery was healthy, tall, and full. The carrotwood tree dripped open pods of tiny orange seeds and the three palm trees in the west corner stood graceful and majestic, like sentinels overlooking the yard. All was calm inside the back fence, which Everett patrolled each day in his wheelchair, looking for signs of rabbits.

In contrast, the canyon weeds and scrub grasses ranged in hues from golden to brown. In a month, it would be fire season. Everett loved the wild openness of the canyon. He knew every bend and incline of its footpaths; he had walked, in past years, every inch of its trails. When Carolyn and he had first moved to Penasquitos, years ago, they'd hiked to the waterfall only three miles away. Everett remembered how startling the sound of the rushing water had been when they first came upon it. Some years, the stream waters gushed with loud force over the rocks of the falls; in dry years, the falls were just a trickle, the sharp stones pushing their stark gray faces toward the sun.

When Everett worked for Inland Mining, he visited local quarries to inspect equipment and often noticed how dry and hard the earth was so close to the ocean. But he enjoyed being out in the open desert. The landscape and the wide blue sky moved him in ways he couldn't explain. Here, in the canyon, there were hawks and ospreys, raccoons and rabbits and, of course, coyotes and rattlesnakes. Everett had even seen a bobcat once, tawny and small, like a large housecat, slinking along the tall grasses that lined the trail. As much as he loved the desert, he felt more at home here in the suburbs, on his acre and a half, with the quiet and lushness of the canyon close by.

The coo of a morning dove broke Everett's reverie. He spun his wheelchair toward the house, working up a bit of speed so he could climb the ramp to the back door. Everywhere in his life there were ramps now, their sharp angles crisscrossing the sidewalk in front of the house, the hospital where he still went for physical therapy, the office of his attorney. He knew most of the ramps in San Diego County and even where some were missing.

Everett navigated his chair up to the sliding glass door and reached for the latch. For a brief moment, his face peered back at him in the glass, more jowly and lined than in the past, although he still retained a full head of hair. Looking down, he noticed that his arms looked muscular in contrast to the slight curve of his belly. Even with workouts with weights three times a week, Everett couldn't get rid of the paunch that had emerged about a year after the accident. All his life he'd been careful about his health, playing basketball at the gym twice a week and watching his consumption of alcohol and red meat. Now he felt helpless as old age nipped at him, wearing away the shield of health he'd worn in his more active days.

Inside the house, Everett leaned his rifle against the wooden rack near the door, then went through the kitchen and into his study. It functioned as his bedroom and workshop now. Even though he'd installed a wheelchair lift to carry him upstairs, he preferred to stay on the ground floor of the house. He and Carolyn had retrofitted the study with a special bed that was low to the ground and included rails. Across from the bed sat a large white table, covered with model airplanes in various stages of assembly.

After the accident and his retirement, Everett had rediscovered a childhood passion for model building. Although he'd built all types of them as a kid—automobiles, trains, the human body, even—he now found himself drawn to warplanes. Carolyn had hung them from every corner of the ceiling in a multitude of colors and styles, some low, some high, their wings spread in a perpetual lift that sent them bobbing with just the slightest gust of air. Everett surveyed them with satisfaction—the slate and black gleam of the Navy Hellcat, the amphibious green spots of the German ME262, the bright red suns on the Japanese Zero.

He wheeled to the desk and picked up the left half of the fuselage of his latest project, a 1:48 scale Huey helicopter painted in Testors olive mat. He worked carefully to cement the tailskid to the fuselage and then glued the rotor on the shaft. The strong odor of cement was sharp in his nostrils. As he reached for one of the helicopter windows, his elbow caught the tail and sent it fluttering to the floor behind him. He moved his chair back to find the piece and then heard the sickening sound of a crunch as his right wheel rolled over the plastic.

Everett looked down to see it crushed. As he leaned over to retrieve the broken pieces, his situation—the car crash, the back injury, his failing marriage—caved in on him in an overwhelming wave of frustration. Nothing was simple any more. His life was complicated and hard and he knew that he and Carolyn would never be the same because of it.

Everett placed his head in his hands and wept.

ONCE CAROLYN WAS INSIDE THE LIBRARY, SHE STRODE PAST THE desk and into the ladies restroom. Pausing in front of the sink, she leaned over to turn on the water. It felt cold on her face and neck. She avoided looking at herself in the mirror; the image seemed too old, too pale, too unwilling to address the questions at the back of her mind, the ones that nagged at her every day. She dried her hands with a paper towel and left somewhat renewed, as if she'd ceremonially removed the uncertainty of the last two hours from her memory.

When she got to the main desk, Mary glanced up at her.

"You okay?" she asked. "We were wondering what happened to you."

"A man helped me take the dog to the vet," Carolyn answered as she set her purse inside one of the cabinets. "I think it's going to be all right."

"Was he a cute one?" Sheryl, the new assistant, asked.

"Yeah, I guess so. Kind of quiet. The least I could do was buy him a cup of coffee."

"I meant the dog," Sheryl said. Mary and Sheryl both laughed hard at this.

Carolyn managed to grin, even though she felt a flush creeping up her neck and across her cheeks. She turned to a carrel of books waiting to be shelved and wheeled them out onto the library floor.

The room had the faint musty odor of old books. High above the alcoves, the stained glass windows threw long trails of purple and turquoise light over the stacks. Carolyn pushed the squeaky cart through the aisles, thinking about Roy Washburn. He had mentioned that he lived at the Pala Reservation, but his last name sounded Caucasian. Perhaps he was only part Native American, although his skin was brown. She looked at her own hands on the cart and noticed for the first time that they were pale and small, like those of a child.

She stopped in front of the shelf numbered 800-811. When she knelt to replace two books, she noticed a volume titled *The Massacre at Sand Creek: Narrative Voices*. Thinking this an odd title for the poetry section, Carolyn reached for it and began flipping through pages. The author was a humanities professor at Wichita State. His black and white photograph grinned from the back cover. The book was about the massacre of the Cheyenne Indians at Sand Creek in the 1800's.

Pushing aside the books she'd been shelving, Carolyn sat back on her heels and read through portions of narrative from both Colorado militia and Cheyenne. Soldiers and native inhabitants appeared before her as she became entranced at the beauty of the language. She devoured each line of the text, until she came to a passage by Ekomina, the granddaughter of a Cheyenne victim:

> *Troubled sleep. She thought she'd be free of it, but no*
> *To begin with, little dancing dreams. So small*
> *you can hear them in the cooking pot. Can see their dust*
> *rising out of a bowl of a pipe.*
> *Too small for comfort.*

Making her remember. The bundle. Down in its deep earth home.
So she can feel. They laid it there, but it's not at rest.

A chill sweat broke out on Carolyn's neck and arms as she lifted her eyes from the page. Dust motes swirled in the air. She had held a similar small bundle in her arms. So solid and sweet, it felt like a heavy doll. The small turned nose, the tiny perfect eyelashes. When Everett had taken the baby from her for the final time, she had reached out in panic, screaming so loudly the nurses had to call the doctor to sedate her. Before she slipped into oblivion, Carolyn saw Everett looking through tears at their stillborn son as if it were the greatest moment in his life.

Carolyn sat on the library floor, breathing softly, her pale, child-like hands gripping the book as if they were holding onto a life preserver. She stayed there, staring, until Sheryl touched her shoulder and told her it was time to close.

ROY TURNED DOWN THE RADIO UNTIL THE ANNOUNCER'S VOICE ON KOGX, the classical music station, was a steady drone. He gazed at the new homes, squatting like a line of pink dragons along the hillside as he passed the exit for Old Highway 395. There was so much new development in San Diego. Even the reservation, where he lived with his twenty-year-old son Luke, was changing. Now a large casino loomed over Hwy 76, its Las Vegas-style signs flashing in derision at the prefab homes of the native tribes across the road.

He and Luke lived in one of those homes. It had belonged to his mother Olivia's family, the Ibanez clan, who were part Luiseno. When Olivia married his father, Jim Washburn, who was half white, they had stayed on the reservation. Olivia had worked at a preschool in Fallbrook; Jim worked construction in the housing developments in Carlsbad and Oceanside.

Roy had never liked working with his hands. His dad would come home, clothes dusty and neck red from the sun, and stare at his son who was usually lost in some book describing the British Parliament.

"All that boy does is read," his father growled one evening, as he washed his hands at the sink.

"So let him," his mother said. "He studies history and all history is important. It's the only way any of us remember where we came from." Small and dark-haired, she always came to his defense. He couldn't argue with his native wife, whose lineage provided a home for them on the res.

Roy smiled as he turned his truck away from the sun and onto Hwy 76. He and Luke argued all the time, in much the same manner as his parents. Luke had inherited his grandmother's love of tribal heritage, and Roy knew his own ambivalence irked his son. Luke viewed all non-native history as the white man's legacy—evil, power hungry, and something to fight with all the energy he could muster.

The truck coughed and sputtered as Roy turned into the dusty driveway leading to his place on Ortega Street. The small gray house sprawled flat and unassuming behind a clothesline dripping with faded jeans and white t-shirts. Roy let out the clutch and watched Luke, who knelt at the end of the drive in front of his Silver Wing motorcycle. Luke's long black hair shone in the sun that beat down on his muscular shoulders. He still looks more like Sonia than me, Roy thought, as he swung open the door of the car.

"That thing still not working?"

"Nope." Luke didn't look up.

"You work today?"

"No one called this morning." Luke glanced at his father. "I went out to the Rock for awhile."

"You shouldn't go up there." Medicine Rock was a sacred area on the reservation and the site of a controversial landfill project.

"Yeah? Well, I suppose there are a lot of things I shouldn't do."

Giving a final twist to a lug nut, Luke rose up beside the motorcycle. He threw the wrench to the ground by his father's feet and straddled the bike.

"Come on, Dad, what are you going to do, stop me?" A slight breeze blew in from the canyon, and Roy caught the scent of motor oil and eucalyptus. What would he do if Luke went there again? He knew that nothing he said would make any difference.

Luke turned the bike's ignition and stomped down on the starter, kicking the engine into gear. Without looking back, he spun the motorcycle in front of Roy and skidded out of the driveway, throwing a cloud of dust into his father's face.

Roy listened to the buzz of the motorcycle engine as his son got smaller and smaller against the horizon. He rubbed the dust from one eye and felt it water as the grit scraped against his cornea. Stubborn kid. Luke never listened to him, and it had only grown worse since Sonia's death.

Roy turned toward the house. He noticed the peeling paint around the doorframe and that one rain gutter was hanging loose over the living room window. Sonia would have made him fix it and paint the trim. In the six years since her death, the house had slowly eroded, bit by bit—a cracked window here, a piece of loose siding there. Raising a son and teaching had taken all that was left of him. There was no room for repairs.

Roy placed his keys near the door and went into the kitchen to boil water for tea. As he filled the kettle, he glanced toward the kitchen window. Two crows balanced like a pair of tightrope walkers on the clothesline outside. Thieves, his wife had called them. Sonia had loved animals and believed that each species had personalities just like humans. When Luke was little, she regaled him with Luiseno lore, her favorites being stories with animals. Roy recalled coming home one evening and finding Luke in Sonia's arms on the floor by the fireplace. She was telling their son the Dance of the Dead, a tale about a man who falls asleep beneath an overturned basket in an empty village and awakes to hear voices.

"He heard the woman-who-was-turned-into-rock as she sang," Sonia whispered. "He heard the man-who-scooped-rock-with-his-hand as he sang."

Roy stood quietly behind his wife and son and watched as the reflections from the flames lit the sides of their faces.

"When he threw off the basket and looked where the dead had been dancing, there was only a flock of birds," Sonia continued. "They flew away, startled by the sound of the basket overturning. The turtle-shell rattle that the dead played as they danced lay on the ground. It was now just a piece of soap root."

"So the man never saw the dead people?" Luke asked.

"No, he wasn't allowed to see the dance of the dead."

"What kind of birds were they?" Luke gazed up at his mother's face, and Roy remembered a lump forming in his throat at that moment.

"They were crows."

The kettle began to whistle, and Roy let it scream. He stared at the birds outside. Turning finally to shut off the shrieking kettle, Roy remembered the woman he had met at the library. How small and bird-like she was. Talking with her had made him feel protective and strong. He reached up and took a china teacup from the cupboard, one of the porcelain ones he had brought back from his study abroad in England, and set it carefully on the sink. He poured the boiling water from the kettle, gazing into the clouds of steam that lifted from the cup and thought about the woman, Carolyn, and his wife, Sonia. As he stirred his tea, the two birds suddenly lifted themselves in unison from the clothesline, flapping and cawing at the world below before sailing toward the hills lining the reservation.

Chapter 2

The clock overlooking the Penasquitos Library main desk said three forty-five. Carolyn, leaning on the counter near the new books section, pulled a white business card out of her skirt pocket and ran her fingers over the lettering. *Roy Washburn, History Instructor, Mira Costa College.* She read the telephone number over and over until she had it memorized, then shoved the card back in her pocket. She was acting like a schoolgirl, she realized, and over a man she hardly knew.

It had been two weeks since Carolyn and Roy had taken the dog to the vet. In that time, the incident haunted her, images of Roy coming into her head at the oddest times: when she was peeling carrots for supper, when she smoothed the sheets on the bed in the morning, while she soaped her hair in the shower. There was something mysterious and strong about him, something that stuck with her, like a song she couldn't shake. She found herself reliving each moment: the sickening thump as the car hit the dog, the warmth of the collie's fur, Roy's hands, brown and firm, lifting the injured animal into his truck. She'd even dialed the shelter once to see if someone had called for the collie, but it was still there. Although she knew there was an owner somewhere who was missing a pet, part of her hoped no one would claim it.

The telephone rang at the circulation desk, and Carolyn saw Sheryl answer it. When Sheryl looked at her and gestured toward the phone, Carolyn knew who was calling. Her heart beat hard against her chest as she approached the desk and picked up the receiver.

"This is Carolyn."

"Mrs. Weedman? This is the animal shelter. We haven't had any calls on the collie, and we need to know what you'd like to do."

Carolyn's mouth felt dry, and her stomach tensed up. Roy had said he would take the dog, but should she contact him?

"I'll come in and get her." Carolyn spoke quietly.

"We close at five o'clock. Would you be able to pick her up sometime tomorrow before then?"

Carolyn paused. "Yes. I'll be there."

She hung up and then stood a moment, biting her lower lip. Her hand inched toward her pocket, where the business card leaned against her thigh. She waited until Sheryl was busy helping a customer before picking up the receiver again.

"IN THE THREE YEARS I'VE KNOWN YOU, I DIDN'T KNOW YOU COULD cook." Everett rolled his wheelchair closer to the kitchen sink, where Ben hovered over a ceramic bowl.

"That's because you never asked me before." Ben opened the cabinet and reached into the spice cupboard, pulling out red, green, and yellow lidded jars of various sizes. He set them on the sink and then ripped the plastic off a package of ground turkey before dumping it into a mixing bowl. He cracked two eggs and added spices, breadcrumbs, grated cheese, and chopped parsley. A trace of Parmesan and garlic scented the air, making Everett remember his mother cooking in the kitchen when he was young.

While Ben mashed the mixture together with his hands, Everett noticed how tall the boy seemed, his legs long and lanky in their faded jeans. Usually Ben came to the Weedmans' early in the morning and left after Everett was bathed and dressed. This morning, Ben had mentioned that summer school was over and that he'd finished his finals last week. He suggested surprising Carolyn with dinner, an idea Everett had immediately agreed to.

"So, do you ever cook for Mrs. Weedman?" Ben held up the meat mixture, now blended into a smooth football shape, and patted it with his large hands.

"Kind of tough to reach the cupboards these days." Everett smiled to let Ben know that he wasn't looking for sympathy. "We used to take turns in the kitchen, but Carolyn does most of the cooking now. It keeps her busy." As soon as he spoke the words, Everett regretted them. He hadn't meant to imply that Carolyn was a bored housewife.

Ben placed the meatloaf in a glass baking dish and covered it with a piece of aluminum foil before throwing it in the oven. Each of his actions seemed effortless and smooth, as if he cooked in this particular kitchen every day.

With his back to Everett, Ben turned on the tap and began to wash his hands. Everett studied him, wondering what this boy's private life was like. They never talked much about Ben and his parents, with whom he shared a home in La Jolla. Most of their discussions centered around school, the weather, local politics, and some sports. Ben kept his conversation professional, never mentioning himself unless Everett asked. As he was about to ask Ben about his family, Ben spoke, raising his voice slightly so he could be heard over the running water.

"Mrs. Weedman seems a little preoccupied lately."

Surprised at this comment, Everett recognized the truth in Ben's statement. Carolyn had seemed more quiet than usual the last couple of weeks. Everett had noticed a faraway look in her eye more than once, even though they'd gotten used to long moments of silence together. Still, the question took him aback. Ben had not made this kind of observation before.

"Well, she's a fairly quiet person now," Everett said. "But when I first met her she was pretty outgoing. And strong-willed. We met at a Sierra Club rally while we were in college. She was quite the activist then. Greenpeace, animal rights groups—you name it, she was involved in it. I was, too." Everett stopped and rubbed his fingers across his palm. "I remember her once outside the Wild Animal Park. We were protesting some animal cruelty incident, I think to the elephants there. A driver went by and honked his horn or gave her the finger, I can't remember. She took off after the car with her sign waving above her head." Everett let out a quiet laugh. "I remember feeling sorry for the driver. If she'd caught him, I don't know what would have happened."

Ben had shut off the water, reached for a dishtowel, and leaned against the sink..

"It all changed after we lost the baby. She was never quite the same after that." Everett stopped. "Neither of us were." He felt a sudden sting at his eyes and studied his hands while he tried to compose himself. After a few seconds, he looked up and forced a smile. "So, you've noticed that she seems a little different?" He swallowed hard.

Ben carefully hung the dishtowel on the handle outside the stove before answering.

"Yeah. She just doesn't seem herself." He glanced out the window over the sink.

Both men were silent for a moment as the clock above the telephone clicked in even, measured tones.

"This has been hard on her." Everett put his hands on the wheelchair arms. "I don't ask her what she's thinking anymore. I figure she's gone through enough."

"I'm sorry. I didn't mean to pry." Ben walked over and put his hand on Everett's shoulder. "It's none of my business, really. I just care a lot about both of you."

"And we you." Everett briefly patted Ben's hand and then rolled his chair over to the sliding glass door. He gazed out the window at the browns and greens of the canyon.

"What about you, Ben?" Everett rolled his chair to face the boy. "Is there some shy girl in your life?"

He was a bit surprised as Ben, rather than rallying to the question with some quick remark, looked down at the floor in silence. His jaw was set tightly, and Everett could tell that he was thinking hard before he answered.

"No, Mr. Weedman, there's no girl." Ben paused, his hand gripping the strap of his backpack.

"Why not?"

"Just haven't been lucky, I suppose." Ben shuffled his feet and shrugged, a slight flush of red emerging across his cheeks. "Well, guess I'll head out. You sure you can make the potatoes and salad yourself?"

"Oh, no problem, now that you've put everything out on the table for me."

"See you tomorrow, then." Ben tossed off a mock salute before half-running out the kitchen door. Everett watched him go, then listened while the clock ticked in loud drum beats above the telephone.

LUKE LET THE MOTORCYCLE IDLE A MOMENT BEFORE KILLING THE engine. He sat on the bike and scanned the sky behind the mission bell tower. Long streaks of thin white clouds scarred the wide expanse of blue that outlined the hills behind the mission. The sun, sitting high above him, heated his arms as they rested on the handlebars. Lighting a cigarette, he inhaled deeply, the strong taste of tobacco reminding him of after-school days, when he and his friends had smoked behind the mission church. They would pass the smoldering joints until the glowing stumps singed their fingers. Laughing, coughing, and speaking in whispers, their twelve-year-old voices swinging between cracks and growls, they had told stories of their ancestors and dreamed about the days when they would be the new heroes on the reservation.

Luke finished his cigarette and tossed it to the ground, then set the motorcycle's kickstand before ambling toward the graveyard entrance. The mission was quiet today. Tourists and locals usually came on the weekends, most of them there for Sunday services in the tiny church. Luke pushed open the wrought-iron gate and headed through the dry dirt and weeds to the far left corner of the yard. There, between the plots of buried Scotts and Yanis, lay his mother's grave. Reaching down, Luke ran his hand over the concrete tombstone and then squatted in front of the raised mound. He righted a small vase of purple silk flowers, the leaves wrinkled and covered with dust, that his aunt Delores had probably left there. They wouldn't have come from his dad. His old man never had time for anything but his history books.

Luke pulled another cigarette from his pocket and shook the flame from the match before tossing it into the dirt by the graveyard wall. He squinted up at the sun, then studied the mishmash of tombstones and markers that dotted the yard. Some of the graves were marked with stark wooden crosses. Others contained carefully placed mementos: flowers, dolls, even bowling pins, and, on one, a San Diego Chargers pennant. Luke recognized most of the names on the marked stones. Salazar, Garcia, Castillo—all were families that had lived on Pala land since the 1800's. He took a drag from the cigarette and gazed at his mother's tombstone. The lettering "Sonia Nagi Washburn, 1952-1996" was faint, shallowly etched in the concrete. He let out a breath of smoke.

"*Noyó*'," he whispered. "Mother, can you hear me?" A slight breeze rustled the leaves of the cedar trees in the yard. Luke hung his head.

"*Noyó*'," he said again. He closed his eyes and waited for the voices. Native voices. They always seemed to come to him from far away, along the edges of his memory.

"'*Ettax*," the voices murmured. Hurry.

Hurry? Where and why? Luke wondered. He kept his eyes closed and concentrated hard.

"*Néqpi*."

The sound could have been the sighing of the breeze or the flutter of a bird's wing. He lifted his face to the sun and listened, but nothing more came to him and he finally opened his eyes. Resting on the dirt of his mother's grave was his cigarette, gone cold. Luke picked it up and stubbed it into the ground at his feet.

As he stood to go, he noticed two dark-haired children, a boy and a girl, standing outside the gate. Clutching their schoolbooks to their chests, they stared in silence, then raced away as Luke headed toward them.

"Defend yourselves!" he shouted after them. "That's what they told me to do."

He stood watching them, the bottoms of their sneakers flashing red and brown as they disappeared into the alley across the street. Nothing else moved except for a battered truck, trundling down Mission Avenue. Luke looked back at the mission and raised his hand, palm forward, toward his mother's grave. Then, straddling his bike, eyes alert and head held high, he rode into the hills behind the reservation.

ROY SET THE TELEPHONE GENTLY BACK IN ITS CRADLE AND WATCHED as the green charging light struggled to come on. What had he just agreed to?

He'd been pleased to hear Carolyn's voice on the other end of the phone, sounding breathless and a bit shy, but was surprised when she said that the dog he'd helped rescue two weeks ago had not been claimed. When she reminded him that he'd offered to take the animal, that whole day washed over him. He couldn't even remember what made him stop to help. The sight of the collie lying on the pavement and Carolyn bending over it, her curly brown hair glinting in the sun, had propelled him out of his truck without even thinking.

He hadn't told Luke about the incident, nor did he have any supplies—no leash, no food, no toys. Even so, he'd stood in his living room a moment ago holding the receiver to his ear and heard himself saying, yes, he was still willing to keep his original promise and he'd be finished with classes by eleven thirty tomorrow. That meant a visitor and a new pet in less than twenty-four hours.

With a mild feeling of panic, he surveyed the shambles of his small living room. The couch was stained and sagging. Piles of books and newspapers competed for the few inches of space available on the dented pine coffee table and the equally worn brown carpet. As he bent down to begin tidying the mess, he heard the front door open and close behind him. Thinking it was Luke, he turned to find his younger sister, Delores, striding past him into the kitchen with two white plastic shopping bags.

In the six years since Sonia's death, Delores hadn't missed a week without stopping by to bring in a few grocery items, wash a little laundry, or, when Luke was younger, help him with his homework.

The first month after Sonia died, Delores had pointed to the boy's muddy and battered tennis shoes and said, "Let's go." They'd returned with Luke wearing outlandishly large white Nike basketball shoes and a huge smile on his face, the first in months. Roy remembered deciding at that moment that he would forever forgive Delores her faults, as tormenting as they could be.

Joining her now in the kitchen, he watched as she emptied the bags onto the counter near the sink. Bulbous, red beefsteak tomatoes and dusty green cucumbers spilled out onto the chipped tile, along with lemons, limes, peaches, green beans, and a casaba melon, looking forlornly dull and wrinkled next to the smooth purple skins of three lanky Japanese eggplants. Two tiny fruit flies spiraled dizzily into the air from inside the bags and Delores caught them both in one thunderous clap of her hands.

"Hey, Brother, I got five minutes to unpack these for you, then I'm off to the council meeting."

Roy caught a lemon as it rolled off the counter while Delores rummaged through the cupboard for a bowl and dumped the fruits and vegetables into it in a careless arrangement. Her long black hair, streaked throughout with wiry bits of white, swung in rhythm as she moved. His sister was never still, her thin brown arms always in motion as she chopped onions for a stew or wiped down the counter top with a damp cloth. Today, her eyes looked myopically luminous and wet behind the tortoise-shell frames of her bifocals. She picked up a peach and rinsed it at the sink. Noisily biting into it, she licked the dripping juice from the side of her hand.

"You need anything else before I go?"

"How about a couple of cans of Alpo and a muzzle?"

The look she threw him through her thick lenses was puzzled at first, then incredulous. "You're getting a dog?" She stopped a minute to finish the last bite of her peach, then expertly tossed the pit into an upright plastic trashcan in the corner of the room. "Are you nuts? You can't even take care of yourself and Luke, let alone a dog."

"It couldn't be helped. A woman hit it a couple of weeks ago, and I took it to the vet for her. No one wants it, so I agreed to take it."

"Must have been some woman. What's she look like?" Delores picked up her purse from the counter and slung it over her shoulder.

"Come on, Delores. I'm just trying to help out."

"Right. A real crusader, you are." Delores turned toward the kitchen door and then paused. "Hey, Luke wasn't at the council meeting last week. They say he's talking to himself again, like he's hearing voices."

Roy hung his head at this news. It didn't surprise him—Luke had gone through episodes like this since his mother died. Roy and his sister had talked about getting the boy some psychiatric help, but both of them feared the stigma that his son would face on the reservation.

"Has he been okay at council?"

"When he's there, yeah, he's been okay." Delores stopped and threw a rheumy glance directly at her brother. "They're filing the environmental impact report this week."

Roy knew the report Delores was referring to. It was a County document the tribe had fought against in the landfill dispute at Gregory Canyon.

"I'm sure that would set Luke off," Roy said.

"It's set us all off, Brother." Delores leaned forward to give him a light kiss on the cheek. As she left the kitchen, he caught the scent of peaches and a trace of mint, making it seem suddenly like early spring rather than the middle of summer.

THE SALES CLERK BEHIND THE COSMETIC COUNTER AT THE DRUGSTORE had the empty gaze of the eternally bored. Carolyn gently cleared her throat, feeling guilty at interrupting whatever was going on in the girl's mind.

"Yes?"

Carolyn was taken aback at the abruptness of the girl's response. She had expected a "May I help you?" Instead, she felt as if the clerk was answering an unspoken question, one Carolyn had not even asked herself.

"I was looking for some new makeup and wondered what you might recommend?"

Without answering, the girl reached down beyond the counter and rifled through the drawers below. Carolyn studied her as she pulled out black tubes of lipstick and round containers of shadows in shades of mauve and ocher. She wore her hair in a smooth black bob that delicately caressed her face. With her finely arched eyebrows and kohl-lined eyes, she could have been an Egyptian princess or a sorceress. She watched as the girl laid out an assortment of blushes next to some tissues and a Q-tip.

"Is this for a special occasion?" the clerk asked, finally gazing directly at Carolyn.

"Yes. I mean, no. It's not special at all." Carolyn felt flustered by the question and the girl's beauty. She could see her own face in the mirror on the counter, the wrinkles in her forehead, how pale her skin looked below the faint smattering of freckles on her nose. Her curly brown hair seemed pathetically wild and untamed. Carolyn felt all the old insecurities of years past, of always being the least pretty in the crowd. She shook it off when she realized that the girl was waiting.

"I mean I'd just like something natural and fresh. An everyday look, maybe."

The clerk picked up a large round container of brownish orange powder and rubbed her finger in it. She reached out and gently swiped a small amount over Caroline's right cheek, then dabbed her finger in a rose-colored container and rubbed it over the left side.

"Either of these might do for you. The tangerine brings out the honey color of your hair."

Carolyn looked in the mirror, turning her face first one way and then the other. Both colors were subtle and gave her face a warm glow.

"They're nice."

"Let's try some lavender on your eyelids; it'll highlight the green in your eyes."

While the girl applied eye shadow above Carolyn's right eye, Carolyn thought about Roy Washburn and how he had sounded when she called. She thought about how carefully he had given her directions, about how she would pick up the dog and bring it to Roy's house tomorrow at noon.

The clerk finished with the left eye and placed her hand under Carolyn's chin to turn her head. Carolyn remembered that she had not bought new makeup in years.

"There. I think that's a nice look with the rose cheek color."

Carolyn glanced at the mirror and winced as her eyes, their normally boring hazel now a wicked green, gazed back at her. You're married, the eyes said.

"What do you think?" the girl asked.

Carolyn looked again at the rose and tangerine-colored cheeks, the lavender- lidded eyes, the curly honey-colored hair framing her face in the mirror. This was the face of a woman she didn't really know at all.

"It's fine," she answered.

Chapter 3

It hit her when she walked through the door. Warm and comforting, like her house when she was a child. Carolyn recognized the scent of garlic and a hint of Parmesan cheese. It smelled like home. She set her purse and store bag on the hall bookstand and went into the kitchen. The table was set for two, with wine glasses and red cloth napkins to match the checkered tablecloth. Here she'd hurried home from the mall, feeling guilty for being out so late after leaving the library, and Everett had dinner already prepared. She glanced into the office, but he wasn't there.

"Hello? Everett?"

The hall door to the garage opened, and Everett wheeled himself into the kitchen, a bottle of red wine lying across his lap.

"Took a while to find it, but I finally did. Look familiar?"

Everett held up the label so she could read it. It was a merlot from Van Roekel vineyards in Temecula.

"It does. What's the occasion for all this?"

"No occasion; just thought I'd make dinner for you for a change. Ben fixed the meatloaf; I managed the rest." Everett wheeled himself to the sink and pulled open a drawer. After rummaging a bit, he found a corkscrew and proceeded to wrestle the cork from the bottle. It came loose with a small pop.

"I found this in the garage, in that box under the workbench. Remember when we bought it?"

Carolyn did. It was right before the accident, three years ago. She and Everett had spent the weekend in Temecula for their anniversary. She recalled the smooth sweet-smelling sheets on the bed at the Temecula Creek Inn. They'd made love in the afternoon and spent the evening in their nightshirts on the balcony overlooking the golf course, sipping wine and nibbling on crackers. A good memory. An old memory it seemed now, making her uneasy at not telling about Roy and the dog. She rubbed her hands on her face to wipe the images away.

Everett handed her the wine bottle, and as she reached for it, Carolyn was startled to see pink, orange, and lavender powder covering her palms in streaks like a child's chalk painting. Reaching up, she quickly rubbed a bit more at her cheeks and eyes and then wiped the evidence on her denim skirt. Everett, busy replacing the corkscrew in the drawer, didn't comment, making Carolyn think that he hadn't noticed the makeup at all.

"Hungry? I've got mashed potatoes, and I even made a salad." Everett spun his wheelchair around the kitchen, pulling potholders from drawers and casserole dishes from the oven. He finally placed the salad on the table and tossed it after drizzling olive oil and red vinegar into the bowl. Carolyn sat down as Everett poured the wine. The full glasses glowed like garnets, reminding her somehow of her trip to the makeup counter at the mall. She flushed, then quickly lifted her glass.

"What shall we drink to?"

"To us," Everett said, lightly touching his glass to hers. The edges met with a gentle clink. Carolyn sipped her wine. This was not like him at all, she thought, wondering if he knew something, if the woman from the shelter had called here at home. She realized she was being ridiculous and decided to concentrate on dinner. Dinner was something she could do, right here, right now. She wouldn't think any more about tomorrow.

Carolyn focused on the items in front of her, passing plates and dishing up lettuce and tomatoes from the salad bowl. For a few moments, there was nothing but the sound of forks and knives against the china. Carolyn, used to the silence, let it envelop her. Then Everett spoke.

"Ben and I had a good talk this afternoon." He didn't look up as he said this, concentrating on cutting his meatloaf into even, bite-sized squares. "We spoke a little bit about him, whether or not he has a girlfriend, which I guess he doesn't." Everett paused here to take a sip from his wine glass. "We also talked a little bit about you."

Carolyn looked up from her plate at this last sentence. The kitchen clock ticked behind her.

"What about me?"

"Mostly about how quiet you've been lately." Everett scooped a bit of potato on his fork. "He really cares about you, you know." He looked at her when he said this.

"Ben's a sweet boy," Carolyn answered, feeling relieved that there wasn't more to it. "There's nothing going on, really. Nothing at all."

"Are you sure?" The clock seemed to tick faster and the air in the room felt thick. Carolyn started to reach for her wine glass, then placed her hand back in her lap. Should she say something? About the dog, about Roy? Telling Everett would make it all seem meaningless and insignificant, a simple event in an otherwise dull and undistinguished life. She didn't want that. She didn't want that, at all.

"Tell Ben I'm fine, Everett. Just a little tired lately, but otherwise I'm fine."

"You sure?"

Carolyn looked at Everett and saw the earnest expression in his eyes. This was a good man, she realized. A better man than she deserved. She reached over and touched his hand, which rested on the arm of his chair.

"Yes. I'm sure."

Through the kitchen window, Carolyn could make out the last quarter of the setting sun, glowing red as it quickly dropped below the horizon. She remembered her sixth grade science teacher telling her and the other students about the green light that supposedly flashed just before the top of the sun disappeared. As always, Carolyn watched for the flash but, again, didn't see it. A childhood fable, she decided.

She picked up her plate and walked over to the kitchen sink, flipping on the light with her elbow as she went by the switch. The bulb struggled momentarily to come on before illuminating the room with a fluorescent hum. Carolyn rinsed her plate, then returned to the table where Everett was stacking his silverware on top of the remaining dishes. As they silently worked together to clean up, the lights suddenly flickered, then went out in a quick burst of darkness.

"Wow. Did we blow a fuse?" Carolyn had jumped a little when the room went black.

"Must be a power failure." Everett glanced up toward the kitchen counter. "The clock's out on the stove, too. I'll go check the fuse box." He wheeled his chair past her toward the garage.

Carolyn stood a moment and listened to the darkness, the normal evening sounds appearing magnified and somehow significant. The clock above the kitchen telephone continued its rhythmic tick in battery-powered oblivion, and the crickets in the yard chirped in loud synchronous beats. The world seemed suddenly mysterious and alive. Everything around her had a message just for her, something important and undefined.

Still listening closely to the nighttime sounds, she moved toward the cupboards in the kitchen, reaching up above the stove and feeling in the darkness until she located a box of matches behind a stack of candles and old napkin rings. She shook out a match and as it flared, turned toward the kitchen window. In the glass she could see herself, looking surprised and small, holding the match in her trembling fingers.

Behind her reflection, in the dark portion of the glass, something moved in the yard.

She shook out the match and leaned toward the window, making out the shaggy outline of a coyote as it nosed quietly along the edge of the back fence. Carolyn watched as it padded around the flowerbed and then trotted toward the house. It stopped suddenly, just as it had the last time, and raised its head toward the window where Carolyn stood. The skin on her neck and arms crawled in an undulating wave, as if a tiny snake was inching its way over her.

She wasn't sure if she cried out for Everett—"Come quick; it's here, just like before"—when the lights suddenly flickered and went on above her, dissolving the view through the window and throwing her own reflection back at her. Carolyn felt her nostrils flare and her breath quicken. After a few moments, she moved to the sliding glass door and slowly opened it. When Everett wheeled himself into the kitchen, she didn't turn around.

"What is it?" asked Everett.

For a moment, Carolyn didn't answer. She let the evening breeze caress her face as she gazed into the darkness. The moon lay ahead of her, on the southern end of the canyon. The coyote was gone.

"Just the end of summer," she said.

She slid the door closed and locked it with a firm snap.

CAROLYN WOKE THE NEXT MORNING WITH A STIFF NECK AND HER right cheek crushed against the unyielding upholstery on the arm of the family room sofa. She had fallen asleep while she and Everett were watching the eleven o'clock news. She sat up and studied him a moment as he lay softly snoring in his wheel chair, the reds and greens of the plaid cotton throw in his lap outlining the thinness of his legs. Quietly getting up off the couch, she tiptoed past her sleeping husband to turn off the television, stopping briefly to tuck in one end of the blanket where it trailed on the floor in front of the chair's right wheel.

She climbed the stairs to the master bath and turned on the shower, then tossed off yesterday's clothes and stepped in. The hot water cascaded over her shoulders and back while Carolyn absently rubbed the soap in her hand. She had told her supervisor that she wouldn't be in today. A first for her in the five years she'd worked at the library. It seemed that suddenly everything was changing. The sameness of her old life had been replaced by new thoughts, new feelings and now, new behaviors.

Carolyn moved the soap over her hands and arms, letting the suds and the fresh citrus smell wash over her. There was nothing wrong with taking a day off to bring the dog to Roy, even though she could have had the people at the shelter call him to pick it up. It was her fault that the dog was injured in the first place; it was her responsibility to see it placed in a good home.

She cranked off the water and reached for a towel. As she dried her legs and feet, she remembered drinking coffee with Roy after rescuing the dog. He had understood what she said about being married, how it changed her, made her give up some of the things she might have done if she hadn't left her single life. He had had a wife himself, lost to cancer.

As she hung up her towel, Carolyn remembered her friend, Joyce, who had battled breast cancer eight years ago. Joyce had prevailed, ultimately, in defeating the disease, but the years of chemotherapy—the hair loss, constant nausea, and weakness—had worn on Joyce's relationship with her husband. She had divorced him and moved to Seattle to live near her sister.

Carolyn wondered if Roy's marriage had weathered the battle or if he and his wife had drifted apart under the strain. She knew how a simple event like an accident or the discovery of an illness could somehow change everything, could stretch the closeness between a husband and wife into first a tiny distance, a drifting apart that crept up slowly. Eventually the space became a gaping hole that no words and ultimately, no action, could bridge.

She left the bathroom and surveyed her clothes in the master closet. Most of the items hanging here were hers now. Since Everett didn't come upstairs anymore, they had moved his things to the closet in the bedroom below. Carolyn slid hangers aside one by one, noticing how thin and soft most of her blouses and shirts were. Like old friends, they were comforting in their familiarity.

Since the day would be hot, she selected a pair of denim shorts and a white t-shirt and was just finished dressing when the doorbell rang. It must be nine o'clock, the time when Ben came each morning to help Everett bathe and dress. Carolyn heard their muted voices in the hallway downstairs as she turned to the bag of makeup she'd brought upstairs last night. It sat on the floor near the vanity in the master bath. Without opening it, she carefully slid it under the sink with her foot and settled for brushing her teeth and combing back her hair into a loose ponytail.

When she came downstairs, she heard Everett and Ben in the bathroom, their voices a low hum. She made a pot of coffee in the kitchen and poured some into a metal thermos before knocking lightly on the door.

"I'm heading out now," she announced, waiting to see if Ben would pull the door open.

"Okay, Mrs. Weedman."

Carolyn felt a moment of envy at the youthfulness of Ben's voice.

"I'll be home this afternoon, around three or so." She waited for acknowledgement, but heard none as the roar of the running bath water drowned out whatever response Everett had cared to make.

Picking up her purse, she rummaged for her keys and headed out the door. Since Roy wouldn't be home until after eleven thirty, she had arranged to work a few hours at the County psychiatric counseling center, where she'd been volunteering for the past eight years. As she guided her car onto the freeway, she remembered how her neighbor, Vicky Suggs, had told her about the program.

"We could sure use your help. And it would give you something to do while Everett's working," Vicky'd said.

They'd been sitting inside Carolyn's living room that morning. She remembered looking up from her cross-stitching at Vicky's words and then quickly turning back to her needle and thread. Everett was not home much in those days. He worked late into the evening, or traveled, often for weeks at a time.

"Everett's not always working." The clock ticked above the mantel as she pushed her needle into one of the corner holes. "He's seeing someone else." She finally stopped and gazed at her friend, who quietly set down her coffee.

"Oh, honey. I'm sorry." Vicky reached over and put her hand on Carolyn's arm. "Are you sure?"

Carolyn nodded, the lines of thread in her hand crisscrossing into a multi-colored blur as tears stung at her eyes.

"Do you know who it is?"

"I'm not sure. I think it's a friend of ours."

"Have you confronted him?"

Carolyn looked up from her needlepoint.

"No."

"Why not?"

"I don't know. I keep hoping I'm wrong, that I'm imagining it."

Vicky was quiet a moment.

"Well, at some point you'll need to talk to him." Vicky reached for her coffee cup, took a sip and set it back down. "In the meantime, think about volunteering. It might be good for you to get out of this house once in awhile."

"I'll give it some thought," Carolyn said. The two women walked to the door, where they stopped and gave each other a firm hug. Carolyn stood in the archway, watching Vicky walk down the porch steps and then called out to her.

"Wait."

Vicky turned, one foot on the bottom step.

"All right," Carolyn said. "I'll do it."

She'd applied as a counselor, listing two college courses in psychology and her father's and brother's struggles with ADHD in the section marked "Experience." The mental health director put her at the help-line desk, where she answered telephone calls for individuals seeking referrals. At first she worried that she wouldn't be able to handle the pressure of dealing with distressed patients and their families. But after her first call from a mother whose daughter was suffering from manic mood swings, Carolyn was hooked. She listened quietly as the woman spoke and then experienced a glow of satisfaction after providing her with referrals to three child psychiatrists who specialized in depression. Volunteering made her realize that she could have a positive effect on other people's lives, even if she wasn't very good at fixing her own.

Today, she was struck by a blast of hot, dry air as she opened the door to the tiny office off of Highway 8. Tony Rens, the Grossmont College student who worked as a part-time administrative assistant, waved at her from a desk in the corner.

"Welcome to the sauna." He fanned a copy of the local psychiatric directory in front of his face, the slight breeze blowing his blond bangs to the side.

"Did the air go out again?" Carolyn asked, as she stowed her purse in a drawer and pulled out a telephone record notebook.

"It's been down since yesterday," he answered. "Lucky for you that you're only here twice a week. You'd die if you had to sweat in this factory everyday."

"Well, I do have a real job, you know."

"Oh right, Miss Librarian. Excuse me for forgetting." He smirked as he picked up his headset and placed it on his head.

Carolyn ignored this last comment and turned on the computer at the volunteer desk. She rubbed her hand across her forehead, feeling the first few beads of sweat form along her hairline at the high heat of the room. The screen lit up as her first call came in.

"Hello. My doctor gave me this number and told me that I need to find someone who can treat my anxiety disorder…"

Carolyn logged in the call, then a few others, and finally looked up at the clock on the wall above her to see that an hour had already passed.

She gazed out the window. The traffic on the freeway outside the parking lot rushed by like a metal river. Was she really going out to this strange man's house alone to bring him a dog that she had hit?

A hand appeared before her face, holding an iced drink from Starbuck's. She hadn't even heard Tony leave the room.

"Here. You look like you could use a cold one."

"Thanks." Carolyn smiled at him, then took a sip from the straw. "It is hot in here."

"Well," he said, perching on the desk next to her and taking a loud slurp from his own drink, "at least you came dressed for it." He raised an eyebrow while pointedly staring at her shorts and t-shirt.

Carolyn felt her face flush even more in the heat. "I'm taking some time off from the library today." She stopped and looked away from him as she took another sip.

"What've you got—a hot date?" He grinned at her under his mop of yellow hair.

Carolyn tried to laugh it off. "Yeah, right."

Tony pointed his finger at her. "You're not fooling me, Miss Librarian. You've got it going on with someone, I can tell."

Carolyn shifted in her seat. "Don't be ridiculous." She set her cup down and turned back to her computer, but her hands shook a little as she settled them on the keys.

"Carolyn's got a boyfriend," he crooned at her like a grade school child.

"Shut up, Tony."

"Come on, tell me who he is. Someone at the library. A friend of Everett's?"

"I said, shut up."

"Whoa. Settle down. I'm just fooling with you." Tony went back to his desk and picked up his headset. "Besides, it doesn't really matter what I think, does it?"Carolyn sat still in her chair, the telephone ringing beside her. Did it matter what people thought about each other? She and Everett had had a similar conversation once before, a long time ago. They'd never been able to answer that question.

She stood up from her seat and pulled her purse from the drawer. "I think this is going to be it for me today. Tell Vicky I'll call her next week."

She stalked out of the stuffy office into the even more oppressive heat outside.

IF IT WAS PAINFUL, IT WOULD ALMOST BE EASIER TO BEAR. BUT THERE was no pain, no feeling at all in either leg. Everett stood above the steel braces, his hands clenched, his teeth clamped down in a tight grimace. The only sensation he felt was in his arms pressing down on the brace handles; the only sweat came from his brow as he struggled to make first one foot move and then the other. His right foot inched forward ever so slowly and then his left, following a minute distance before he collapsed and sat back in his wheel chair. Charlie Simpson, the bulky intern who'd played football at San Diego State, patted Everett on the shoulder.

"That's the way, my man. That's the way. You be tough, you know, like a warrior. Keep trying and you'll get it. You'll see."

Tracy Warner, Everett's physical therapist, stood tall and blond behind Charlie, her black reading glasses at half-mast on her nose. She silently marked a few notes on a chart before tucking her pen into the pocket of her scrubs.

"Okay, Charlie. That's probably enough for today." She came up behind Everett's chair and grabbed the handles. Charlie made a fist and pointed it at Everett.

"Warrior. Remember that."

Everett weakly met Charlie's fist with his own, then rested his head in his hand while Tracy wheeled him toward the windows near the left wall of the PT floor. On the other side of the room, he noticed a lanky, pale teenager, sitting alone in a wheelchair watching a television mounted on the wall above him. He hadn't seen this boy here before. Everett wondered where he came from, what freakish accident had landed him in this sterile hospital room where all the exercise machines had metal handles and rubber grips and none of the clientele walked in on his own. Everett watched for a moment, but the boy never looked away from the television set.

While Tracy stopped to take a call on her buzzing cell phone, Everett turned his gaze to the window overlooking the hospital parking lot. From his second floor view, he could see people crossing the walkway to enter the lot. The hot noonday sun shimmered on the roofs of the automobiles hunkered in tight even rows across the concrete. At the far end of the lot, an older man with a red baseball cap slowly made his way toward the hospital entrance on unsteady legs. Even this old creature could beat him in a foot race. He watched as the senior wandered amongst the automobiles, a wounded rat lost in a maze.

"So, how are we doing?" Tracy's gravelly voice boomed as if it was projected from a loudspeaker.

"We? Gee, let's see. One of us is standing and one of us is sitting down." Everett gave her a weary smile. "How's that for an assessment?"

"I see." Tracy let this phrase hover in the air for a moment, then looked Everett directly in the eyes. "You're making good progress, you know. The nerves in L4 injuries take a while to regenerate. But remember, yours is only a partial injury. You will get sensation back. It's just a matter of time." She peered down at him through her glasses. "And will power."

"I know, Tracy. I know." Everett directed his gaze toward the window.

"How's everything else going?"

Everett sat up straighter in his chair.

"Ben is coming every morning. No bladder infections this month."

"How's your emotional state? Are you feeling okay?"

"For those parts of me that feel, yes. I'm feeling okay." Everett smiled when he said this.

"And Carolyn? How's she doing?"

Through the glass below him, Everett watched a woman walking hand-in-hand with a small dark-haired girl dressed in pink overalls. The child's tiny fist clutched the end of a yellow balloon, bobbing behind her in the afternoon sunlight.

"Everett?" Tracy's voice brought him back to planet PT.

"What? Oh, Carolyn. She's fine." Everett tried to smile when he said this but stopped when he saw the look on Tracy's face.

"I've known you for three years," she said. "You're not fooling me one bit, you know."

Everett turned again to watch the yellow balloon bounce here and there amidst the cars in the parking lot until it finally bobbed out of sight.

"Hey." Tracy knelt down next to his wheelchair and put her hand on his arm.

"Do you want to walk again?"

He hung his head. What wouldn't he give to walk again, to reach into a cupboard above sink level, to stand in the shower and feel the water running from the top of his head to the bottom of his feet, to walk so long and so far his calves ached with exertion, to lift Carolyn in his arms and carry her up the stairs. What wouldn't he give?

"Yes." His voice was so quiet it was almost a whisper.

"Then you've got to be present," she said. "You've got to be strong." She gave his arm a squeeze. "And you've got to stop feeling sorry for yourself."

Everett gazed across the room, where a therapist and an aide were helping the teenage boy to stand between two parallel bars. Above the boy's head, on the television screen, a cowboy was firing behind a stand of trees toward a group of Indians brandishing bows and arrows. The camera zeroed in on one warrior, done up in full native garb, an enormous row of feathers cascading down his back from his elaborate headdress. The actor raised his bow above his head and let out a fierce war cry before charging forward, the sounds of gunshots echoing around him.

"Who is that?" Everett asked.

"His name's J.T. He was in a motorcycle crash three months ago. He's an L4 like you. Want to meet him?"

Everett's first impulse was to say no, he wanted to be left alone. But as he watched, the boy struggled to stand, his thin arms trembling so hard his body shook like a sapling facing a strong wind. Everett rolled his chair over to the bar and waited until J.T. sat down.

"Hey," Everett said. "You're doing pretty well, there. A lot better than I did this morning." The therapist, Marcy, and the aide, Eileen, both knew Everett. They smiled at him and waited for the boy to respond. J.T. hung his head sullenly, his red-rimmed eyes still wet with tears of exertion.

"Aren't you going to answer Mr. Weedman?" Marcy asked.

The boy shrugged, then looked up at the television. The white posse was in retreat, their native opponents standing tall on a ridge above the plains watching as the horses galloped away in billowing clouds of dust. The lead Indian raised his bow above his head and released a loud cry of victory. Everett and the boy watched together as the image on the screen lingered for a moment and then faded to the gray background of scrolling credits and the grazing lilt of a western theme song.

IN THE BACK SEAT OF THE HONDA, THE COLLIE SLID BACK AND FORTH on the upholstery. The sound of the dog's nails scraping the leather reminded Carolyn of mice scrambling behind the walls at her house. She hadn't thought to get a pet carrier. When they left the shelter, the dog had happily jumped into the back seat as if she was used to riding in cars. Carolyn had realized then how unprepared she was for this rescue mission. She drummed her fingers nervously on the steering wheel and fiddled with the radio, rapidly changing stations as she glanced at the directions she'd scribbled on the back of a realtor's notepad. The blue and white image of "Dan, the Real Estate Man" beamed in blissful oblivion above the black scrawl of cryptic "rights," "lefts," and "exits" that made up the treasure map to Roy's house.

When she passed the 395 exit, she worried that perhaps she'd gone too far. Even though she'd lived in San Diego for twenty-five years, she had never been to this part of the County. Finally settling for the pop music station KPRI, she pressed the button to turn up the volume. She hummed along to Bonnie Raitt's "Something to Talk About" and then, recognizing the content of the song, pressed the off button, banishing Bonnie and thoughts of infidelity to the back of her mind.

"It's okay, girl," she said. "We'll be there soon."

She glanced into the rear view mirror to study the dog in the back seat. The collie was thin-boned and delicate, a long white star emblazoned from the top of her head to the tip of her nose. She seemed friendly, wagging her tail each time Carolyn made eye contact with her. When the people at the shelter had brought her out to the waiting room, she'd greeted Carolyn in a frenzy of barking and pawing, as if finally being rescued by an old friend. When they'd left the office, she wiggled her entire body in anticipation while Carolyn dug in her purse for the keys, leaping forward with joy when Carolyn had opened the car door.

The Hwy 76 exit sign finally appeared, lit like a roadside beacon by the morning sun. Carolyn breathed a sigh of relief. She was surprised at how empty the horizon was as she followed the highway towards the mission area. After living in the suburbs for so long, it seemed strange to see nothing but scrub brush and blue sky on either side of the road. She passed a roadside vegetable stand advertising lettuce and strawberries. Only a few cars stood outside the tables stacked high with ears of corn and piles of dark round watermelons.

Carolyn drove by an abandoned dairy farm, its concrete milking station sitting stark and empty alongside a field overgrown with tall green grass. The hills behind it rolled on, carpeted by even rows of orange groves, the green leaf clusters lightly dotted with tiny orange fruit. She passed large outcroppings of washed out boulders and silvery rock formations and then experienced a jolt of recognition when she went by the barricaded gates of the Inland

Mining Company. Everett had worked for that company for years before his accident. Carolyn had visited him at his office in Mission Valley, but had never been to this plant. She thought it ironic that here she was, driving past a spot that Everett must have frequented as an employee of the mining firm.

A finger of guilt poked at her, but she brushed it aside when she rounded the curve in the highway and found herself approaching the Pala Casino. The roadside signs loomed large and imposing and rows of expensive cars glittered in the concrete parking lot. She was surprised at the size of the brown and maroon hotel. European in style, it seemed overly stylized and out-of-place next to the tawny golden colors of the canyon gorge that sat just outside it.

Across from the casino, she turned onto Mission Street and listened to the dog's nails scuff against the seat as she slid into the turn. The houses were diminutive and tired, the road dotted here and there with small trailers and gravel driveways. When she came to Ortega Street, she slowed until she found Roy's address, then parked the car in the dirt drive. She studied the small gray house for a moment, noting the chain link fence that encircled the yard and the clothesline hung with white t-shirts in an air of total surrender. The setting seemed a bit rustic for this elegant, high-strung dog. Carolyn could picture it sitting pampered and brushed out on a pillow inside a Victorian mansion; this dusty yard seemed more suited for a wolf hound or Rottweiler, any breed that was masculine and tough.

She got out of the car and opened the door to let the collie check out its new surroundings. The dog sprang from the back seat and padded over to the chain link fence, looking up at Carolyn expectantly. She pushed the gate open with a metal squeak and the dog followed her to the steps where she knocked on the battered screen door.

"Hello. Guess you found it okay." Roy pressed the door open and waved her inside. They both turned to look at the collie, which ignored them while it nosed around the periphery of the yard, its tail wagging vigorously.

"Your directions were great," Carolyn said, as she set her purse on the wooden table in the center of the room and took a seat on the sofa. The house smelled of furniture polish and Pine Sol. "Are you sure you're ready to take on this dog?"

"She seems manageable." Roy watched the animal through the window. Carolyn studied him as he stood with his hands on hips before the glass. His long hair was pulled back as before and he looked strong and relaxed in his white shirt and faded jeans. She put her hand up to her ponytail to adjust the knot at the back and then surveyed the room. She didn't know what she had expected; perhaps some native artwork or typical bachelor pad sports posters or magazines. Instead, she found the walls covered with British paraphernalia: the English flag with its stripes of red, white, and blue, framed prints of Queen Elizabeth and what looked like Henry VIII, a wooden plaque with a mounted document that read "Magna Carta." She felt as if she had suddenly stepped back in time and was sitting in a British cottage outside of London, rather than a thirty-year-old tract home in northern San Diego.

"Would you like something to drink? I've got tea and can make some coffee, although I don't drink it myself."

"I'm fine, thanks." Carolyn lifted a framed photo of a woman and a small boy that was sitting on the end table next to the sofa. The photograph was black and white, the woman holding the boy closely to her, her face soft and serious. The boy stood chubby and wide-eyed at her side. "Is this your wife?" she asked.

"Yes, that's Sonia. And my son, Luke. That picture was taken years ago." Roy came over and lifted the photo out of her hands to gaze at it. His voice took on a reverent tone. "Luke was eight-years-old in this picture. He's almost twenty-one now."

Carolyn was surprised, somehow, that Roy had a son. She hadn't thought about any children when he'd told her that his wife died.

"You must love England; there's so much British art here," she said as Roy gently set the photo back down on the table. He paused a moment and looked around the room before answering.

"Art is a kind term for it. I spent some time in London years ago on a post doc. Now I teach Elizabethan history." Roy smiled at her and shook his head. "Classes start next Monday. The fall semester seems to come earlier every year."

"What is it you like about Elizabeth?" Carolyn asked.

"She had a great spirit," Roy answered. He smiled again, this time in a way that seemed to light up his entire face. "Not unlike that dog out there."

Carolyn glanced at the living room window and saw that the collie had latched on to one of the shirts hanging from the clothesline and was whipping her head back and forth in an effort to pull it to the ground.

"Hey!" She and Roy shouted in unison as they flew through the front door and separated the dog from the shirt, which was stretched and showed tiny teeth marks along its frayed edges.

"So, what do you plan to name her?" Carolyn asked. Roy squatted next to her, his face so close she could reach out and touch it. They both ran their palms over the dog's soft fur.

"Good question. What do you suggest?"

"Well, you said she was spirited. I agree with you on that." Carolyn noticed that Roy wore no jewelry and that his hands were a smooth, even brown against the collie's white ruff. A teacher's hands.

"In my mother's language, we would call her "tóowish ′áachish." That means "crazy spirit."

"Tóowish," Carolyn repeated. She stopped a moment and looked at the dog. "Somehow that seems right."

They took a tour of the area, Roy driving them in his truck down Courser Canyon Road and parking off the concrete on a small, unpaved turnout. He and Carolyn picked their way across the rocky bed of the canyon floor, Tóowish running on ahead of them to nose amongst the brush that stretched across the canyon. The sun was bright and relentless. Carolyn noticed its glint on shiny bits of sediment and rock as she walked in unison with Roy, their footsteps making identical crunching noises in the gravel. It felt good to be walking beside a man, to feel her arms swinging freely and the sun beating down on her neck.

A hawk circled lazily above them against the pale blue of the sky and Roy paused a moment to watch it. Carolyn stopped also, as its circling pattern became tighter and tighter until it arched its wings and dove toward the mesa in a quick swoop. Tóowish lifted her head and gave a short bark before dashing toward the spot where the bird had descended. Carolyn and Roy stopped next to a flat smooth block of washed out granite. They sat and watched as the dog circled back toward them, her nose pointed toward the canyon floor.

"It's beautiful here." Carolyn gazed at the gold and green foliage that dotted the hardscape before them.

"It won't be for long," Roy replied. He pointed toward a rise in the canyon across from where they sat. "See that area to the east of us? That's Gregory Canyon. The County is putting in a landfill there. Pretty soon you'll see nothing but garbage on the horizon."

"What?" Carolyn followed the direction of his finger. "Who would do such a thing?"

"A consortium of developers put an initiative on the ballot a few years ago. Even though our tribe fought it, the measure passed. There was one attempt to stop it in the state legislature, but that failed, too." Roy paused to pick up a rock from the ground at his feet. He studied it for a moment before continuing. "After the environmental impact report is approved and all the regional boards file their permits, it'll be a reality."

Carolyn looked at Roy in disbelief. "Can't anything else be done to stop it?"

Roy smiled wearily. "We'd like to think so. There are a number of environmental groups that plan to challenge the approval. Our tribal council is working with them; my son and my sister are members."

Carolyn felt another jolt of surprise at the mention of Roy's son. "What about you? Are you part of that group?"

Roy looked again at the rock in his hand. He turned it over once and then tossed it out into the brush near Tóowish, who was digging under a bush. The dog barked happily and took off after the rock. "Once Sonia died, I kind of had my hands full raising my son and teaching. As much as I love this area, I've always been more interested in exploring other places in the world." Carolyn noticed that a wistful expression flitted briefly over his face as he spoke. He turned and smiled at her again. "Besides, Luke seems to be the activist in the family. I'm happy to leave that role to him."

Carolyn was quiet. His references to Luke reminded her that Roy was part of a family, something that she and Everett had never had.

"What about you?" Roy asked. "Do you have any children?"

Carolyn thought a moment. Should she describe the child that she'd lost years ago? The thought of doing so seemed as painful as reliving that moment all over again.

"No," she said, staring off into the distance of the canyon.

"Any plans for them in the future?"

Carolyn looked at Roy. The sun bore down hot and hard on her head and her tongue suddenly felt swollen. She tried to envision the future with Everett, but the only image she could conjure was an empty room, sterile and white. At an open window, a shutter banged futilely in dull, even strokes. A brown hand reached up to close it. She shook the image away.

"My husband was in an auto accident three years ago. He suffered some paralysis." She spoke quietly and firmly. "He had severe back trauma and has been in a wheelchair ever since." She stopped and looked at Roy. "He's capable of ..." she paused a moment, took a deep breath, and then continued, "... of being with me." Her voice faltered. She gazed a second at the horizon. The air became suddenly thick and still while the sunlight glinted on the sand. She turned to Roy. "But he hasn't tried in two years." After studying her hands for a moment, she shrugged and forced what she hoped looked like a brave smile. "So, we won't be having any children."

She could feel her lip trembling as her eyes welled up. Turning her face away from Roy, she wiped at the hot tears that spilled over her cheeks. I'm a fool, she thought, a ridiculous fool.

There was a touch on her shoulder.

"Here."

When she turned back toward him, he was holding out a handkerchief and looking at her in the same self-assured manner that she had noticed in the Starbuck's two weeks ago. She paused a moment, her hand raised to her cheek, then took the white cloth and mopped at her nose and eyes.

"You keep a handkerchief in your pocket?" Carolyn sniffed and tried to smile as she handed the damp cloth back to him. "What man in San Diego carries one of these around?"

"Someone who's been to England," he said, flashing a quick grin and offering her his hand as he stood up.

She placed her hand in his and, rising too quickly, slipped on the gravel under her foot. Roy reached up to steady her and when he did, they both stopped, holding onto each other's arms. Neither of them let go. Carolyn felt the sun on her head and the warmth of Roy's hands and for a brief moment she felt connected and whole. The ground was firm under her feet and a man was standing next to her, looking into her eyes and holding her as if it meant something. Carolyn studied Roy's face, noting that his eyebrows arched just the slightest bit on either side and that his eyes were the same soft brown as a piece of suede. There was kindness in them, and concern, and something else. Was it desire? Or did he regret any involvement with her and her pathetic life? She didn't care; she only knew that she wanted to be here with him in this hot rocky field. She reached out and touched his cheek, briefly, with one hand, then stepped back, her other hand still in his.

"You're feeling sorry for me, aren't you?" she asked.

"No. Not at all." He leaned closer, as if to kiss her, and Carolyn closed her eyes. Just then she heard frantic barking and a strange strangled cry. She and Roy turned toward the sound and saw that it was Tóowish, straining forward, front paws to the ground, growling at an outcropping of rocks. They ran forward, still holding hands, and then broke free of each other as they came upon the dog.

Coiled near the rocks, raised back as if to strike, sat the largest rattlesnake that Carolyn had ever seen.

Its small oval head tapered off into a pile of thick curves, a trail of enormous black diamonds cascading down its back. An amber-colored rattle at the tip of its tail shook at regular intervals, giving off the familiar warning hiss. The snake watched the three intruders. Carolyn shuddered. When snakes appeared in their yard at home, she let Everett deal with them, preferring to watch from behind the sliding glass door.

"Don't move." Roy put his arm out and pointed at the snake's head. "Snakes are more afraid of us than we are of them. If we stand still, it'll go away."

"What about the dog?" Carolyn asked. Tóowish stood two feet from the snake, paws forward, tail protruding straight out from her back.

"Tóowish," Roy commanded. "Sit." They watched in surprise as the dog reluctantly sat back on her haunches. "Stay."

The three of them were still, frozen like statues before the massive reptile, which continued to stare at them with beady black eyes. Finally, after what seemed more like hours than minutes, the snake lowered its head and turned toward the outcropping of rocks. As it slithered away, Roy slowly reached down and picked up a couple of tiny stones that lay at his feet. He tossed one and then another toward the snake, causing it to inch forward with greater urgency. When it was about three feet from them, Roy motioned to Carolyn to back away slowly. The dog followed. As soon as Tóowish was near, Roy leaned down and ran his hands over her fur, feeling for wounds.

"She's okay," he said. Carolyn felt a surge of relief. On the way back to Roy's house, she reached behind the seat to rub the fur on Tóowish's neck. Below the silky strands she could feel the warmth of the dog's skin. She studied Roy as he drove, letting her eyes linger on his brown, bare arm. Although he wasn't overly muscular, his body was compact and strong. She wondered what his skin would feel like lying next to hers, belly to belly, cheek to cheek. The thought of being that close to him made her face burn.

Roy turned at the sound and gave her a quiet smile. She smiled back, and wondered where they would go from here. Would he ask her to come back to visit? Or should she bring it up herself? As if eavesdropping on her thoughts, Roy spoke.

"Will you be able to come back sometime and visit us?"

Her heart gave a funny little thump at these words and she was about to answer, yes, but stopped short. They had pulled into Roy's driveway and there, standing next to a large silver motorcycle, was a muscular tanned man with long black hair, a younger version of Roy. Something about the way he stood facing them made the hair along her arm stand up on end.

"Who is that?' she asked.

"That's Luke." Roy answered. His voice sounded tight "He's supposed to be working."

They pulled up and Carolyn opened her door to let Tóowish out of the back seat. The dog bounded forward, then stopped and carefully sniffed at the edge of Luke's frayed blue jeans. Luke reached down and patted her, then glanced up at Carolyn and his father.

"Míiyu, noná´."

Roy ignored the greeting. "This is Carolyn Weedman," he said. "What are you doing home?"

"What are you doing with a dog?"

Carolyn winced at the defiance in the young man's voice. She was certain that his question was about her and not the dog at all.

"It's nice to meet you." Carolyn stepped forward and extended her hand. Luke stared straight at her, his eyes small and black. She felt a chill up her spine and then a jolt as he took her hand. His grip was hard and unyielding and his hand felt like a stone in hers. The handshake was brief and perfunctory. Carolyn stepped back and looked at Roy.

"Thank you again, for all you've done. I'll come back and visit, I promise."

Roy smiled and held his hand out to her. She took it, feeling the warmth and strength that now seemed familiar. When they finally let go, he turned toward his son, the smile banished from his face. Carolyn walked over to the yard and whistled for Tóowish. The dog bounded from the side of the house and wagged her tail as Carolyn petted her.

"Take good care of this man," she whispered into the dog's ear.

As she walked back to her car, she could hear Roy and Luke talking in hushed voices, one sounding flat and firm, the other raised in contention. As she backed out of the drive, she turned toward the house and saw that the two men were standing face to face, like a matching pair of warriors carved in stone. Neither looked up as she pulled away.

Chapter 4

Sunlight poured in through the bedroom window, bathing the sheets in a blinding patch of white. Carolyn pushed aside the pillow she'd been gripping and checked the alarm clock on the nightstand. Seven thirty a.m. She'd have to leave for work in an hour. She reluctantly swung her feet to the floor and stumbled downstairs. At the office door she paused and checked on Everett, who snored lightly on his twin bed, his head turned toward the wall. His model airplanes hung silently above him like shadowy winged sentinels. Carolyn carefully shut the door. She would let him sleep until Ben came at nine o'clock.

In the kitchen, the teakettle worked itself up to a shrill whistle as the clock ticked off the start of the day in slow, even beats. She poured boiling water into a one-cup coffee filter and closed her eyes at the heady aroma that drifted up from the dark roast grounds. The smell reminded her of Starbuck's and the afternoon when she and Roy had first sat and stared at each other over the twisting steam as it evaporated between them. Where was he now? Just waking up? Watching the hawks as they circled the reservation above his front door?

She brought her cup to the table and sat down, absently staring at the fingers on her left hand. There was still a faint strip of white where her wedding band had once sat on her third finger. She hadn't worn her ring in over a year, abandoning it in the polished abalone shell that gathered dust on her dresser upstairs. Everett had asked about the ring the first time she forgot to wear it; after about a week, he stopped asking and she left it in the shell to mingle with the other jewelry she rarely wore—gold hoop earrings, tear-drop pearls, and a single diamond stud, its mate inadvertently washed down a shower drain while she and Everett were on vacation in Hawaii.

Carolyn sipped her coffee and then forced herself upstairs to the shower. When she reached in to test the running water, small beads shot up into the sunlight streaming in from the shower window. The water drops glistened like jewels. Carolyn cupped her hands and marveled as the water tumbled over her fingers, seeming somehow radiant and pure. As she soaped her hair, she recounted the events of yesterday on the reservation—watching the hawk circle overhead, feeling the tears on her cheeks, stumbling into Roy's arms. It had all seemed so easy and simple.

She dried herself with a towel, noticing that the sunlight wove its way through the blinds above the shower window, lacing her body with bands of light. She hummed a few bars of a romantic tune that had been her favorite a long time ago and left the bathroom to dress, feeling so warm that her skin seemed to glow. Somehow, her clothes fit better today than they had yesterday, hanging in just the right folds, tucking in where they should. Her hair seemed to glisten, her shoes slid on easily. She reached into her purse and there were her keys, this time right where they should be. The car started on the first try, and Carolyn glided through every traffic light without having to stop once on her way to work.

SOMETHING COLD AND WET PUSHED ITSELF AGAINST THE SKIN ON Roy's back, causing him to sit up so suddenly that he and Tóowish both jumped in surprise. The collie stared at him over the bedclothes, her head tilted slightly to the side as if she had a question for him. When Roy plopped back down against the pillows and turned over, the dog began barking, first a short yap and then louder until Roy finally roused himself and mumbled, "Okay, okay." Tóowish headed toward the bedroom door and then turned back, her tail wagging eagerly, as if leading the way to something momentous. Roy struggled out of bed, reaching around the floor until he found the jeans he'd been wearing yesterday. He shook them out with a loud snap and then pulled them on, all the while watching the dog as it paced back and forth in the bedroom doorway. He'd heard Luke let her out early this morning, so he thought she was taken care of but, obviously, she had something she wanted to show him.

Roy discovered what it was as soon as he stumbled behind her into the kitchen. A rolling carpet of black ants converged on the bowl of dog food sitting on the floor next to the kitchen counter. The trail led all the way from the bowl, where the ants spilled in a mad frenzy over the grayish lump in the center, up the cupboards to the window over the kitchen sink. Roy shook his head in disgust at himself; he hadn't thought about how vicious the ants could be in the summer. He knew what Sonia would have said to him at this moment. "They're just foot soldiers, searching for food and water to prepare for the winter." Well, foot soldiers or not, these troopers were about to die.

Roy rooted around under the sink until he found an empty plastic spray bottle. He filled it with water, smiling to himself at the kindness he was about to show in his administration of death. His wife and son had always been adamant about not using pesticides to deal with ants. Even though neither one was here at the moment, he paid them each a silent tribute, before turning the spray on the seething column that scrambled up the kitchen counter. He coated the dog dish, the counter top, even the windowsill where they were coming in, until the majority of them swam in the pooling liquid. Those that escaped the water scattered. Roy let them go. He'd learned that with ants, you just had to disturb their trail and clean up the casualties and the rest would disappear.

He pulled out a ribbon of paper towels and mopped up the small black carcasses. The dead ants fell around his feet on the floor as he held the small kitchen trashcan up to the sink and wiped the wet mess into the plastic liner. After going through the majority of the paper towel roll, he finally swept the last black specks into the trash. Once he'd rinsed and refilled the dog's bowl, he reset it on the floor and watched as Tóowish sniffed at it and then dug in. She ate daintily, her small head bobbing and her tail wagging whenever she paused in her chewing to look up at Roy.

He liked this dog. He didn't know why. His offer to keep her had been an impulse, one that he'd wondered about after helping

Carolyn get her to the vet the day of the accident. But there was something delicate and sweet about Tóowish, something that reminded him of all the women, fictional and otherwise, that he'd admired over the years. When he'd first lifted her into the truck that day she was hit, he'd marveled at how light and soft she felt. Now, watching her lick the empty bowl, her pink tongue narrow and quick, he wondered how whoever owned her could give her up. Carolyn said that no one had claimed her, but Roy found that hard to believe. This dog seemed too special. It was hard to imagine that anyone who had once known her wouldn't have worked hard to find her after she was missing.

When Tóowish finished eating, Roy let her out and then sat at his dining room table to prepare for the first day of school on Monday. He opened a three-ring binder, which contained notes for a new course he'd be teaching entitled *Kings and Queens of England.* The bulk of the course was finished; he just needed to outline the last three weeks of the class, which would cover the House of Hanover through the time of George III and the founding of the American colonies. As he scribbled notes on a lined pad of paper, he caught himself whistling softly, a native tune that his mother had taught him as a small boy. He hadn't felt like whistling in a long time; the events of the past few weeks had brought him a feeling of contentment that he hadn't experienced since Sonia died.

He glanced up to watch Tóowish through the living room window. Seeing her outside in the yard reminded him of the hike through the canyon with Carolyn the day before. When he closed his eyes he could see her chestnut colored curls shining in the sun and felt all over again the urge to kiss her that had overcome him when she stumbled against him. Would she consider returning to see him? Luke hadn't given her a warm welcome, The kid would just have to get past his distrust of anyone white, especially this woman.

Roy didn't know how it happened, but he found himself picking up the telephone that sat on the dining room table and dialing information. He heard himself ask for the number for the Rancho Penasquitos library, then watched his own hand, as if he didn't even own it, dialing the number. When Carolyn's voice came on the line, he smiled and suddenly was back where he belonged.

"It's good to hear your voice." Carolyn sounded happy; he could picture her small hands cupping the receiver on the other end of the line. "How is Toowish holding up after her first night at your house?"

"She's doing great," he replied. "Acts as if she's lived here all her life."

"Somehow that doesn't surprise me."

There was a slight pause, then Roy cleared his throat and asked the question that had been in the back of his mind since yesterday afternoon.

"I was calling to see if you wanted to get together next week. We could go for a ride or maybe have lunch somewhere. I'll be teaching on Mondays and Wednesdays; I wondered if any other day would be good for you." Roy looked down and found that he was gripping the phone cord tightly with his other hand. He hadn't felt this anxious about making a date since he was in high school.

"Lunch would be nice. I think I could get away on Thursday."

Roy relaxed his grip and rubbed his hand against his forehead, which had broken out with sweat in the early morning heat.

"Thursday it is. How about if we meet halfway? Are you familiar with Chan's in Escondido?

"If you mean the restaurant across from the Arts Center, I know exactly where it is. How about twelve thirty?"

"Sounds good; I'll see you there."

They said their goodbyes. As Roy hung up the phone, he noticed that a dead ant clung to the fibers of his t-shirt near the pocket that rested above his heart. He flicked the insect away with a quick snap and whistled as he turned back to his notebook.

WHENEVER THERE WAS TROUBLE COMING, DELORES HEARD DRUM beats. It was almost as if her ancestors were warning her, in their own obtuse way, to pay close attention to what was about to occur.

This time it was the roar of Luke's motorcycle as it pulled into her driveway that set the sounds off. The putt-putt-putt of the engine as Luke shut off the ignition echoed in her mind like a tom-tom beat. Before answering the door, she closed her eyes for a moment, letting the sound subside until the pounding in her head matched the beating of her heart.

"Míiyu, Nephew." Delores noted with pride that Luke was getting muscular and bronze from his summer work on the Pala construction sites.

"Míiyu, Aunt." Luke put his arms around her and lifted her off the floor. She chuckled as he set her down; it was only in the last five years that he'd grown tall enough to do this.

"Why aren't you working today?" Delores peered up at him through the thick rims of her glasses. She'd heard rumors of her nephew's absence and was worried that he was headed for one of his spells.

"Why is everybody so concerned about whether or not I'm working?" Luke's face clouded over. "You're starting to sound just like Dad."

"Even if I tried, I could never sound like your father. Come, let's sit in the backyard and talk."

They walked through the tiny living room into a kitchen only six feet across on either side. Even though it was eighty degrees outside, this part of the house was cool and dark. Large bundles of dried herbs, tied with pieces of twine, dangled from the ceiling. Traces of seeds and bits of bark dusted the tiny stove's surface below the slowly twirling bunches. Chaotic piles of leaves and twigs covered the sink.

When they reached the back doorway, Delores pushed aside a silvery green batch of lavender suspended in front of it. The herb's lemony-sweet fragrance filled the room. Luke held the back door open for her as they left the house. Without speaking, they sat down next to each other in the sun on the steps of the cement porch.

The yard stretched out before them in a crazy quilt of weedy brush and dusty patches of earth. Along the back fence, tall stalks of coreopsis stood like slumping soldiers, their heavy heads bursting with seeds that spilled onto the dry ground below. Delores waved her hand toward an unusually high stand of plants with broad, gray leaves.

"I can fix you some *qáaṣil* before you go. White sage is good for clearing your sinuses."

Luke shook his head and gazed at the horizon beyond the fence.

"So, your father's found a woman?" Delores reached into her shirt pocket and pulled out a handful of sunflower seeds. She offered some to her nephew, then set the pile down on the concrete between them and proceeded to crack a kernel between her two front teeth.

"How did you know about that?" Luke asked. He held a seed between his fingers, turning it over until the salt came off on his skin.

"He told me." Delores squinted up at the sun. "Have you met her yet?"

"Yeah. Yesterday."

"What's she look like?"

Luke paused a moment. He shrugged and made a face. "I don't know. Kind of small, thin. White." He turned and looked directly in his aunt's eyes. "Like a ghost."

"Ah." Delores smiled at Luke's description. "Well, he hasn't dated much, you know. There were only two since your mother passed away. Remember that Cupa woman, Anna Santos? The one with the big mole on her face? And then the woman from the school? She didn't last much longer than the first."

"Yeah, well, I don't blame them. He doesn't have much to offer any woman who isn't related to the Queen of England." Luke flipped the seed onto the sandy patch of ground in front of the steps.

Delores chuckled, then sat quietly for a moment. What her nephew said was true, Roy hadn't seemed interested in anything but his teaching since Sonia had died. But Delores hoped her brother would find someone new; he deserved that happiness.

"You need to give him a chance, Nephew. When the right person comes, we should wish the best for him."

"Just like he does for everyone else, eh?" Luke emphasized the intended irony of this statement with a brief smirk.

"What is it with you? Always going on about your father as if he's 'aláxxwish? He did the best he could to raise you." Delores cracked another seed between her teeth. "He lost Sonia, too, you know."

"Yeah, poor Dad. Let's all cheer him on in his search for a white woman." Luke tossed another seed to the ground.

Delores turned a bit to study her nephew in the hot sun. She knew that the loss of his mother had been devastating. Even so, Delores wondered when this preoccupation with blaming his father would end.

"What do you want from him?" she asked.

The sun glowed in the sky as the shadowy brown figure of a hawk circled in slow motion overhead. Luke sat motionless, his dark head bent as if in prayer.

"Nothing he can give me, Auntie." He glanced up at Delores and gave her a tight smile. "Nothing anyone can give me anymore." He placed his hand briefly on his aunt's arm then stood, watching the hawk as it sailed low over the horizon and disappeared into the clouds. As he turned toward the back door, she reached up and took his hand.

"Come to Council, Nephew. We need you there."

He looked away from her without answering.

"Please. We need you."

Luke gave his aunt's hand a squeeze, then leaned down and placed a kiss on the top of her head. The door banged once behind him.

Delores listened as his footsteps faded into the depths of the house, then recognized the unmistakable roar of the motorcycle engine. She gathered the remaining sunflower seeds left on the porch and dropped them into her pocket. As she reached for the back door knob, the drumbeats started. At first as soft as a heartbeat, their dissonance grew into a steady pounding rhythm, until Delores could ignore them no longer.

She closed her eyes and recited a short prayer to the guardian spirit, Taakwic, then went into the house to call her brother.

WHEN CAROLYN PUSHED OPEN THE HEAVY RED DOOR TO CHAN'S, she felt as if she was stepping into another world. The heat of the midday sun disappeared behind her while the door slowly closed, and there she stood, facing an enormous dragon, its fiery eyes flashing above sharp golden claws. The statue loomed above her, just inside the entrance, daring her to cross its path. Its malevolent glare made her shiver. The restaurant lobby was cool and dark, with red chairs lined up like rows in a jury pool and Chinese prints framed in black lacquer on the walls. The air smelled musty and rich. Underneath the faint odor of fish, Carolyn caught the scent of something frying.

There was no one at the counter, and the tables in the dining area appeared empty. Carolyn resisted the urge to flee and rang the small silver bell on the glass counter. Next to the cash register sat a shiny redwood Buddha, his face glowing in the smoke from two joss sticks that burned in an adjacent rice bowl. The incense reminded her of going to church when she was a child. The memory of her parish priest's admonishments –"thou shall not commit adultery"—flashed into her thoughts. She felt her face burn with guilt. She was about to turn away when a small Asian woman, dressed in black silk, suddenly appeared behind the smoke. As if signing for a deaf person, Carolyn raised two fingers to indicate that someone would be joining her for lunch. She followed the woman who, gliding forward on the tips of tiny black slippers, led her to a table within eyeshot of the door.

Carolyn became engrossed in the menu, its plastic-covered pages preserved like a sacred tablet in embossed black leather. She didn't see Roy until he was standing right in front of her. Glancing up, she caught her breath. There he stood, in the same leather jacket and white jeans that he'd worn on the day she met him. He looked familiar and, at the same time, foreign. She felt a tiny jolt of excitement and then remembered that she had no business here, meeting a single man for a date. This made her smile less broadly than she would have liked, and she held her hand out to him almost formally, as if to shake it. He took it with a brief smile and sat down, continuing to gaze at her.

"I feel like I'm interrupting some serious studying," he said.

"Well, this is a big decision I've got to make." Carolyn smiled back at him. "I mean, order the wrong thing, like Peking duck when it should have been Kung Pao chicken, and then what would we do?"

Before Roy could answer, the woman in black materialized. They placed their order and then watched as the waitress poured cups of jasmine tea and set out bowls of crispy noodles. Carolyn noticed that Roy had ordered beef with broccoli, which was Everett's favorite. She wondered what her husband was doing right now and then realized that he would be home, as always, puttering around the yard or working on his model airplanes. She suddenly felt his presence, as if he was sitting right next to her, watching.

Roy reached out across the table and touched her briefly on the hand.

"You seem kind of distant. What were you thinking about?" he asked.

She decided to tell him the truth.

"My husband."

Roy didn't blink at this.

"Do you wish he was here?"

"No," Carolyn answered. "Although, to tell you the truth, I feel that he is here, in some ways."

"Do you still love him?"

If it had come from any other man, this question would have bothered her. But she was certain that this was something Roy really wanted to know. Their future relationship, whatever that turned out to be, would hinge on it.

"Yes," she said. "I think I still do. But not in the way I used to. So much has changed between us. Everything seems different now." She sipped at her tea and then shook the liquid at the bottom of the cup. The leaves swirled into a small pile, but the arrangement revealed nothing to her. "Do you understand what I mean?"

"Unfortunately, I do," Roy answered.

A shadow seemed to pass across his face. She was about to ask him about his wife, but at that moment the waitress arrived with their soup.

"Hot and sour," she said.

They watched as the woman set two small bowls in front of them and ladled the hot liquid from a large tureen. She left the remainder on the table before silently vanishing.

Carolyn picked up her white porcelain soup spoon and stirred the thick brown broth before tasting it. The soup was tangy and hot and might have burned her tongue if she hadn't swallowed quickly. This was another of Everett's favorite dishes. She tried to wipe the image of his face from her mind.

"You haven't asked about Tóowish," Roy said.

"Oh, you're right. How is she?"

"Terrific. She spent the morning digging holes in every corner of the yard. That was after she chewed the garden hose. Ate straight through it." Roy chuckled and shook his head.

"What will we do if someone claims her?" Carolyn asked. "I keep thinking that, at some point, the shelter will get a call from her original owner."

Roy didn't hesitate.

"If her true owner surfaces, we'll have to give her back," he said. "Makes me kind of sad to think about it, though. I guess she's really just on loan to us." He smiled and looked up at Carolyn. "We'll have to make the most of our time with her."

Carolyn wondered what he meant by this. Was he asking her to come see him at home again? Before she could ask, their main courses arrived and both of them were lost momentarily in the shuffling of plates and passing of dishes piled with food. While Roy sipped his tea, she looked around the restaurant and realized that it had slowly filled up with a sizable lunchtime crowd. After a pause, she took the opportunity to voice a question that had been at the back her mind.

"You asked me about my husband and my feelings for him. I'm wondering the same thing about you and your wife." Carolyn spoke these words shyly, feeling a little awkward about asking such a direct question. "Do you miss her?"

"Very much," Roy replied.

Somehow, Carolyn knew that this would be his answer. It made her envious, that he had had a good marriage and loved his wife. At the same time, she felt reassured. This was a man who was loyal to those he loved.

"It wasn't always easy," he continued. "Marriage never is. But when you face losing the person who's been with you for so many years, all the petty differences between you seem to fade away. The most important thing is staying together. And staying alive." He paused a moment, a faraway look in his eyes. "And then, when that isn't an option, you learn to say goodbye and mean it."

Carolyn sat still, gripping the chopsticks in her hand.

"For us, Sonia's leaving wasn't something we got to choose. I don't really know where exactly you are with your husband, but I do know that every relationship has its challenges." He gazed directly at her. "When the time comes to make a decision about your future, you'll know what to do. Both of you."

Carolyn thought about this for a moment. She realized that what he said was true. She also knew that some relationships were more challenging than others.

As she filled his cup with tea from the silver pot on the table, she made a decision. It was time to stop skirting the main issue.

"So, where do we fit in with all of this?" she asked. Then, without thinking, she reached out and placed her hand on his.

Roy might have said something. In fact, she was sure he did, but his answer was lost in a loud crash of china plates. Carolyn turned to face the back of the restaurant. There, in a clutter of commotion, two servers hovered above a mass of silverware and broken crockery that the waitress had dropped from her serving tray. A baby wailed over the waitress's broken apologies. It took a few moments before the other diners in the restaurant settled back to the business of eating.

When Carolyn turned around to face Roy, something made her glance toward the restaurant door. There, standing at the counter, stood Ben. He was digging into his wallet to pay for what looked like a take-out order.

He glanced up suddenly and their eyes met.

At first, it seemed that he didn't recognize her. Then, she followed his gaze toward Roy, who had turned around to see what she was looking at. Ben bowed his head slightly and gave her a brief wave before picking up his bag and hurrying out the door. Carolyn suddenly realized that her hand was still in Roy's. She pulled it away.

"Was that someone you know?" Roy asked.

At that moment, the enormity of the situation hit Carolyn in full force. Ben had seen her holding hands with an unfamiliar man. She placed her palms first on her face, then on her hair, then grabbed her purse and stood up.

"I'm sorry," she said. "I have to go."

She rummaged through her bag, searching desperately for her wallet and keys. Roy reached up and placed his hand, again, on hers.

"It's all right," he said. "I'll get it." He felt for his back pocket. When he pulled out his wallet, she noticed that it looked as worn and battered as it had on that day they first met, when he'd opened it to give her his card. The sight of it made her want to weep.

"I'm sorry," she repeated again. "You are a beautiful man. This is all my fault. It really is."

With that, she closed her purse and headed toward the entrance. At the door, the dragon statue towered above her, its thick red lips leering in disgust. She pulled the door open and fled the dark restaurant, blinking in confusion as she stumbled into the blazing sunlight.

THE SMALL FINGER OF GUILT THAT HAD POKED AT CAROLYN FOR THE last few hours became a full-fledged hand, shoving her from behind when she entered the library, slapping at her head when she turned on her computer, forcing itself around her brain and squeezing until it ached. She'd been exposed and now panic set in. What had she done? She'd never cheated on her husband before. Never. She would have to talk to Ben, tell him it was all a mistake, explain what she'd been doing there.

And what about Roy? He must think horribly of her for deserting him so abruptly. The hand curled itself around her neck. Call him, it urged. Call him now. Carolyn rubbed at her eyes and leaned her head back trying to ease the tension and doubt. She pulled his card from her purse, then reached for the phone. At that moment a customer stepped up to the desk.

"I'm sorry to bother you, but could you tell me where I might find a listing for San Diego real estate offices?" The diminutive gray-haired woman smiled at her sweetly. Carolyn reluctantly released the receiver and focused on her customer.

By the time she'd helped the woman and two more individuals doing research, it was four o'clock. Mary brought over a pile of hard covers that needed to be entered into the library system.

"Go ahead and take your break now," she told Carolyn. "I'll wait until you get back."

"That's all right. I'll just stay here and use the computer. You can go ahead, if you like."

"Suit yourself," Mary answered before shuffling toward the break room.

Carolyn fingered the white card, which was lying on the desk where she'd laid it hours ago. Roy would think she was an idiot if she called now, after leaving the way she had today. She set it back down, then pushed aside the pile of books Mary had left and turned to the computer screen. If she couldn't bring herself to talk to Roy, she could find out more about him. After typing in her password, she brought up her Internet account and typed in his name. Only two links came up, both of them at the college with listings for his history courses. She entered the words "Pala reservation landfill" in the search line. More than a dozen sites came up. She clicked on the first entry, the Pala Indians' site, and began to read. The landfill had been an ongoing issue since the early 1980's, when developers first proposed using the Mount Gregory site but were stymied by the native tribes and the County planning staff. Carolyn felt first shock and then indignation as she read how the tribes and local officials had fought the development. The proposed site was on sacred ground.

Opening another link, Carolyn discovered that the developers, having gotten nowhere with the tribes, environmentalists and local communities, decided to place a proposition on the ballot in the 1994 election. It passed, forcing the tribes to sponsor an assembly bill in 2000 that would protect tribal sacred sites from desecration. The state governor vetoed the bill. The landfill, Carolyn realized, was going to happen unless someone could stop the developers.

She felt a poke on her shoulder and heard a voice, sounding faint and insistent, as if it was coming from far away.

"It's time to close," Mary said.

Carolyn sat up, stretched, and looked at the clock. It was ten minutes to five, which was closing time on Thursdays. She'd been lost for the last hour researching different websites and hadn't noticed the time passing.

"I think I'm going to stay for a while longer," she told Mary. "I'll lock up when I leave." She wasn't ready to face Everett after the events of the day. She also wanted to know more about the landfill project.

"We'll see you tomorrow then," Mary said. A shadow of concern passed over her face that Carolyn chose to ignore. She waved at Mary as the older woman walked through the detectors and out the glass doors.

For the next two hours, Carolyn clicked through websites that covered the landfill. She read testimony from tribal leaders and lawyers regarding the failed assembly bill. She studied maps of Gregory Canyon and reviewed the draft environmental impact report. As the sun went down and the library lights came on around her, Carolyn lost herself in the battle faced by Roy's tribe. Her fear and trepidation at being seen by Ben began to diminish as her sympathy grew for the plight of the Pala natives.

She had just clicked on a site owned by one of the environmental watchdog agencies, when the telephone rang.

"Rancho Library," she answered.

"I wondered if you'd run away somewhere." Everett's voice sounded kind and cheerful, although he must be worried if he was calling her at work.

"Everett, my gosh, I'm sorry. I decided to stay late to get some research done. What time is it?"

"Just seven-thirty. Are you going to be awhile or should I fix something for us?"

"Oh, don't bother with anything. I'll be home in a little bit."

There was an awkward pause.

"Are you—? Everett's voice was suddenly silent on the other end of the line. "Oh, never mind."

"Am I what?" Carolyn felt the icy hand of guilt circle her neck again.

"Nothing. It doesn't matter. See you in a bit." The buzz of the dial tone seemed to echo the hum of Carolyn's computer screen.

She hung up the receiver and was about to sign off on her computer when she noticed a line of copy at the bottom of the screen. She scrolled down to the final page of the environmental website. There, in the middle of a list of developers, was Inland Mining Company. Carolyn leaned closer to the computer screen to make certain she was seeing correctly. Next to the Inland listing, under the title "Principal Contact," was the name Everett Weedman.

EVERETT STUDIED THE PIECES OF GREEN PLASTIC SCATTERED ON THE tabletop before him. The broken fuselage had sat for three weeks while he drummed up the courage to try to piece it back together. He turned the desk lamp so its halogen glare focused directly on the broken bits, then picked up the two largest pieces and tried fitting them against each other. The edges were sharp and the uneven shards of the crushed plastic made gluing them difficult.

He held his breath as he worked, concentrating on keeping his hands steady. The strong smell of the cement and the fierce light seemed to close in around him, shutting out the world so thoroughly that it wasn't until the garage door banged shut that he turned around and saw her standing in the office doorway, appearing slightly disheveled and wild-eyed.

"I didn't hear you drive up," he said. He carefully set two just-glued pieces on a piece of wax paper lining the tabletop before turning his chair toward her.

Carolyn stared at him, saying nothing.

"Is something wrong?" Everett asked.

"You knew about the landfill," she said.

"What landfill?"

"The landfill on the Pala reservation. You knew about it, and you let it happen."

"Pala reservation? What are you talking about?"

"I can't believe you'd do it."

"Do what, Carolyn? You're not making sense." Everett ran his hand up to his forehead and wiped at the cold sweat that had formed there.

Carolyn gazed up at the ceiling, tears welling in her eyes. Her voice cracked a bit as she spoke.

"The thing is, you've always loved nature. At least, that's what you told me. 'It's the most important thing in the world, Carolyn.' That's what you used to say. But it was all lies. Everything about us is a lie." Everett watched as tears spilled down her cheeks.

"What is this about? You're upset, and I don't have a clue why." Everett heard a pleading tone come into his voice, but he didn't know how to stop it. "Tell me, what have I done to make you so angry?"

"You signed off on the landfill development. At Inland Mining. You let them put it in and now it's going to happen."

A light seemed to go off in the back of Everett's mind when she said the words "Inland Mining." He suddenly remembered visiting a canyon sight for the company about eight years back.

"Are you talking about the Gregory Consortium? That happened years ago. Why bring it up now?"

"Because its still happening and you were involved. How could you?" Her voice had become a whisper.

He remembered the whole deal now. The ballot measure and the battles with the community and the tribes. He hadn't liked working on it then. In fact, he'd put it out of his mind. It was one of the many land use incidents that had made him glad to be rid of his job when he was forced to retire.

"I do remember something about that," he said. "But you have to understand that I was working for a company, Carolyn. It was part of my job to preview that sight."

"So all your talk about environment and principles, was that all a lie, Everett?" Her voice was low and calm.

Everett drummed his hand on his wheelchair armrest, then glanced up at her. He couldn't believe they were having this argument.

"No, I've always meant what I said and you know it." He stopped and bit his lip, then spoke slowly and clearly, trying to keep his voice even. "Sometimes you have to sacrifice to make progress, Carolyn. That's something that I'm not sure you would understand."

"I don't know anything about making sacrifices?" Her voice, flat and hard as flint, made him flinch. She stared at him, her arms wrapped around her chest, her back straight and tall. "After giving up any hope of a career years ago to be your vision of the little woman? After all those years I sat home waiting for you, while you were out on business trips, while you were out fucking your best friend's wife?"

Everett froze, the long unspoken truth pinning him against the back of his chair. He watched as she swiped at a tear on one cheek.

"What I've sacrificed for our joke of a marriage would fill a landfill, Everett."

He looked at her a moment before turning the wheels of his chair so he faced the table top again. He could feel his heart thumping in his chest. The smell of cement rose up sharp in his nostrils, making him nauseous. He heard her clothes rustle as she walked away behind him and then the sound of the garage door slamming and the car engine turning over.

Everett sat still for a moment, trying to shake off the echo of her footsteps as she'd walked away. The long days of travel, the years with Lorena, the landfill deal—they were all in the past. He was through with all of that, they both were. At least that's what he'd let himself believe these last three years.

He reached for the two pieces he'd been trying to glue when Carolyn first came in, but they'd separated, strings of drying cement clinging like a spider's web between them. He tried to force them back together, but they wouldn't hold. Exasperated, he threw the pieces at the pile on the table, causing the entire mess to scatter onto the floor. With an angry slap, he snapped off the desk lamp and sat breathing quietly as he listened to the stillness of the gathering dusk.

CAROLYN FELT AS IF SHE WAS COMING APART, PIECE-BY-PIECE. Every inch of her body seemed to move on its own, as if her mind was a separate entity that none of the rest of her obeyed. Those were not her hands on the wheel, steering the car down the freeway. This was not her heart beating frantically in her chest. These were not her lips whispering the words, why, why, over and over as she watched the lights on the freeway signs flash by. She tasted salt as the tears slid down her cheeks and let them flow without wiping them. She heard the wheels of the car rumbling over the concrete below as if from far away. Moving forward into the dark summer night, she no longer knew who she was or where she belonged. All she wanted was to escape the pain and disappointment of the last twenty five years, the last two weeks, the last hour.

When the exit sign for the Pala reservation flashed before her, she almost missed it. Spinning the gravel under her tires, she veered onto the ramp, steered the car toward Roy's house, and parked in the driveway behind his white truck. The moon hung round and low over the rooftops and the crickets sang softly in the grass. Carolyn climbed out of the car and strode toward the door, letting her keys and purse fall from her hands as she knocked. She could hear Tóowish bark and then Roy opened the door, his face luminous and pale behind the screen. He said nothing when he saw her, then inched the door shut behind him so that only the two of them stood facing each other on the porch.

"You left so quickly today," he said. "I didn't know what to think."

"I'm sorry." Carolyn reached up and touched his brow, running her finger just above his right eye. She traced the hair that lined the side of his face and brought her hand down to his chest. He stopped her there, placing his hand over her own.

"I'm not sure what you want from me," he said. His eyes were bright and round in the dark.

"I just want to be here," she murmured. "With you." She rested her head against his shoulder for a moment and then looked up toward him. His shirt felt warm and he smelled of soap and cedar. He brought his hand to her hair then leaned down and kissed her, gently at first and then hard, without stopping. She felt the shock of his mouth on hers, so different and yet so familiar, rough and smooth at the same time. Her lips, her tongue and then her whole body melted against his and suddenly she came together, all of her responding as one entity, deliciously separate and yet whole and alive.

When he stopped and pulled away, she felt as if she were falling, caught short by the suddenness of losing contact with him.

"What is it?" she asked.

He gazed down at her in the darkness, stroking her hair with his hand.

"I don't know. I guess this is happening a little fast for me."

She didn't answer. Taking his hand, she turned and led him off the porch. On the grass at the far end of the yard they stood close, holding hands.

"When I came here tonight, I thought I was going to split apart," she said. "I don't know why I feel so safe here with you, but I do." She stopped and looked back at the house. "If you want me to leave, I will."

"I want you to be certain about this." He cupped her face in his hand, rubbing her cheek gently with his thumb.

"I am."

"Are you sure?"

"Yes." The word was just a whisper. As their arms entwined, Carolyn felt herself lean back into the soft grass. The ground seemed to wrap itself around her. She bent back like the supple branches of the trees. She felt herself lifted by the wind. She heard her own voice cry out, slowly at first and then quickly, lost in the echoing chorus of the crickets' song. She and Roy were one, bow and arrow, flesh and bone, earth and sky.

For the first time since she could remember, Carolyn felt no fear as a coyote sounded its long and lonely lament in the distance.

Chapter 5

Carolyn woke to the feeling of something sharp scraping against her left ankle. She reached down under the sheets, which were slightly coarser than her own at home, and felt near her foot. Her hand brushed against a thin point, like the tip of a needle. After pulling a bit she extracted a small white feather of goose down. She let it float to the floor and then looked up in the graying light that filtered through the curtains on the window. The alarm clock on the nightstand next to her blinked a warning signal of red sixes and zeros on its digital display. Carolyn felt a moment of panic as she realized that she'd been there all night. She had to get home.

On the floor lay Tóowish, stretched along the foot of the bed, her sides puffing in and out as she quietly snored. The only other sound was Roy's breathing, faint and shallow, next to Carolyn. It was too dim to see much of the rest of the room, but she remembered the wooden rocking chair in the corner with her clothes piled on the seat. She vaguely recalled dropping them there in the dark last night, when she and Roy had finally tiptoed into the house.

Careful not to disturb him, she pushed back the sheets, and tiptoed over to the chair to dress. The movement woke Tóowish, who raised her head and then sat up, tail thumping on the floor. The dog shook herself loudly, causing the tag on her collar to clatter just enough to force Roy to stir. Carolyn pulled her blouse over her head and then leaned down to pet the collie, quieting her. Tóowish calmly sat down next to Carolyn, who seated herself in the chair to put on her sandals. As she adjusted the straps on her right foot, she noticed a patch of tiny bumps on her ankle.

"You're awake." Roy sat up on his elbow, his hair falling over his shoulder, looking sleepy and relaxed. At the sound of his voice,

Tóowish began a drumbeat with her tail and then ambled toward the bed to be petted.

I'm sorry, I didn't mean to disturb you." Carolyn finished putting on her other sandal. "I have to go." She stopped to check the ankle on that foot. It, too, was covered with a series of finely raised blisters.

"What is it?" Roy asked.

"Nothing, just a rash. I'm allergic to grass. This happens all the time in the summer."

"I've got something for it. Wait here a minute." Roy sat up and rooted around on the floor next to the bed. Carolyn watched the muscles flex back and forth on his back as he pulled on a t-shirt. He stepped into a pair of shorts before padding out the door and returned a moment later, holding a small dish in his hand. Tóowish trailed him in and out of the room like a shadow.

"Let me see," he said, kneeling in front of the chair. He lifted the hem of Carolyn's jeans above the left foot and cradled her ankle in his hand. "This should help." He dipped a finger in the bowl and spread a wet pulpy mass over the bumps on each ankle.

"What is that?"

"Yerba mansa. My sister grows it in her yard. If you grind the roots and soak them in water, they're good for all kinds of skin irritations."

The poultice felt cool and soothing. He set the dish down on the floor and placed his hands on her legs. She ran her fingers over his hair and then pulled his head toward her and kissed first his forehead, then each cheek and, finally, his mouth. Roy reached up and kissed her back then tried to pull her toward the bed.

"I can't. I have to go." They stood above the blankets and sheets, holding each other close. "I don't want to leave."

"Stay."

"I can't. I'll call you."

She gave him one last hard kiss and pulled away, stumbling out the bedroom door and into the kitchen. On the table sat her purse and car keys. Carolyn stopped short when she saw them there. She remembered dropping both on the porch when she'd arrived last night, but she hadn't brought them inside. Roy hadn't either, she was certain. They'd crept into the house with their clothes and shoes in their hands. She surveyed the room and seeing no other signs of explanation, picked up her things and went out the front door.

The sun was rising, tinting the dawn sky with streaks of pink and gold. As Carolyn opened her car door, she noticed that Luke's motorcycle was parked on the other side of Roy's truck. It hadn't been there when she'd arrived last evening. Carolyn started the engine and backed the car out of the drive. Her heart beat hard in her chest and her stomach churned as she tried not to think about what she would face at home.

ROY EMERGED FROM THE SHOWER DRYING HIS HAIR WITH A TOWEL that smelled slightly of mildew. He glanced at the tiny bathroom and tried to remember if Carolyn had used it last night. He hoped not; the dust at the back of the sink and the gray soapy residue in the tub were evidence of how rarely he cleaned this room. He hung the towel on a hook behind the door and lathered his face with shaving cream. After wiping the steam off the mirror, he slowly dragged a razor over his chin and thought of Carolyn. Her visit had caught him by surprise, but it was a delicious one. She had seemed so vulnerable and beguiling when she appeared at his front door. All of his instincts, which had cautioned him to go slow with this married woman, had melted away at that moment. As he rinsed the cream off his face, he thought about how smooth her skin had felt, how wonderful it had been to hold her in his arms. Her tenderness and desire surprised him and delighted him at the same time.

As he searched for a clean shirt and jeans in his closet, he wondered if she was going to be all right when she got home. He didn't know much about her husband. What if the man was violent or abusive? He'd never been involved with a woman who was still married, although he'd dated a couple of divorced women in years past. He resolved to call Carolyn when he was finished teaching his classes at the college.

As he entered the kitchen, he found Luke sitting at the table, holding a bowl at arms length in front of Tóowish. The collie was lapping at what looked like the remnants of Luke's cereal. Roy noticed the hint of a smile on his son's face and realized that this dog had charmed him, too. Pulling a bowl from the cupboard, Roy nodded his head in Tóowish's direction.

"Isn't it a bad idea to give dogs milk?"

"There wasn't much in here. Besides, I don't think it'll hurt her. She seems agreeable to everything." Luke ran his hand gently over the dog's head and then moved to the sink to rinse out the bowl.

"When did you come in last night?" Roy asked. He figured he'd get the conversation about Carolyn over with as quickly as possible.

"Late," Luke said.

"Where were you?"

"At Donny's." Luke paused, still facing the sink. Without turning around he asked, "How was the white woman?"

Roy thought he heard a forced casualness in his son's voice.

"You mean Carolyn," Roy answered. "She's nice. I like her." He stopped a moment to crack open a new carton of milk. After pouring it on his cereal, he carried the bowl to the table and sat down. "I want you to be polite to her when she's here."

"You mean she's coming back?"

"Yeah. Got a problem with that?"

Luke paused to shut off the running tap water, then turned to face his father.

"Maybe I do. Maybe I'm tired of the fact that you spend so much time studying white man's history, teaching in the white man's world, chasing the white man's women. When are you going to realize that you're not a white man, Dad? You have your own culture, and you act like it doesn't exist." He grabbed a towel off the sink and slapped it over his hands.

Roy was silent for a moment.

"Do you really think that my seeing a mómgwish is going to change anything for our tribe?" Roy asked. "Does what I do in my private life make that much of a difference to the rest of our people?"

"It makes a difference to me."

"Hell, Luke, my father was white and it didn't matter. Not to my mother and not to me." He stopped and looked at his son. "You have white blood in you. Does that weaken your loyalty to the Pala nation?" Roy pushed his chair back in exasperation. "Of course it doesn't, son. You're still a true Luiseno and you're still your mother's child, whether I date a white woman or not."

Luke turned toward the sink and silently hung the dishtowel over the faucet. Roy knew that this non-response indicated acquiescence. He began to regret his outburst and tried a change of subject.

"Why don't you come down to the college with me today? It's still the first week of school. You could crash that Poly Sci class you were interested in," Roy said.

"No thanks. I've got things to do." Luke picked up his keys from a hook above the kitchen sink. "Wám´ nóo ´angéey, father."

"See you." Roy raised his hand in a goodbye gesture, but Luke had already disappeared through the doorway.

Carrying his bowl to the sink, Roy rinsed it and watched the water as it swirled down the drain. For so many years, he felt that his quest to study another culture had disappointed his father. Now he was disappointing his son. He wiped off the counter with a towel, then gathered his keys and canvas briefcase, which were lying on the sofa in the living room.

As he headed toward the front door, something small and black on the floor near the couch caught his eye. It was one of his socks, which he must have dropped when he and Carolyn came in last night. He reached down and grabbed it, stuffing it into his pocket before stepping outside. He wondered if Luke had seen it on his way out and then decided it didn't matter. What his son thought of his love life was not something he wanted to think about. All he wanted to focus on was Carolyn and what she might be doing at this moment. He tried to imagine her at home, facing her husband, but all he could conjure were images of her hair in the moonlight, the sound of the crickets chirping in the darkness, the scent of grass and white sage. He tried to shake the memories away but they lingered in the air before him as he started his truck and headed toward the highway.

CAROLYN STEPPED CAREFULLY OUT OF THE CAR TO AVOID A RABBIT hole at the side of the driveway. No matter how diligent Everett's efforts, the rabbits overran the Weedman's home on the canyon, appearing on the lawn as soon as the evening sky turned dusk in the summertime. This morning, she noticed that there were small, scattered piles of droppings along the edge of the concrete, looking almost intentional in their randomness, as if they were marking the way. Go forward, they seemed to indicate. Today Carolyn would rather have sunk down one of the holes.

She studied the house and noticed that nothing looked different, even though she, herself, felt changed and new. The front door had the same three chips in the enamel above the keyhole. The rose bushes hung their petaled heads below the windows. It was still hers and Everett's in name, the place that they had chosen together to start a life and a family. The family had never come, and their life was certainly not what they'd intended. Like the ivy that curled itself around the edges of the front porch, the disappointments had slipped into every crevice of their relationship. But the house was the same.

The key resisted a bit as she struggled to put it in the lock. As she wrestled with it, she pictured herself standing at Roy's front door again. The thought made her freeze, for just a moment, and then her knees went weak. That knock on his door had changed everything. For the first time in her life she felt outside herself somehow, as if she had shed her skin and emerged a new person, raw and radiant at the same time. There was a kernel of calmness deep inside her that she hadn't felt in years.

When the key finally ground into the lock, she paused a moment, then pushed open the door slowly, trying to make as little noise as possible. The house was still. Tiptoeing into the kitchen, she found Everett asleep in his chair in front of the table, the cordless telephone and the phone book in front of him. His head rested to the side, mouth slightly open and snoring softly. She noticed how shot with silver his hair was now, blazing white in the early morning light. Something about his position struck her as boyish and innocent; her heart wrenched at the thought of what last night must have been like for him.

Even though it was warm, she pulled a cotton throw from the couch in the family room and carefully laid it over his lap. The clock clicked rhythmically above the sink. The sound made her wish for a moment that she could reach inside and wind the hours back. How far would she take herself? To before Everett's accident? To Roy's house, under the moonlight? Even though there was no going back, the thought made her smile.

She crept upstairs to shower feeling almost like an intruder in her own house. Hopefully, Everett would sleep until Ben came and she could leave for work. After toweling her hair and putting on a blouse and skirt, she sat a moment on the bed and then leaned back onto the comforter, gazing up at the ceiling. She closed her eyes and remembered lying in the grass, looking up at the moon and listening to the crickets chirp. Roy had called them "chilíkmay," a word he'd whispered so softly into her ear that the feel of his breath had made her tremble.

She fingered the buttons on her blouse, then ran her hands over her stomach and breasts, feeling her body to see if it was really the same flesh and blood that had been hers last night. She wished she could capture the sensation of floating, of being transported above the moon. She wanted to bottle it up inside her, to dispense it in small drops every day for the rest of her life. The thought made her feel warm and drowsy, until with a start she realized that she was falling asleep and would be late for work if she lay there any longer.

When she got to the bottom of the stairs, Everett was no longer in the kitchen. His absence brought her up short until she noticed that the sliding glass door to the backyard was open. She stood in the doorway and watched as Everett wheeled himself along the sidewalk. The cotton throw sat across his shoulders like a king's robe, and he sat erect and vigilant, as if inspecting the fruits of the green and gold landscape before him. He held a handful of California poppies in his hand, their bright orange heads making a cheerful patch in the center of his lap. She walked down the ramp and stood at the base of it, feeling like a defendant in court, about to receive a sentence.

Everett spun his chair toward the door and noticed her for the first time. His face was blank. She came to his side and knelt down near the chair's right wheel so that her gaze was level with his.

"I'm sorry," she said.

Everett's face tightened. He said nothing.

"I shouldn't have run off like that. It was crazy and wrong and I'm sorry." She hung her head again. "I don't know what came over me last night."

"Where did you go?" His voice sounded hoarse, almost like a whisper. He gazed back at the canyon beyond the far wall of the fence.

"I drove around for awhile." She paused and looked at him. The urge to tell him what happened welled up in her and then she realized what that would do to him. To them. She couldn't bring herself to speak the words. Instead, she stretched the truth until it hurt. "I stayed with a friend," she continued. He wouldn't ask whom. There were only a handful of people it could be and Everett knew them all.

"I was worried when you didn't come home. I even called the Urgent Care Center to see if you'd showed up there." Everett fingered the petals of one of the poppies, then wiped his hand on the thigh of his pants. "I must have fallen asleep around midnight or so." He looked away. Carolyn noticed the salt and pepper stubble of his beard on the edges of his chin.

She placed her hand on his knee and rubbed her thumb against the soft denim fabric. She knew these clothes as if they were her own, had folded them a hundred times, had helped him put them on. The thought of her husband's life and what it had come to washed over her and she felt herself opening up to the pity and sadness that she thought she'd overcome after all these years. She wanted to cry, but she felt strangely empty. The emotion of the night before had drained her of all other feeling. Without thinking, she placed her head on his knee and waited, for what she wasn't sure. Judgment? Normally, he would have stroked her hair or said something soothing. Instead, he sat still as a stone, clutching the crumpled poppies in his lap. She finally raised her head and studied his face, but he was staring at the canyon, his jaw working as if he wanted to speak but was holding back.

Carolyn watched two white moths as they chased each other dizzily up and down the yard, then patted his knee one more time and stood. At that moment the doorbell rang. She grabbed the handles on his chair and began to push him toward the house. He brought a hand to the right wheel and stopped her.

"It's all right," he said. "I'll just sit out here awhile."

At that moment, Carolyn knew that her husband understood everything that had happened to her. Suddenly, she felt as if a chill wind had blown through the yard. A surge of energy coursed through her, causing the hair on her arms to stand up straight. Carolyn felt her nostrils flair and her stomach tighten. She resisted the urge to bolt and instead walked slowly up the ramp, poised to make her escape once she'd let Ben in the front door.

LUKE BENT DOWN AND STUBBED OUT HIS CIGARETTE IN THE GRAVEL on Courser Canyon Road. He checked his watch and gazed at the skyline above Mt. Gregory. Nancy Meza was supposed to meet him here at eleven o'clock. It was ten minutes after. He wondered if she would show.

Clumps of patchy scrub oak covered the hills and the sagebrush and thistle in the valley below were still in the sunlight. Even though it was Saturday morning, there were no hikers in the canyon and nothing stirred in the meadow at the base of the hills.

Luke paced a bit beside his motorcycle, then turned at the sound of a car coming up the road. It was Nancy in a silver Honda, the paint on the hood glistening under a recent wax job. She parked the car next to his bike and gave him a quick salute from behind the windshield. He could make out a small dream-catcher swinging from the rear view mirror as she rooted around in the seat and then emerged, a large black camera hanging from a strap around her neck and a yellow notepad in her hand.

"Míiyu, Luke." She held the camera away from her body and wrapped one arm around his neck to give him an enthusiastic hug. "I can't believe the last time I saw you was at graduation."

"Míiyu." Luke felt the thinness of her shoulder blades through her shirt. They separated and looked at each other for a moment, Nancy's brown face beaming. Luke noticed that she wore her hair in a chic black bob now, its shining plaits gently framing her high cheekbones and flat nose. She had been tall and gawky in high school, but standing here in crisp khakis, her long legs leading to a pair of shiny leather hiking boots, she seemed sophisticated and grown up.

"So, you're a big-time reporter now," Luke said.

"Yeah, right. I wouldn't call *The Corridor Times* big-time, but it's a step up from writing the high school newspaper." Nancy pulled the lens cap off her camera and stuffed it in one of her pockets, then checked the F-stop before looking back at Luke. She pointed the camera at him and snapped his picture. "I do get some freelance work from the *Union*. Mostly Native stuff."

"I know. That's why I called you." Luke put his hand on her elbow and pointed toward the base of Mt. Gregory. "Want to take a walk out there?"

"Sure. Here, hold this." Nancy handed him the tablet of paper and then rooted in her shorts pocket for a pen. "So this is where they're putting the landfill?" She reclaimed the notepad and jotted something across the top. Her feet crunched on the gravel next to his as they picked their way across the canyon.

Luke pointed to the left of the mountain. "Out there. They're planning about three hundred and eight acres. It'll hold a million tons of waste per year."

Nancy made notes on the tablet as she walked. "How long can they continue at that rate?"

"About thirty years." Luke swatted at a fly that buzzed by his head. "The impact report says they're using only seventeen percent of this entire site, which is about seventeen hundred and seventy acres. What the report doesn't say is that it's on sacred ground." He lifted his hand and pointed to an outcropping of rocks at the base of the foothills. "Remember the rock paintings in that grove? There are even more of them as you climb up the mountain."

"I remember seeing them as a kid." She held her hand up to her forehead and squinted into the sun. "Man, it's been a long time. Can you show me one?"

Luke nodded and led them toward the cluster of rocks. As they got closer, the buzz of katydids and blue bottle flies made the air hum. Luke motioned toward a low-lying copse of sumac and prickly pear cactus near the outcropping they had sighted earlier.

As they picked their way through the lower chaparral, he stole glances at Nancy. She seemed happy to be back on the res, her long arms swinging in rhythm with his as she walked. They had never been close in high school, but she was one of those girls who was friendly with everyone. Luke had thought about calling her after she moved to east county to go to San Diego State. He never had a reason to until recently, when the council members asked him to see if she would do a story on the environmental impact report. He was surprised that she remembered him when he called. Even more surprising was her willingness to do the story. When he'd called to get her number, her mother told him that Nancy was tired of being pegged as a Native American writer and wanted to specialize in more mainstream features.

"So, do you ever get back here to see your parents?" he asked.

"Once in awhile. Now that I'm working full-time, I don't come up as often."

She looked over and smiled at him as she walked. "What about you? Are you working now or still in school?"

"I took a couple of classes at Mira Costa, but didn't have much interest in them." Luke pulled at a sage bush as he walked by and rolled the leaf between his fingers. "I do some construction work here and there, when I can." He tossed the balled up leaf into the tall grass ahead of them. "It doesn't make my dad happy, but it keeps me busy."

"How is your dad?" Nancy asked. "I remember taking his history course the summer before I went to State. He's a great teacher." She gave a quick laugh and looked over at Luke. "All the girls in the class had a crush on him."

"Yeah, he's a real Casanova." Luke pointed to the boulders up ahead. "If we go around those rocks, the paintings are on the other side."

Now near the base of the mountain, they skirted a large outcropping of granite, the slabs' dark edges pointing jaggedly toward the sun. Luke led the way to a wooded area north of the giant boulders. The air was cooler here in the shade of the trees. They followed the edges of the stones, until they came to a cluster of larger rocks, fallen together so that their smooth gray sides were facing each other like walls in a hidden room. Luke bent down and ran his fingers along the edges of one slab, searching until he found a small opening in between the stones. He beckoned to Nancy, then crouched down and pointed toward a rectangular patch of reddish markings.

"Remember this one?" He reverently traced the rock outside the edges of the petroglyph with his finger.

Nancy crouched down beside him and studied the panel, which was barely visible in the dark gray background of the basalt. It was painted in a brick colored substance, the geometric pattern shaped in a maze-like series of connected letter H's. She lifted her camera and adjusted the lens. After snapping about six photographs, she stopped and wrote a few lines on her notepad. When she finished, she looked up at Luke, her brows drawn in a worried line below her forehead.

"There are more of these, aren't there?"

Luke nodded. "All the way up the mountain. I can show you some, if you like."

"It's all right." She bit her lower lip, then let out a sigh. "You know, I remember reading all the articles that came out a few years ago when the consortium formed and the proposition passed. Even though I grew up out here, it didn't hit me until now how beautiful this area is. Guess we take what's in front of us for granted, don't we?" She set her camera down and leaned back against one of the rocks. "So, what does the Council want me to do?"

"Get a story out on the sacredness of the site. Write about the rock art. Interview the elders on the ceremonies that still go on at Medicine Rock." Luke reached out and touched the edge of the petroglyph. "Help us remind everyone how much we stand to lose."

"Does the Council still meet once a month?"

"The second Tuesday. Can I tell them you'll come to the next meeting?"

Nancy was quiet a moment, then extended her hand. "I'll be there."

He took it and helped her up from the sandy ground. They walked quietly out of the sanctuary of the alcove and into the heat of the canyon. The sun was high above them. Luke recognized the soft chirp of a chickadee and the melodic trills of a group of cactus wrens as he and Nancy headed back through the chaparral.

When they reached Courser Canyon Road, she pulled her keys out of her pocket and opened her car door. After placing the camera and notepad inside, she turned toward Luke.

"So, how is it that someone your age is on our tribal council?"

"There are a few young people there. You can't hold office until you're twenty one, but you can be a member if you're eighteen." He put his hands in his pockets and ran his foot over the gravel on the road. "To tell you the truth, my aunt talked me into it. I guess she thought it would be good for me to do something constructive besides fight with my old man."

"Yeah? Well, your aunt's a smart lady," Nancy said. "Tell her I said so." She stepped into the car and waved at him through the window as she drove away. Luke raised his hand in farewell and watched until the vehicle disappeared down the road. He wondered if she was seeing anyone, but hadn't found the nerve to bring it up. Now he'd have to ask around.

He straddled his motorcycle and adjusted his helmet before snapping on the strap. Gunning the gas pedal, he pulled out on Courser Canyon and headed toward Ortega Street. He was glad to turn away from all the traffic on Mission Avenue, the line of cars ahead of him streaming toward the casino parking lot. When he pulled into his driveway at home, he noticed the white woman's car parked next to his father's truck. He felt his stomach clench in a hard knot as he eased back on the throttle and turned off the engine. He didn't know why this relationship bothered him so much. There was nothing especially bad about this woman, yet he sensed somehow that her being here would have a negative impact on his family's future.

As he put his key in his pocket, he heard voices coming from the open screen door to the living room. He stopped just outside the gate and listened.

"I'd wanted to tell you about him. I just never had the chance, really." The woman, Carolyn, was speaking. Luke thought her voice sounded quiet and sad. "He's a good man," her voice continued. "He would never hurt me or betray me. Not the way I've betrayed him." There was a pause. "But I found out something the other day that made me hate him for the first time ever." Another pause. "It has to do with you."

"With me?" Luke heard the puzzlement in his father's voice.

"You know the canyon you took me to the other day? When we talked about the landfill?" Her voice sounded shaky. "I spent some time at work researching the area and the proposition. While I was looking through the articles on the consortium, I found the name of my husband's company on the list of members." She paused again. "Roy, Everett was one of the principals who helped push the legislation through. He was an engineer at Inland Mining when the consortium was formed."

"Your husband was involved in the landfill planning?" Roy's voice sounded small and far away.

"Yes, I'm certain about it. I confronted him when I got home last Thursday, and he confirmed that it's true. I still can't believe it. We were both environmental activists when we first met. I never would have thought that he could be involved in something like this." Her voice trailed off.

Roy must have said something to her, but Luke couldn't make it out. He stepped away from the gate and stood in the driveway, his hands in his pockets, the tightening at the pit of his stomach coming back. So his instincts were right. This woman was married to one of the developers. Luke felt his face flush with anger as the muscles knotted on his arms. What was wrong with his father, that he would pick this kind of person for a relationship? As Luke turned toward the house, he heard voices again, this time from inside his head.

"*Néqpi*," they whispered. Defend yourself. Luke closed his eyes and tried to shake the voices away, but they persisted. "*Kwáavichu cháami chóo'onmi.*" Protect us all.

Luke rubbed at his eyes with both hands and then lifted his face to the sun. After silently voicing a prayer to Taacwic, he climbed back on his motorcycle and gunned the engine hard. His tires spit gravel toward the house as he sped out the driveway into the road leading to the mission.

EVERYTHING SEEMED TO BE SLOWLY SLIPPING OUT OF CONTROL.

First his wife was acting strangely, lashing out at him in anger and disappearing whenever she had a free moment. Then, at his physical therapy session yesterday he'd fallen, landing hard on his left elbow and wrist. The incident had left him feeling emotionally as bruised and sore as his arm. So much so, that Everett cringed just thinking about it. Now, as he surveyed his yard on Saturday morning, he saw that what had started out as a small corner of chewed grass had become an enormous patch of raw dirt. The rabbits had eaten their way through the west end near the fence, turning the lush green carpet into the equivalent of a cow pasture.

Everett rolled his chair along the periphery of the lawn and noted the brown stubble where the grass was chewed to the roots. Even though he'd tried to thwart them by lacing the turf with naphthalene pellets and snail bait, the rabbits had simply moved, undeterred, to newer portions of the yard. On some evenings, he'd watched them emerge from the canyon and hop from spot to spot, oblivious as they gnawed away at his manicured lawn. Their latest efforts had expanded all the way into its center. Everett felt helpless as he surveyed the most recent assault on his main source of solace.

A shadow fell across the scarred grass and Everett raised his head and squinted into the sun. Ben stood beside him, cradling a basketball in his hands.

"How about some one-on-one?" Ben slapped at the ball, a look of encouragement on his face.

Everett ignored the question. "Look what these bastards have done," he said, waving his hands toward the damaged corner of the lawn. "A few more weeks and this yard will look like a strip mine."

"Well, you could turn it into a baseball diamond," Ben said. "You know, build it and they will come." He smiled at his own joke. Everett didn't respond to the humor.

"Nothing would show up here but rodents," he said.

"All the more reason to shoot some hoops," Ben responded. "Come on, Mr. Weedman, it'll help you forget about your gardening problems."

They headed out of the yard through the wooden gate and down the sidewalk toward Creek Village Park. Even though it was only ten o'clock in the morning, the sun hovered above them, high and hot in the sky. Everett winced every time the basketball hit the sidewalk. Normally he loved the slap of the leather against the concrete, but today the sound seemed to slam against his skull whenever Ben bounced the ball.

Ben loped alongside Everett's wheelchair, methodically dribbling the basketball with the careful attentiveness of someone who has never played the sport. Everett tried not to smile at his caregiver's clumsiness. He remembered his own first attempts at shooting baskets when he was a small boy. His father had encouraged him, shouting "Come on, Evvie, that's the way," each time the ball had thunked against the rim. When he finally made his first successful shot, his father had jumped up and down and hollered as if he'd made the winning points at an NBA playoff game. Everett remembered the feel of the ball in his hands, his fingers pushing against the rubbery leather as he heaved it toward the basket. When it circled the rim and slid through the net, he'd felt victorious and capable of anything. As he and Ben waited on the corner for the traffic signal to change, he wished he could recapture a shred of that feeling again.

They crossed the street in silence. Everett maneuvered his chair through the access ramp at the park entrance and followed Ben along the central field toward the courts at the eastern end. The scent of newly mown grass hung in the air and the trees seemed to hum with the sound of the traffic on Creek Village Road. A group of small girls chased a soccer ball in one corner of the lawn, while a Middle Eastern family picnicked at the far side near the canyon. Everett stopped a moment and studied them. A tall dark-haired man helped two boys set up a flying model rocket, while two women set out plates and cups on a blanket on the grass. The older woman wore a billowy silk sari, its pink and yellow folds gently moving along with her in brilliant contrast to the green and brown hues of the canyon foliage. There was a gracefulness and unity to the movements of the two women. When the man left the boys and rejoined them, the younger one held her hand out to him as he sat down next to her on the blanket. Everett felt a strange mix of longing and envy as he watched them. It took Ben, yelling at him from the edge of the court, to distract him from his reverie.

Normally, Everett would have enjoyed humoring Ben in his attempt to play a game of ball, but today he could have done without it. Ever since Carolyn had accused him of betraying the Native Americans in the landfill deal, the space between them had been full of tension. These last few days, Carolyn had been silent and distracted, barely speaking to him when they were together. This morning, she'd left suddenly, saying she had to go somewhere and would be back later in the afternoon. Her absences weighed hard on Everett even more than the silences between them.

Watching Ben as he gamely tried to toss the ball toward the rim, Everett took a deep breath and rolled his chair through the chain link gate leading into the court. Under the basket at the far end, a group of teenage boys grunted and swore as they wrestled each other in a half-court pick-up game. Everett rolled past them in his chair and lifted his hands toward Ben. When he got the ball, he bounced it a few times, noticing that it needed some air, and took aim toward the open net. The shot swirled inside the rim and ricocheted out. Ben chased after it, then ran back smiling.

"Nice shot. Try again."

Everett weighed the ball a moment in his hands and then tossed it up, this time using the old flick of the wrist that his coach had taught him in high school. It arched up in the air and then swished through the net, barely making a sound before hitting the concrete below. Ben recaptured it and dribbled down the court a few times before heaving up a clumsy shot that bounded off the edge of the backboard. He caught the ball again and tossed it to Everett.

"Best two out of three?"

Everett hefted the ball lightly in his hands and squinted in the sunlight at Ben.

"You're humoring me today, aren't you?" He heaved the ball up toward the backboard and watched as it banked through the net. Ben caught it and tossed it back.

"What do you mean?"

"Exactly what I said. You're feeling sorry for the old man. I can tell." Everett aimed the ball at the hoop and watched as it careened off the edge of the rim. "Did Carolyn put you up to this?"

Ben fished the ball out from the corner of the court and then stood a moment, bouncing it carefully in front of the basket. He looked up at Everett.

"Mrs. Weedman doesn't talk much to me anymore," he said, keeping his eye on the ball as he dribbled it on the concrete. "I don't know why. She's just been different lately."

Everett was quiet. Then he reached over and stole the ball from Ben on an upward bounce.

"It's okay," he said. "She doesn't talk to me lately, either." He cradled the ball to his chest for a moment and then tossed it back to Ben. "I guess you could say that we've hit a rough patch in our marriage."

"I'm sorry," Ben said. He stood a moment, tracing the curves with his finger as he balanced the ball in his hand.

"It's alright. Not much you can do about it. Not much I can even do about it."

"Have you talked to her at all?" Ben asked.

Everett sat still in his chair, studying the canyon beyond the court's chain link fence. "We spend most of our time avoiding each other," he said. He noticed the look of concern on Ben's face and something about it made him feel guilty, as if he was unloading his personal burden onto the shoulders of an innocent bystander. He gave Ben what he hoped seemed like a broad smile and held out his hands. "Don't worry about it," he said as Ben tossed him the ball. "We'll be alright."

Ben seemed to be struggling to smile back. Everett shifted the ball around in his hands and then released it lightly up into the air. It floated toward the basket and fell through the net with a delicate swoosh. The satisfaction of making the shot was marred by the sudden ache in his left wrist. Thoughts of yesterday's fall reminded him that he was no longer the man he used to be.

"Let's head back," he said.

Everett kept the ball in his lap as they retraced the path to his house. When they reached the driveway, Ben dug into his pockets for his car keys.

"I hope the rest of your weekend is okay," he said. He stood for a moment, as if there was something else he wished to say.

"What is it?" Everett asked.

Ben shrugged. "Nothing," he said. "I was thinking about something I wanted to ask Mrs. Weedman. I'll wait until I see her on Monday."

Everett thought this was odd, since Carolyn seemed to have little interaction with Ben lately. He let it go, though, and lifted his hand in farewell as Ben backed his VW down the driveway.

Once he was inside the house, Everett stopped a moment to listen to the stillness. The empty rooms seemed to almost reverberate, as if they were bound and couldn't speak. He went into the study and spent some time trying to work on the Huey model, but the effort to pull out the paints and brushes was too much for him. He finally threw the pieces down and wheeled himself to the gun rack near the sliding glass door. He pulled out his rifle and rolled his chair outside into the glare of the noonday sun. The August heat bore down on him like a laser gun. For a few moments he sat with his eyes closed, his face toward the sky, feeling the full force of the solar rays. He tried to imagine what it would be like to burn alive. How long would he be able to stand it, the flames scorching his skin and the smell of burning flesh filling his nostrils?

When he opened his eyes, he caught a movement in the far corner of the yard. Without thinking he shouldered his rifle and took aim in that direction. A gardenia bush quivered below the palm tree in the corner and then something small and brown emerged. The gun seemed to fire itself and Everett felt an incredible rush of energy course through his body. It was immediately replaced with an overwhelming sense of shame as he realized that he had hit some kind of animal, which rested, immobile, beneath the palm tree. He wheeled his chair closer and saw that it was a squirrel. It lay curled up on one side, its tiny head crushed by the blow of the bullet that had pierced its eye. Everett wanted to reach out and touch it, to run his fingers over the soft fur, but he didn't move. He sat, instead, for a long time in the gnawed, brown patch of remaining grass, keeping watch over this unlikely victim and wishing he could take its place.

CAROLYN PICKED HER WAY THROUGH THE CHAIRS AT THE STUDENT center and across the lawn to the back end of the Mira Costa campus. Even though it was a Wednesday, when she would normally have been working, she had traded some hours with Mary so she could surprise Roy with a picnic lunch. On her left shoulder hung a canvas backpack, stuffed with sandwiches and apples and a couple of bottles of water. The water made a soft swishing noise as she followed the concrete walkway leading to the back cluster of buildings where his History 140B class would be finishing in a few minutes. She found the humanities cluster and followed the signs to H6. Carefully opening the back door of the classroom, she stepped inside and leaned quietly against the back wall.

Roy stood facing the blackboard at the front of the room, his hair tied in a ponytail that hung like a question mark across his back. On the board were three columns in white chalk. Squinting, Carolyn could make out a list of names under the heading "Intellectualism," including Thomas Hobbes, John Locke, Thomas Hardy, Robert Boyle and Sir Issac Newton. Under the heading "Economics," she read that in 1603, England had exported raw wool and cloth; in 1714 began the development of trade and colonization, along with the import of root crops, tea, coffee, sugar, and tobacco. Roy was standing in front of the third heading, entitled "Culture." Carolyn sidled over to an empty seat in the back row and sat down to listen.

"In 1611, the King James version of the Bible was released," Roy stated. The tiny piece of chalk he held made hard tapping noises as it danced across the chalkboard. "Johnson and Donne were writing poetry, and Shakespeare emerged as one of the popular Jacobean playwrights. Milton wrote *Paradise Lost* and Bunyon finished *Pilgrim's Progress*. Other writers, like Dryden, Swift, and Defoe, were emerging as major figures in literature. Van Dyke was the court painter to Charles I and Inigo Jones was the architectural painter of the royal family." Carolyn watched as Roy turned toward the class.

"Sir Christopher Wren, who I know some of you remember from our 140A class, designed the new St. Paul's Cathedral. We'll see some photographs of his work when we meet next time." Carolyn could see that Roy made eye contact with each of his students before looking back at her. Although he gave no outward gesture, she thought that his face lit up a bit in recognition.

A student's hand shot into the air.

"Wasn't there a lot of controversy over James' being crowned when Elizabeth died?"

"Yes, actually, there was," Roy answered. "When Elizabeth's reign ended, the country was at war and there was a great deal of discontent. Everyone had high hopes for James. The courtiers expected more patronage, while the Puritans hoped for an increase in Calvinism. Since he was the son of Queen Mary, the Catholics expected he would be lenient toward them. Merchants hoped the war with Spain would end so more trade could go on, although some merchants were profiting from the war." Roy stopped and turned around to glance at the clock at the front of the room. "We'll talk more about that and how James ended the Spanish war when we meet next time." He picked up a notebook, paging through it a moment. "Go ahead and read the next twenty pages in your text. Be prepared to discuss *The Law of the Monarchies* and what it has to say about the divine right of kings. See you next week."

Carolyn watched Roy while listening to the slapping of books as they were closed and the whirr of backpacks being zipped shut. As the class shuffled out of the room, she noticed that he waited to gather his things, nodding to some of the students, making brief comments to others as they passed his desk. When the last student left, he gave Carolyn a big smile before leaning forward to gather the books in front of him.

"Planning on crashing this course?" he asked.

"I don't know. The teacher seems pretty hard core to me." She smiled, then slid out of her seat and stepped slowly up the aisle until she stood in front of the podium. Being this close to him made her heart beat fast. "I actually came to see if you'd like to have lunch. It's not very fancy, but I brought some sandwiches and stuff." She looked up at him. "If you're free."

He had moved away from the lectern and was standing next to her, a smile forming below his always-serious eyes. She noticed how soft and brown they were and forced herself not to reach out and touch him. She knew that if she did, she wouldn't be able to stop herself from going further.

"I could go for some sandwiches. And stuff, too," he added, a look of amusement on his face. "There's a grassy spot right outside the library. We can eat out there." He reached for her hand and led her out into the sunshine. The August sky was full of cottony clouds and the sun burned high above the Oceanside campus. Carolyn felt lightheaded and young again as they passed individual students milling along the concrete walkway. When they reached the open area next to the student center, Roy pointed toward a shaded area on the lawn. They sat beneath a small carrotwood tree and pulled out the items in Carolyn's backpack. Although it was warm, there was a slight breeze in the air and the sound of traffic on Hwy 76 hummed faintly in the distance.

The two of them unwrapped their sandwiches and opened their water bottles. .

"So, did you like the history lesson?" Roy asked.

"Yes, very much." Carolyn watched as Roy took a bite of his sandwich. "I wonder, though, why you teach British history and not your own."

Roy smiled. "By my own, I suppose you mean Native American history?" He set his sandwich down and gazed out at the college lawn. "Well, it's complicated for me. I've always loved stories about England. Ever since I was a boy, I was fascinated with all of it—the pageantry of its kings and queens, the wars at home and overseas, the British navy. As I grew older, the changes that took place in the United Kingdom over the centuries resonated with me. I think maybe because of what our own people went through." He looked at Carolyn. "I'm sure you're familiar with our history and the trail of tears, when the Supreme court forced the Cupas out of Warner Springs a hundred years ago. Even though my family came from the Luiseno tribe, which was already here, the Pala nation has had to struggle to survive. I always felt that studying the history of England might help me understand my own."

He pulled at a small clump of grass and then twirled a leaf in his fingers. Carolyn noticed the set look on his face and wondered if his choice of profession had made living on the reservation hard for him.

"Do your friends and relatives like that you're a British history professor?"

"Some of them don't. My father never did. Neither does my son." He tossed the bit of grass aside. "But most of those who know me understand that I have a lot of pride in my tribe and what we're doing for our people. Take the casinos, for example. Most Californians are against having them in their communities. They believe that they're symbols of a lot of evils in our culture—gambling, alcoholism, financial greed. What they don't realize is that our tribe will use that money to make itself better. We're building a new administrative center and sports complex for our citizens. We're giving jobs to a lot of people who didn't have work. We're also giving them hope." He stopped and picked up his sandwich again. "I'm not against any of that. But we have to accept that some of the progress we make is going to change things. Our land will look different. We'll lose some of our tribalism. We'll become more mainstream." He paused, as if searching for words. "More assimilated. Some of our members don't like that."

"Like Luke?" Carolyn asked.

"Yes," Roy answered. "Like Luke."

There was silence for a moment, and when Roy spoke again, his voice was quiet.

"He overheard our conversation last Saturday."

Carolyn felt her spine stiffen. She knew that Luke didn't like her.

"How do you know that?" she asked.

"I thought I heard his motorcycle start up outside while we were talking. He asked me about it later when he came in." Roy twirled the cap on his water bottle back and forth. "It wasn't a good conversation. But then, most of them aren't."

"What did he say?"

Roy looked up at her, his eyes serious and his mouth set in a firm line.

"He doesn't like that I'm seeing you. Partly because you're white, partly because Luke is never happy about anyone I'm seeing." He picked up an empty sandwich wrapper and crumpled it into a ball. "He's also pretty immersed in fighting the landfill deal. Your husband's involvement doesn't sit well with him."

"It doesn't sit well with me, either," Carolyn said. She put her hand on Roy's arm. His skin felt warm and soft. "I don't want to cause problems between you and your son."

She stopped and bit her lip. "Luke seems so intense and angry. Has he ever been seen by a mental health professional?"

Roy said nothing at first, then leaned back on his elbows, his gaze suddenly distant and serious.

"After his mother died, he was pretty depressed for awhile. We both were." Roy stopped a moment. "My sister and I talked about taking him to see someone, but we were worried about what people on the reservation would think." He glanced up her. "It's not something that's embraced by our culture. We prefer to turn to our tribal leaders and our ancestors for help when family members are troubled."

Carolyn nodded, encouraging him to continue.

"He's been better the last few years," Roy said, "although lately the landfill deal has preoccupied him more and more. I'm sorry he was rude to you the other day."

Carolyn realized that this was a difficult subject for Roy. It must have been hard for him raising a son alone after losing his wife. Reaching into the backpack, she pulled out an apple and held it for a moment, rubbing her finger across the shiny red peel. Of course Luke would hate her. She hated herself for what she was doing to her husband and her marriage. This thought reminded her that while she was here, with another man, Everett sat home alone. A mental picture of him pushing himself forward in his chair buzzed in her head, like an angry bee trying to bump its way through a windowpane. Carolyn struggled with the rush of guilt she felt and then pushed the image aside.

With a firm twist, she pulled the stem from the top of the fruit and held out the apple to Roy. He cradled it in his hand for a moment.

"Please don't blame yourself for anything Luke says or does," Roy continued. "He fights a lot of demons. And if anyone is responsible for them, it's me."

Carolyn watched as Roy raised the apple to his lips and bit into it. No, she thought, the responsibility doesn't belong only to you. And as for demons, she felt certain that some of them hovered above her own head at this very moment, watching over her and her lover as they shared forbidden fruit in their own unlikely garden.

THE AIR IN THE GARAGE HUNG THICK AND HOT AS LUKE POKED among the dust-covered crates stacked along the perimeter. He felt a thin line of sweat slithering down the center of his back like a snake as he peered through the dim light at the labels on each box in the stack. After rummaging through three of them, he finally located the one he wanted. It was a medium-sized box, coated with spider webs, his grandfather's first name, "Lucas," scrawled across one end in thick black marker. After brushing off the dirt on the top, he carried it to the corner of the garage, seated himself on a pile of carpet remnants, and pulled the box top open.

Inside lay a bundle of letters, tattered from years of being opened and refolded. Luke knew their contents well. As a child, he had followed his grandmother into the garage and watched as she sat with this same bundle, pouring over the thin pages, her brown hand covering her mouth as she silently read. Luke had snuck into the garage in later years to read through them himself, marveling at his grandfather's strong hand and the stories he told about working in the Conservation Corps as a young man in Tennessee. Luke knew him only through these letters, for his grandfather had succumbed to a brief and brutal bout with lung cancer the year his only grandson was born.

Luke set the letters aside and pulled out a photograph that lay on top of a small carton at the bottom of the box. He spent a moment studying the image. The eyes gazing back at him were those of his grandfather, standing next to another young man in a forest of pine trees. The two youths slouched next to each other, wearing identical work shirts and baggy pants. Lucas Washburn grasped the wooden handle of a shovel in his one hand, looking defiantly at the camera, the stub of a cigarette hanging from his mouth. Luke had poured over this picture a number of times, running his finger across the glossy black and white surface. He knew that his father had never gotten along with his grandfather and guessed that he and the older man would have been friends.

He set the photograph aside and reached inside the box to retrieve what he had been looking for all along. It was a smaller box the size of a cigar carton, its black cover faded to a dull slate color. Luke fingered the yellowed label on the top, then lifted the cover and removed his grandfather's Colt .45 pistol from inside. It lay heavy in his hand, its blued finish gleaming slightly in the dim garage light.

The checkered grip in his palm reminded him of the times his father had taken him out to the canyon to shoot when he was a boy. On one occasion, they had hiked into the hills, carrying this same gun in an army surplus backpack. When they reached an open field, Roy had pointed to a large boulder at the edge of the meadow about thirty yards away.

"Take a bead on that rock," he'd told Luke.

Luke remembered lifting the pistol and squinting his left eye to gaze down the sight on the barrel. When he had the stone in focus, he looked up at his father.

"What do you see?" Roy asked.

Luke shrugged. "Just a rock," he answered.

"Does it look the same through the gun site?"

Luke squinted past the gun again, until the rock was right between the fixed points of the site.

"It looks small," he said.

Roy took the pistol from his son's hand and balanced it in his palm a moment. He looked over at Luke.

"I want you to remember that," Roy said. "Everything is small when it's at the other end of a gun." They had gone on to set pinecones on the rock for target practice. Every time Luke sighted down the barrel, his father's statement echoed in his mind.

The words came back to him as he sat in the dusty heat and gazed at the pistol in his hand. Luke closed his eyes and leaned back against the row of boxes. More words sounded in his head, but this time they were the voices of his ancestors.

"*Ngé''i*," they whispered. Revenge. "*Háal póyk.*" Find him.

Luke waited for more, but the words faded in a breath of air.

When he opened his eyes, he was still gripping the pistol in his hand. It felt heavy and warm from the heat of his palm. He laid it on the ground and placed the factory carton, letters, and photograph back in the cardboard box. After returning the box to its place along the garage wall, he retrieved the pistol and stepped outside into the August sunlight. His mission was clear. The white woman's husband would know what it was like to be small at the other end of his gun.

Chapter 6

The lizard appeared suddenly on the corner of the porch, just as Delores knocked on her brother's door. She watched as the small reptile paused for a moment, its tiny head bobbing slightly before it darted across the concrete just past the tips of her shoes.

Qaṣilla, she thought. *–Pómkilawish lóovilut*. Lizards, for her, were always a sign of good luck.

She heard muted sounds and then a shuffling noise before the door opened. Inside the doorway, her brother's dog barked sharply behind a small white woman with curly brown hair.

"I was looking for Roy," Delores said. "Is he home?"

"Oh, yes, he's in the shower." The woman appeared flustered for a moment, then seemed to recover herself as she pulled the door open wide. "Please, come in."

Delores strode inside, holding two plastic shopping bags out in front of her as if they were leading the way to the kitchen. She dumped the bags on the counter, then turned to study the woman who had followed her and taken a seat at the table. This must be Roy's new girlfriend. Delores smiled a little to herself. She could see why Luke had called her a ghost.

"I haven't seen my brother take too many showers while company was here," she said. The white woman sat up straight at the word "brother," which made Delores smile again. Perhaps Roy hadn't told his girlfriend that he had a sister.

"You must be Delores," the woman said. "I'm Carolyn Weedman." She held out her hand and then dropped it in her lap when Delores didn't move to take it. "I'm a friend of Roy's," she continued a little lamely, as if she wasn't certain how to label herself.

Delores ignored the last statement and busied herself emptying the bags. She pulled out a number of large tomatoes and knobby cucumbers, rolling them into a pile on the sink. Out of the corner of her eye, she saw that the woman sat quietly at the table, perched on the edge of her chair as if she was ready to flee. *Tóovit*, she thought. Scared rabbit.

"The tomatoes came in so fast this summer they outnumbered the worms," Delores said, holding up an enormous beefsteak variety in her hand. "Do you garden?"

Carolyn looked surprised. "No, not much," she answered. "My husband used to enjoy it, but he doesn't-" her voice trailed off.

Something in her manner made Delores feel sorry for her. This rabbit was *úmi*, she thought to herself. Trapped.

"Here," Delores said. "Try this." She plunked the large tomato on the table in front of Carolyn and then sat down across from her, first grabbing a cucumber for herself along with a shaker of salt. Both women ate silently for a moment, listening to the faint sounds of water running in the rear of the house.

"So, you must have met my nephew, Luke, by now," Delores said. "What do you think of him?"

"I don't really know," Carolyn replied. "We haven't had much of a chance to talk." She pulled at the edge of the tomato where she had taken a bite. The red juice ran in thin rivulets over her fingers. Suddenly straightening her shoulders, she looked directly at Delores and continued. "I don't think he likes me," she said. "In fact, I'm pretty certain of it."

Smart rabbit, Delores thought. This one might last longer than the others.

"You're probably right about that," she said. She took a hard bite of her cucumber and crunched loudly for a moment before continuing. Then she gave Carolyn a quick wink behind her thick glasses. "But you're not the first one he didn't like."

Carolyn sat up straight in her chair at this remark, a weak smile on her face. Delores felt another wave of sympathy for this woman, who obviously felt uncomfortable facing a new family member.

"Be careful around Luke," she said, tapping the saltshaker slowly over the remaining bit of vegetable in her hand. "He's like the *šóowut* rattlesnake—okay while he's sleeping, but quick to strike when he's disturbed." She popped the last bite into her mouth and chewed noisily.

Carolyn seemed to catch her breath at this. She looked as if she was about to speak when Roy appeared in the kitchen door. Delores noticed the quick glow that lit Carolyn's face when her brother entered the room and knew that trouble was coming. She felt it as surely as the sound of the drumbeats that were beginning to pound at the back of her head.

"*Míiyu*, sister," he said. "I wasn't expecting you today." He moved toward Carolyn and stood behind her chair.

"*Míiyu*," Delores replied. "I know." She looked over at Carolyn, who was staring at the floor. "There are some tomatoes for you on the sink." Delores rose from the table, grabbing the saltshaker and placing it back in its usual spot on the counter. She stopped in front of Carolyn.

"Watch out for rattlesnakes," she said. Turning to her brother, she added,

"*'Óm 'axánnax.*" You, too.

By the time Delores reached the front door, the pounding in her head was so loud it made her feel dizzy. As she stepped out on the porch, she looked for the lizard, but it was nowhere to be found.

IT ALWAYS STARTED WITH A BITTER TASTE, AS IF SOMEONE HAD placed a dime on his tongue. On some occasions a sound set it off, like the screeching of a tire or the honk of a horn. Even a simple noise, like the creak of a door closing, could send Everett into a trance. Today, sitting before the third story window while he waited for his physical therapy session, it was the knock of a bird against the window. Everett had jumped at the loud thud and the fluttering of wings directly opposite him. He tasted the familiar metallic sensation in his mouth and suddenly he was back in

Mexico three years ago. The steering wheel was hard under his hands and he remembered hunching over it, barely keeping his eyes on the road, his breath hot and sour-tasting. Carolyn sat rigid beside him in the front seat of their Toyota Camry, her eyes staring straight ahead, her hands clasped together in her lap, as if in prayer.

They were returning to San Diego after meeting his coworker, Warren Fox and Warren's wife Lorena, for dinner at La Tapitia Restaurant in Puerto Nuevo. Once he'd eased the car onto the highway, Everett gripped the steering wheel and glanced at Carolyn, who did not return his look. He recognized the signals. When she was angry with him, she froze him out with a wall of silence, withdrawing to a place inside that sometimes took him days to break through. Normally, he could wait her out, but the margaritas he'd drunk made him impatient and edgy. He knew his behavior at dinner had bothered her. Part of him didn't care; he felt obligated to be more himself and less the good husband when he was with his friends. But another part of him wanted forgiveness. The past Monday had been the tenth anniversary of the death of their son and he knew the memory was still tugging at both of them.

"Maybe the checkpoint won't be too bad at this hour," he said.

Carolyn was silent, her gaze never wavering from the direction of the windshield. He swallowed hard and tried again.

"It was good to see Warren and Lorena." Everett regretted the words as soon as he spoke them. Carolyn had said once that the Foxes were like perpetual college students, forgoing children by choice and living from party to party. Everett felt that her assessment was unfair. Warren was a man's man, focused on sports and heavy equipment, skipping lightly over anything that reeked of deeper feelings. Most of the engineers Everett worked with were like that; they spent their days figuring out how to carve out the earth. Dynamite and Ashland Scrapers were their weapons of choice. They had no tolerance for anything they deemed weak or insipid.

Everett steered the car through the darkness, the tires pushing against the Mexican pavement with a dull, thrumming sound.

Carolyn still hadn't spoken. He wondered how long this bout of silence would last.

She had not said much during dinner. Warren had tried to shake her out of her quiet mood.

"Come on, Carolyn. Have another Corona; it'll lighten you up a little," he'd urged, when the waitress returned to take their order. The restaurant had been dark, the glow from the bare red bulb over their table seeming to pulsate above the spinning blades of a nearby ceiling fan. In the dim light, Everett had watched his wife's back stiffen and knew the effect Warren's words had on her.

"Leave her alone, Warren. Maybe she doesn't want to lighten up," Lorena said, with the slight Castilian lisp that Everett always found intriguing. He remembered her shaking her dark hair so that it seemed to swirl around her shoulders, making her look exotic and dangerous. "Maybe she just wants to be left alone."

Glancing at his wife now, Everett knew that Lorena had been right. Being alone was something of a sport for Carolyn. She had become good at it.

The lights on the other side of the freeway seemed to fly up toward them and then melt away as they moved forward into the night.

"Why do you try so hard?" Her words, spoken quietly against the backdrop of the tires rolling against the road, startled him. He knew exactly what she meant, but his pride wouldn't let him acknowledge it.

"What do you mean? Try so hard at what?"

"At proving to everyone that you're important, that you matter." She spoke without turning her head, her eyes seeming to focus on the tiny drops of mist that were beginning to condense on the windshield.

As he was about to answer the right front tire caught a dip in the road, causing the car to swerve slightly. He gripped the wheel and turned it to compensate.

"I'm not trying to prove anything to anyone." But he knew that he had been trying hard that evening. There had been too much tequila and too much time to himself, and when his best friend's wife had tilted her head back to laugh, he had wanted her to be laughing for him and no one else. Everett gripped the steering wheel hard and tried to think of a response that would be right, but the road ahead looked dark and mysterious and there were no answers in the weak beams of light illuminating the mist before them.

"You do matter." Carolyn finally spoke. "Even if you don't believe it, you do."

Everett heard the sincerity in her voice and for a moment, his eyes welled up with tears. The thought of her loving him was not what made him sad; it was his uncertainty about whether he still loved her that suddenly filled him with anguish. I don't deserve you, he thought, but he bit back those words.

"I believe it," he said. "There isn't much else to believe in anymore."

Out of the corner of his eye he saw her turn toward him, her eyes wide and her mouth opening as if to speak. It was the last thing he remembered before seeing the headlights of the white station wagon careening toward them. There was a loud bang and the sound of glass shattering, and he was lying on the pavement on his back, a ringing sound in his head and their Toyota upside down on the shoulder of the road a few yards away from him. Its wheels were still spinning, and inside he could make out Carolyn hanging from her seatbelt like an insect caught in a spider's web. He had lain there a long time on the wet pavement, unable to move or speak until the world went black. When he awoke, there was something covering his mouth and someone was shaking him, saying his name over and over.

"Everett. Everett."

He jumped, just as he had when the nurse tried to wake him in the emergency room in Tijuana, just as he had when the bird hit the window, only now it was Tracy shaking his shoulder and calling him back to the present for his physical therapy session. Charlie waved at him from the balance beams as Everett covered his mouth with his hands to disguise a wave of nausea.

"How often does that happen?" Tracy asked as she pushed his chair over to the beams.

"Less than it used to," he answered. Drained and sheepish, he watched Tracy make some notations on his chart as he waited for the bitter taste in his mouth to subside.

"Does Dr. Osterman know about it?"

Everett nodded. His psychologist knew more about him than he knew about himself.

Tracy seemed to study him a moment, then waved her hands toward the balance beam.

"Okay, Charlie, let's give it a go. Everett, I want you to concentrate hard this time. Remember to move from your hips and use your upper arms to swing forward."

Everett felt his shoulders lift as Charlie reached up under his arms and dragged him to the apparatus. Gripping the poles, Everett stiffened his arms and balanced himself against the bars. So this was his penance for believing he mattered. He bit his lip and focused on the muscles in his stomach, trying to force his pelvis to move forward. Nothing happened and he collapsed against the rails. Charlie stepped up to support him, while Tracy nodded approval.

"Good. Try again," she said.

Everett straightened his arms again and focused on his hips, willing them to respond, visualizing movement in his legs. There was a tiny shift forward in his left foot and then he gave up, relaxing his arm muscles and leaning into Charlie again.

"Excellent!" Tracy said. "I saw movement there." She made another notation in her chart. "Rest a minute and then let's give it one more try."

Everett took a deep breath. He straightened his arms again but, this time, instead of visualizing his pelvic muscles, he pictured his hands on the steering wheel and Carolyn turning toward him, about to say the words he had been waiting for. I forgive you, he heard her say, for all that we have lost. He saw his hands tightening on the wheel and his arms straining above the poles and then, looking down, he saw his right foot inch forward in front of him before he collapsed onto the ground.

Tracy cheered and Charlie yelled, "My man!" while the other patients in the room turned to stare at them. Everett looked up from the floor toward the window and saw a small bird, its wings fluttering just outside the glass. It must have been his imagination but, for just a moment, it seemed to hover there before soaring into the blue of the San Diego sky.

IT HAD BEEN SO LONG SINCE SHE'D BEEN AT LAKE MIRAMAR THAT she drove by the entrance without recognizing it. After turning around a few blocks up, Carolyn circled back and caught sight of the entrance, which was paved with fresh concrete. A shiny aluminum guardrail now separated the entry and exit lanes. The old wooden sign listing opening and closing times had been replaced with a metal marquee announcing that the lake was still open to visitors despite recent construction. Carolyn pulled into the driveway and parked near the boat dock on the western end of the water. After stowing her purse in the trunk, she reached into the front seat of the car and pulled out a large shopping bag full of day-old bread. Mary had forced it on her at work, begging her to take some of the bags that her husband brought home from the bakery every week.

Carolyn walked out on the dock and searched the horizon for other patrons, but the lake was quiet. There were few visitors on Thursday afternoons in the August heat. A chain link fence surrounded the lakeshore and notices were posted every few feet announcing the water district construction that would continue until September. Fishing season was over, and the few rowboats tied to the dock on the other side of the shore bumped forlornly against each other on the shifting lake surface.

Carolyn reached into the bag and pulled out some slices, the dough warm and damp in her hand from sitting all afternoon in the hot car. As she walked toward the edge of the dock, two large geese swam toward her honking loudly, followed by a flock of ducks and a few coots. The birds dipped their heads forward as she tossed bits of bread onto the lake, the smaller ducks waiting until the geese had turned away before darting toward the soggy remnants floating on the water.

As Carolyn pulled more bread out of the bag, she thought about Roy. Normally she would be seeing him this afternoon, but today she'd chosen to come here instead. After meeting his sister last week, there had been a tension between them that wasn't there before.

As she dropped tiny bits of dough toward the feeding birds, she noticed a hovering black shape, about two feet long, below the water. In a second there were more of them, and Carolyn realized that they were catfish. She watched as the fish schooled before her, swimming in graceful arcs over each other as they reached for the chunks of bread that were falling on the surface of the water. At one point, she threw a handful of pieces into the center of the school and watched the water churn as the fish fought each other for the floating bits, their large mouths gaping open. Their long whiskers and sleek black bodies made them look dark and sinister, causing Carolyn to shiver despite the August heat.

She tossed some bits to the birds that were now clustered near the shore by the edge of the dock and then shook the remaining crumbs over the water. The surface quivered as the catfish fed and then the lake was still, the dark forms circling quietly below the surface. As Carolyn went to throw the empty bag in the trash can near the pier, she noticed two men standing under the trees next to a building at the end of the parking lot. The one with his back to her was wearing jeans and a red t-shirt that looked familiar. Carolyn walked toward them and then stopped short as she realized that the two of them were holding each other in an embrace. She was about to turn away, but something made her stay. After pulling back from his partner, the man in the jeans moved his face slightly toward her and she recognized him immediately. It was Ben.

He must have seen her because he said something to his partner, who struck out toward the parking lot, moving hastily in long loping strides. Ben waved to Carolyn and then walked toward her, his usually smiling face looking serious and difficult to read. Carolyn stepped forward and greeted him, her hand over her forehead in the bright sun.

"I thought that was you," she said, "but I wasn't sure."

Ben smiled at her and then waved his hand in the direction of his friend, who had disappeared behind the building near the park entrance.

"We like to bike here in the afternoon after class gets out," he said. He looked shyly at her, and Carolyn sensed that he didn't want to say anything more. How odd, she thought, that we've managed to accidentally find each other out. She pointed to a bench that sat on a rise above the lakeshore.

"Do you have some time to sit for a while?"

He nodded, smiling at her in the old way that made him seem more like himself. They walked over to the bench and sat down, each of them gazing out at the lake. Ben leaned forward, resting his elbows on his thighs, then turned to look at her.

"This is funny," he said, "being here, the two of us." He squinted toward the water and then stared down at his hands. "We see each other almost every morning, but we don't get to talk the way we used to."

"I know," Carolyn said. "I haven't been around much." She stopped for a moment and then turned her head toward the pier. "It's been a strange summer."

Ben rubbed at a spot on his jeans and then glanced up as if to speak. He stayed silent, and Carolyn suddenly felt a rush of sympathy for him. How hard his life must be, she thought, with the secret he's been keeping. She put her hand on his arm and then placed it back in her lap.

"I want you to know," she said, "that Everett and I love you. You've been an enormous help to us." She and Ben were silent for a moment as a blackbird flew by and skimmed the surface of the water. A slight breeze blew over the lake, rustling the leaves of the trees that lined the shore. "And no matter what happens with Everett and me, you are always welcome in our house."

"What will happen with you and Everett?" Ben asked. He looked up at her, his face seeming serious and full of innocence. Carolyn noticed that his eyes were gray in the sun and that his lower lip looked scraped and raw in one corner.

"I don't know," she said. A cormorant cried out in the bushes below them, and Carolyn caught the scent of eucalyptus on the breeze. She traced the edge of the wooden bench, noticing how smooth and worn the wood was below her fingers, and then watched as her hand began to shake. Her eyes filled with tears and before she knew it she was weeping openly into the shoulder of Ben's red shirt. He held her there, like a father cradling a child, while the breeze blew softly over both of them and the lake lapped at the shoreline above the shadows circling beneath the surface of the water.

AFTER FOLLOWING HWY 76 ALL THE WAY OUT TO THE COAST, HE arrived at Harbor Beach at three thirty in the afternoon. The daytime crowds, sunburned and bedraggled in their wet bathing suits and salt-covered hair, were just beginning to leave. Luke snagged one of the last remaining fire pits at the north end of the beach, its blackened center littered with sandwich wrappers and empty plastic soda bottles. He cleaned out the debris, carrying it to an already overflowing trashcan near the edge of the parking lot and then unloaded the wood, wrapped tightly in a large black garbage bag, from the back of his motorcycle. The pieces were remnants from the construction site where he worked this week. Laying sawed off two-by-fours and chunks of lumber in an A-shaped pile in the center of the blackened fire ring, Luke pushed small handfuls of crumpled newspaper underneath the pile. He did everything but light it; Nancy would be meeting him at five o'clock and he wanted to save the wood until it was dark.

While he waited, he pulled a cigarette from his t-shirt pocket and lit it, discarding the smoldering match in the center of the fire pit. White cigarette smoke flew up in front of him like small disappearing ghosts each time he exhaled. Luke watched the waves swell in regular, even lines against the shore, the last few body surfers and swimmers trying to catch each rising crest before it broke in rolling foam upon the sand. Even as a kid he'd loved this time of day at the beach the best. He liked the quiet, when the crowds left and the sun began its slow descent toward the horizon. The sand seemed to stretch out longer and wider, the sky turning from blue to gold as the sun came closer to setting.

Luke caught the spicy scent of charcoal and grilled hotdogs as other visitors lit fires in the row of cement rings strung along the east side of the dunes. He leaned back into the warm sand and watched a pair of seagulls as they circled high in the air above him and then settled on the beach a few yards away. They cocked their heads sideways at the humans circling the fire pits and waited for a chance to snatch at the remnants of food being served at each campfire.

One of the birds was stalking the young couple to the right of Luke, carefully placing one yellow claw before the other on the sand as it edged around the bags of hot dog buns and potato chips that lay on their beach blanket. Just as the gull was about to swipe at a plate of exposed grapes, Luke spotted Nancy near the parking lot, her hand to her forehead as she searched the beach for him. He stood up and waved both arms in the air until she saw him. She stepped lightly over the drifts, carrying a store-bought bundle of wood in one hand and a small cooler in the other. Under her arm was a woven blanket, which he took from her and spread out on the sand near the fire pit.

"I wondered if I was going to be able to find you," she said. "Parking's terrible here. My car's all the way at the other end of the lot."

She set the wood down beside the remnants stacked outside the ring and then opened the cooler and removed two bottles of beer, wrapping each of them with a white napkin. The paper felt damp and cool in Luke's hand as he twisted off the caps. He handed one bottle to Nancy, noticing as he did that her hair was pulled back on each side with small metal clips shaped like butterflies. She wore a pair of khaki pants and a plain white blouse that made her look more like the Cupa girl he knew in high school. He noticed that she'd tied a sweatshirt around her waist and was glad she remembered that the ocean air would be cooler later.

"So, what happened to Tuesday?" she said. "I thought I was supposed to come to your Council meeting."

Luke took a drink of the beer and let the sour taste roll over his tongue a moment before swallowing. He listened to the waves rumbling against the shore and then looked over at her.

"I'm sorry," he said. "They wouldn't let you come."

"What? Why not?"

Luke hung his head. "It's different now. They've become really careful about who attends these meetings." He picked at the wet paper around his beer. "It's nothing personal. Even I had a hard time getting in there."

"But you did," she said. Nancy took a hard pull on her beer and gazed out at the shoreline. "Your family always had more clout on the res than mine. Must have been that old Washburn mystique." She playfully poked him with her foot as she said this.

"What mystique? My family never had anything over any other family out there," Luke answered, ignoring the nudge. "My grandfather was half-white and drunk most of the time. There were no special privileges for being a Washburn."

Nancy shrugged. "Whatever you say." She took another sip from her beer. "You going to light that?" she said, nodding her head toward the fire ring.

"Sure." Luke dug into his pocket until he located his matches, then struck one and tossed it toward the newspaper clustered underneath the lumber. A small flame licked out at the wood, then disappeared a moment before igniting the newspaper, red-edged and billowing small plumes of black smoke. Luke pushed at the smoldering wads until they finally caught.

"So, what do you want me to do?" she asked. "I can interview locals about the landfill and get background on the EIR. Will that help?"

"Maybe." Luke ducked as a puff of smoke blew past his head. He picked up a stick from the woodpile and poked at the flames inside the pit. "It doesn't really matter now, so do whatever you like."

"What do you mean by that?" Nancy's voice sounded small and high above the distant boom of the crashing waves. "I thought this was important to you. To our tribe."

"There's nothing our tribe can do. You've seen the report. The voters let it happen, and now it's a reality. There's nothing our Council can do about it, either. I'm through listening to them."

"This is a surprise, Luke. You seemed so passionate about the whole thing when you called last month. And when we went out to the canyon, you urged me to take this on." Nancy rubbed her hands over her arms as the evening air began to cool. "I'd like to cover this story," she continued, "but if you know something new, you need to tell me."

"There's nothing new to tell," Luke answered. "And there isn't anything you or our Council can do to make it better." He picked a small bit of seaweed out of the sand and threw it into the fire. "In fact, I'm through with our Council. I'm not wasting my time there any more. I've got other plans for fixing this situation."

"Other plans? Like what?" Nancy asked.

"Never mind," Luke answered. "They're not important."

"Wait a minute. You didn't invite me all the way out here to call off the landfill story. What other plans are you talking about?"

Luke gazed past the surf break toward the yellow-orange ball of the sun, which was just about to touch the edge of the horizon. Should he tell her? he wondered. Would she understand? He watched as she unwound her sweatshirt from her waist and pulled it over her head. The GAP logo stood out in thick white letters across her chest.

"Tell me," she said.

Luke closed his eyes and the voices began to murmur in his head.

Ngé''i, they whispered. Revenge.

"Luke?"

Tó$$u muiróppax cham'éexi. Revenge our land.

Luke stared at her through the dark plumes that rose up from the campfire. The smoke shifted and, suddenly, visions of native men and women appeared before him. Their bodies, shaped in swirling clouds of gray, seemed to twist and dance until they evaporated in long thin wisps of white haze.

"Luke." Her hand, cold and smooth, suddenly touched his arm. He shuddered and felt his breath come short and fast.

"What is it?" she asked. "What do you see?"

Luke gazed into the fire and saw his grandfather's gun in the palm of his hand. He saw his arm as he lifted the pistol and fired bright yellow light and blue smoke from its barrel.

"Lóoviqup," he said. He looked at Nancy, whose wide cheekbones and flat nose seemed to flicker with reflected firelight. "I see the way."

She asked him what he meant, but he said nothing, staring into the pit while the Green Corn Moon rose above them and the sand turned cold beneath their feet.

Chapter 7

Everett pulled his braces out of the van and held them upright against the arm of the wheelchair as he rolled himself into the house. It was one o'clock; another three hours and Carolyn would be home from work.

Once he was inside, he placed a brace around each arm and positioned the rubber bottoms on either side of the chair. He struggled to stand up, but the chair slid forward; he'd forgotten to lock the wheel. After setting the brake, he tried again, but it was awkward pulling himself up from a sitting position. He sat back and took a deep breath, then focused all his effort on his stomach and back muscles. It took two tries, but he finally did it. He was standing up inside his own house.

It had taken days to get to this point. After the first small movement had come an awkward sliding step. A few days later it was just a tiny motion, then a few more days and another shuffling step. Everett learned to ignore the sweat that dripped down his neck and his hands, which shook with exertion. His world had suddenly telescoped, becoming a single lens through which he saw only his foot sliding forward, felt only the muscles in his stomach and groin as he strained to move his legs. As if from far away, he heard Tracy urging him on and felt Charlie clapping him on the back every time he had some small success, but he didn't see them. All he saw was the top of each foot as he willed it forward.

After a week he had taken three steps. Today he had stumbled across the physical therapy room floor before collapsing against Charlie.

And now he was standing in his kitchen, in front of the sliding glass door. He sat down suddenly and pulled the braces into his lap. After opening the slider, he steered his chair down the ramp into the backyard, the braces clattering as he rolled out onto the grass. The sun beat down on his arms and shoulders as he took another deep breath and pulled himself forward, the brace footings slipping a bit in the turf. He was standing. Again.

He gazed over the back fence and found that he could now see the trail that he and Carolyn used to walk on so many years ago. It meandered dusty and brown along the streambed, a line of trees and bushes shading it in parts. The canyon floor lay golden before him, its fields of weeds and wild grasses tall and still in the afternoon heat. If he turned his head to the west, he could see all the way to the far end of the preserve, where the horizon met the sea in Del Mar. The familiar sight filled him with such joy that he momentarily fell off balance and sat down suddenly in his chair.

He laughed at his own clumsiness, then lifted his braces to the sun and let out a victory whoop.

THE WATER TRANSFORMED FROM A ROARING STREAM TO A THIN dribble as Roy cranked down the faucet and stepped out of the shower. He had just begun drying his hair when he heard the trill of the telephone in the kitchen. Wrapping the towel around his waist, he stepped carefully down the hallway, trying not to slip on the linoleum with his wet feet. It had been dusk when he started his shower, so he had to fumble a bit in the dark for the kitchen light. He reached the phone on its fourth ring, knocking over a bowl of his sister's summer squash and dropping the towel as he leaned over the sink for the receiver.

"Míiyu, brother. I'm not interrupting anything, am I?"

Roy ignored the hint of sarcasm in Delores's voice.

"Míiyu, sister." Roy reached for the towel and did his best to dry himself off with one hand as he spoke. "You pulled me out of the shower, so it'd better be important."

"It is." There was a pause and then the sound of a loud thump and something rustling in the background before he heard his sister's breath again through the receiver. "It's about Luke."

Even though it was a warm evening, Roy felt a sudden chill, as if a gust of wind had blown through the kitchen. He held the towel to his chest.

"What's happened?"

"They want to kick him off the Council," Delores answered. "He came in all agitated and angry and then he left in the middle of the meeting." Her voice faded out as if she had stepped away from the phone and then came back again, a little too loudly. "He was muttering and speaking *chamtéelay* when he left. Made no sense at all." Delores' voice sounded suddenly small and soft. "He scared me, brother."

"What did he say? Did anyone talk to him?"

"He was hearing the voices again. Something about revenge and saving our people."

The muscles in his stomach tightened. Luke had had episodes like this in the past, where he claimed that voices spoke to him. The worst instance had been after his mother died. Roy knew that his relationship with Carolyn had upset his son recently, but Luke never had adjusted well to new situations. The scene Delores was describing sounded much more serious.

"When did this happen?" Roy asked, glancing up at the kitchen clock. It was almost nine p.m. Luke had left for the council meeting a little before seven.

"About a half hour ago. I stayed to talk to the members, but they were angry at him. They don't want any more disruptions during the meetings." Delores made a snuffling sound. "I tried to reason with them, but they said they're tired of his absences and erratic behavior."

Roy wrapped the towel around his neck and leaned onto the counter.

"Well, let me know if he shows up at your place. I'll watch out for him here." He paused a moment. "Try not to worry, nopíit."

"It's that white woman," Delores said. "It's too much for him, watching you run around after all these years."

His spine stiffened as he stepped away from the counter. He moved his free arm across his chest and gripped the phone tightly.

"What I do in my private life is not your concern, Delores. And if that's what's bothering Luke, he'll have to learn to live with it."

"That may be true for all of us, brother," she answered.

The sharp whistle of a teakettle blew over the phone line, followed by the sound of cups rattling. He waited until he heard his sister's breath against the receiver.

"Tell Luke to call me when he comes home," she said.

"I will," he replied, but the line had already gone dead.

He dropped the receiver back into its cradle. There in the dark of the kitchen window was his reflection. The sight of his naked body startled him, as if he was seeing someone else in the room. Against the blackness of the glass his body gleamed, pale and ghostly. As he straightened his shoulders, the face staring back at him looked eerily like his father's. He flipped off the light switch, banishing the image, and hurried into the bedroom to dress.

He pulled on a t-shirt and a pair of shorts. He'd most likely find Luke at his friend Donnie's house or maybe at the Rest Stop, a bar on Hwy 76 where Luke and his pals hung out. Roy hunted under the bed for his running shoes. After tightening the loop on the second lace, he stopped and sat back on the bed. He knew where Luke would be.

Roy whistled for Tóowish, who appeared from the direction of the living room, tongue wagging and toenails tapping lightly on the hallway floor. He shut off his bedroom light and headed down the hallway. When he got to Luke's room, he noticed through a crack in the door that a light was on. Normally he wouldn't venture into his son's space unless invited, but he stopped and pushed the door open and looked inside.

On the corner of a small oak desk, a single desk lamp cast a sullen orange glow over the room. Next to the lamp sat the monitor for Luke's computer, the words *churó″ i otéelay*—keep your promise—scrolling across the screen. On the floor near the single bed, with its disheveled mess of sheets and an old Indian blanket, lay pieces of paper, lined up in a deliberate spiral pattern. Roy recognized the grassy smell of marijuana and cigarette smoke. He picked up one of the papers and then gathered them all together, paging through them one by one. The pages were printouts from different Internet sites. Some of them contained information on the landfill, including sections of the environmental impact report and updates from different watchdog agencies that were investigating the legality of the site. There were copies of county road maps and a number of pages from the Inland Mining Company website.

When he got to the last page, Roy was about to set the sheets down when something caught his eye. It was a small circle of black ink around a name and a photograph at the bottom of a page of Inland Mining employees. The circled name was Everett Weedman. Carolyn's husband.

He stared at the photograph. The white hair surprised him; he wouldn't have guessed that Carolyn's husband was older. He had pictured him as cold and somewhat stern, but the face in the picture was that of a pleasant looking man with a warm smile and kind eyes.

Suddenly feeling dizzy, Roy set the pages down. It disturbed him to find that his son knew who Carolyn's husband was. Almost as disarming was the fact that her husband looked normal and decent. During their affair, Roy had tried not to think about Everett, but now that he had seen his photograph, it would be harder to ignore the fact that he existed.

The cold thrust of Tóowish's nose against his palm reminded him that he needed to find Luke. As he moved toward the desk to turn off the light, his foot brushed against something under the corner of Luke's bed. Roy saw that it was the edge of some kind of box. He reached down and pulled it out and then felt the same cold wind blow over him that had breezed by him in the kitchen when Delores called. He knew this box without even having to open it. Carefully fingering the National Match end label on the lid, he flipped it open. There was nothing inside but a yellowed sheet of shooting suggestions and one of the original test targets, the black circle in the center torn through with bullet holes. Roy felt his breath flow out of him as he knelt down and placed the box back under the bed. Tóowish nuzzled the underside of his chin. He sat there for a long time in the dim glow of the desk lamp. As he absently stroked the dog's fur, he marveled that he had come to love another man's wife and wondered where his son was and what he was doing with his grandfather's gun.

When he finally stirred, he found that his right leg, curled beneath him while he sat, had grown numb. He stretched it out gingerly, noticing the first few tingles as the numbness subsided. Bee stings, Luke had called them when he was a little boy. Roy checked the clock on Luke's night stand: ten p.m. He stood up and stretched and then whistled for Tóowish to follow him outside.

The air was still warm on the Pala Reservation, and the moon, slightly on the wane from being full two nights prior, shone brightly. Roy noticed that the neighborhood was quiet on this Tuesday night. He snapped the leash on Tóowish's collar and tapped his hand against his thigh, signaling to the dog that it was time to move. Together they jogged out onto Ortega Street, Roy's tennis shoes making crunching noises in the gravel. The houses along the side of the road glowed a ghostly gray in the moonlight. Roy noticed flashes of light and color from the television sets through the drapes in the windows. He knew most of these families, having lived in this neighborhood all his life. As he trudged along the road, his breath blowing quickly in and out, he pictured the neighbors' faces—Mrs. Okuma, Mr. and Mrs. Nunez, Anna Luna, Eleanor Hayes, Elena and Harvey Nejo—as if they were lined up before him, watching him run.

Their eyes seemed to follow him all the way to Mission Road, until he reached the Pala Community Center. The small brown building sat dark and deserted, the Council meeting over at least an hour before. Roy ran past the center and stopped at the entrance to the Mission graveyard, leaning his hand on the rusted bars. Tóowish sat on her haunches, her collar jingling as she scratched at her shoulder. Roy leaned over a moment to catch his breath, then peered into the yard. It appeared to be empty. He pushed the gate open and stepped inside, tugging on the leash so the dog would follow him.

The moon's rays fell in streams through the pepper trees, painting the scattered wooden crosses and tombstones with random splotches of light. Roy stepped quietly through the knee-high weeds that lined the gravesites, moving slowly until he came to his wife's plot at the far corner of the yard. He stopped and studied the small pile of dried flowers that his sister had most likely placed there. The sight of the mounded earth and small gray headstone sent him spinning back to the day that they had buried Sonia. He had stood numb as a block of granite on this very spot, his hand on his son's shoulder, watching the mission workers as they scraped shovels of dirt onto his wife's coffin.

He hung his head, wishing Sonia was here to tell him what to do with their son, when suddenly he had the odd sensation that someone was watching him. He wheeled around and gazed at the trees lining the yard's back wall, but there was no one there. As he turned back toward the gravesite, he noticed a small bit of white next to the flowers. He leaned over and retrieved it, a cigarette butt, still warm at the tip. Luke. He tossed the butt and whistled to Tóowish, who wagged her tail at the sound. Stepping quickly through the yard, they broke into a light jog as they headed out onto Mission Street.

They ran until they reached the Stop and Go Market at the west end of the block. Weak light from the dimly lit entryway cast a haze over the empty parking lot. Roy opened the battered screen door and stepped inside. A small circular fan blew hot air across the racks of snack chips and beef jerky, and light jazz droned from a tiny boom box behind the cash register. In the far corner sat the manager, Russell San Miguel, counting a pile of cash on the counter. A cigarette hung from his lower lip, framing the blue bandana across his forehead in a hazy halo of smoke.

"It's dangerous to count your money in public," Roy said.

Russell didn't look up until he finished laying the bills, one by one, in a green stack on the counter. He wrapped the bundle with a rubber band and set it inside a drawer below the glass countertop.

"You're not supposed to bring your dog in the store," Russell replied as he pulled a key chain from his pocket and locked the drawer with a noisy jangle.

Roy ignored this remark as he studied the contents of the refrigerator case. He and Russ had gone to high school together and had been close friends until Roy went to England to get his master's degree. In the years since, their friendship had drifted until it was nothing more than a series of awkward meetings, like this one.

Roy pulled a bottle of water from the case and put it on the counter. He felt in his pocket for his wallet and removed a dollar bill.

"Luke been here tonight?"

Russell punched the register open and dropped the bill inside.

"Everyone's been here tonight. Our Council chairman, Loma, Jones, your boy, everyone." He stopped and pulled the cigarette stub from his mouth, blowing blue smoke into the air. "Everyone except your woman friend. She only comes in the daytime."

Roy felt a chill as he removed the water bottle from the counter, the plastic cold and wet in his hand. He hadn't thought about his relationship with Carolyn being public. The urge to defend her surged up in his throat, but he fought it back with a swallow.

"What time did Luke come in?" he asked.

"About a half hour ago."

"Did he say where he was going?"

Russell raised an eyebrow before taking a pull off his cigarette and dropping the stub to the floor. He gave it a hard stomp and then looked at Roy.

"The voices were talking to him tonight," Russell said. "He mumbled something about being on some kind of mission, but he didn't say where." He pulled a tribal newspaper from behind the counter and set it out on the glass. "Wherever he went, he won't be thirsty. He took two sixes with him." He opened the paper and began to read.

Roy stood a moment, noticing the gray streaks in his old friend's hair as he bent his head over the paper. In the warm breath of the store fan, he felt the lost years blow over him. He wished he could reach out and gather them and make them come back, but they were gone forever.

Roy gave Tóowish's leash a tug, and together they left the store. Just outside the parking lot, he stopped and cracked the cap off the bottle and let the liquid slide down his throat, then lifted the container and poured the water over his head. The cold rivulets dripping down his back reminded him of the shower he had taken earlier that evening. Delores's phone call seemed as if had happened a long time ago. Feeling naked and chilled, he signaled to the dog, and together they began the long trek home.

WHEN CAROLYN OPENED HER DOOR ON WEDNESDAY MORNING, SHE almost missed the plastic grocery bag. It sat like a large white rabbit, its handles sticking straight out in two corn-shaped ears, huddled on the corner of the porch in the small bit of already disappearing morning shade. Picking it up, she was reminded of old nursery stories about babies being left on doorsteps and wondered who would have deposited it there. Inside were several large zucchini, a couple of long hothouse style cucumbers and tomatoes of varying sizes in shades of green and red. She knew Roy didn't have a vegetable garden, but as she stepped into her kitchen, the bag cradled in her arms, Carolyn recalled that his sister had brought a similar gift to his house a week ago.

She set it on the kitchen counter, emptying the contents while Ben and Everett watched from the breakfast table.

"Someone left us some vegetables," she said, careful not to look at either of the two men as she searched the cabinets for a wooden bowl.

"Cool." Ben looked back down at his newspaper. "Do your neighbors garden?"

"No," Carolyn replied.

Everett said nothing.

In the car on her way to work, Carolyn wondered why Delores would have left the bag there. Was she trying to send a message?

The gesture almost seemed kindly, but Carolyn knew otherwise. As she turned into the library parking lot, it struck her that someone in Roy's family had found out where she lived, which gave her the uncomfortable sensation of being scrutinized. Roy probably gave his sister enough information that she could locate the house. Did that mean that Luke knew, too?

She pulled into a parking space next to the library entrance and stopped a moment before getting out of the car. This was the same spot where she'd met Roy six weeks ago. Images of Roy's hands—lifting the dog from the pavement, passing her a cup of coffee at Starbucks, administering salve to her bitten ankles, moving his hand over her leg and up to her thigh—made her grip the steering wheel tightly, suddenly flush with heat. She glanced up at the rear view mirror and instead of her own face she saw Everett's clear gray eyes gazing back at her. His silence this morning had stricken her more than if he had reached out and slapped her. The enormity of what she'd done this summer suddenly held her pinned, paralyzed, to the car seat, and she knew then that she couldn't go on with the deception any longer. She would have to let Roy go.

When she opened the library door, an air-conditioned gust of wind almost blew her back into the parking lot. She waited for her goose-bumped skin to adjust to the frigid air, then stepped into the employee's lunchroom to put her lunch, thin slices of tomatoes and cucumbers from the unknown garden, into the refrigerator. Mary and Sheryl sat at the break table, smoke from Mary's cigarette curling in lazy spirals above their Styrofoam coffee cups.

"I took Shedaisy a bagful of carrots yesterday," Mary was saying. "Wouldn't even look at them. Has some kind of stomach virus." She blew a mouthful of smoke out over the table and slurped at her coffee. "Damn horse is costing me a fortune."

"I want to come out and ride with you again," Sheryl said. "Maybe I'll try Licorice this time." She stabbed at her coffee cup with a thin red stirring stick. "I think I could handle him now."

"Yeah, well you'd better wait awhile. We're having him gelded next week," Mary said. She looked over at Carolyn, who was refilling the coffeemaker with water. "You want to come ride with us sometime?"

"Oh, no thanks," Carolyn said. "Horses make me nervous."

Mary shrugged. "Whatever." She stubbed out her cigarette into the bottom of her cup and hoisted her bulky body from the chair. As she pulled the rest area door open, she called over her shoulder to Carolyn.

"Speaking of studs, some Indian guy came looking for you yesterday."

The door swung shut before Carolyn could reply. She looked over at Sheryl who was gathering cups and napkins and tossing them into the metal trashcan at the end of the counter. Sheryl glanced up and gave her a nervous smile.

"He seems nice," she said, before hastily exiting the break room.

Carolyn listened a moment to the buzzing of the lights above the linoleum table. Her coworkers knew about Roy. Ben knew. Roy's son and sister knew. Carolyn could picture them all lined up in a jury box. At the judge's bench would sit Everett. In her mind's eye her husband lifted his arm and brought down a gavel, hard, against her head, as two bailiffs dragged a protesting Roy out of court. In the background, she imagined she could hear Luke laughing, his harsh cackle eventually fading into a rattlesnake's hiss. Carolyn shook her head, the hiss drifting away until it was indistinguishable from the hum of the break room lights.

She stuffed her lunch bag into the crammed refrigerator and slammed the door closed.

At the main desk, Carolyn loaded up her cart with books, taking care to avoid the curious eyes of Mary and Sheryl. Let them wonder. She was about to push the cart out into the stacks, when she felt a soft touch at her elbow.

"Excuse me, miss. Could you please help me?"

Carolyn recognized the elderly lady she had assisted a few weeks ago. The woman's soft white curls had a tinge of pink to them, and there was a hint of elegance to the lilac shawl that hung on her thin frame.

"I was wondering if I might post this notice on your bulletin board." She waved a sheet of white paper in the air. As she took it,

Carolyn noticed a web of spidery blue veins sprayed across the old woman's hand.

"Why, certainly, no—." Carolyn stopped mid sentence as she gazed at the photograph in the center of the page. Below the heading, which read "Lost Dog" in shaky black marker, was a picture of Tóowish.

"—problem." Carolyn spoke the word in a whisper. "It's no problem at all." She suddenly felt cold and hot at the same time.

The woman smiled, her eyes watery above their wrinkled lids.

"Lacey was a gift to my husband," she said. "We've had her for three years." She paused for a moment, as if seeing something far away. "My husband died last year, and since then she's been a bit too much for me at times. I thought about giving her away, but you just can't do that with a gift, can you?" Her wet gaze probed at Carolyn. "Since she disappeared, I actually find I miss her." She pulled a tissue from her pocket and dabbed delicately at her nose. "It's funny, isn't it, how we take what we have for granted until it goes away?" Her voice trailed off into the quiet of the library.

Carolyn looked down at her hand and saw that she was clutching the page so tightly that it was starting to crumple. She forced herself to smile back at the tiny lady.

"I'll be sure to post this for you." She shoved the paper into the pocket of her denim skirt and hurriedly pushed the cart away before the woman could say anything more. When she had found a quiet place in the stacks, she pulled out the sheet and studied it. The black and white photo showed Tóowish, sitting with streams of ribbons around her neck in front of a Christmas tree. Below the picture were the words "Missing pet collie. Answers to "Lacey." $100 reward. If found, please call Elizabeth Arman at 555-484-3709."

A cold wind blew over Carolyn as the library air conditioner kicked once again into life. She had been so taken aback by the woman's request that she hadn't known what to say. Now, standing alone in the stacks, the walls of books towering over her in silent judgment, she knew that she had to do more than tell Roy their relationship was over. She had to ask him to give up the very thing that had brought them together.

Crumpling the paper into a tight ball, she shoved it deep into her pocket, where it poked against her thigh like a reproving finger for the rest of the day.

IT WAS ALL A PACK OF LIES. EVERETT WAS CERTAIN THAT WHEN Carolyn brought the bag in from the porch, she knew exactly who the "someone" was who had left it there. While Ben blindly continued to read the newspaper, Everett wheeled his chair toward the kitchen counter. He'd been making slow progress with the braces, so he continued to use the wheelchair when he was at home. He also thought he'd wait until he was good at walking and then surprise Carolyn with the news. Now he wasn't so sure that it would matter to her at all.

He stopped at the bowl of vegetables and plucked a tomato from the pile. Its smooth skin was the color of blood, and it had the sunny smell that only comes from homegrown fruit. He ran his finger across the taut surface and then cupped it in the palm of his hand. It would feel good, he was sure, to launch it at the kitchen window, to shatter the glass into tiny bits and leave it for Carolyn to clean up. What would she think of her gift then, he wondered. The image of his wife on her knees surrounded by broken glass didn't please him as much as he thought it would. Feeling suddenly tired, he placed the tomato back into the bowl and spoke for the first time that morning.

"I'll take my bath now."

Without waiting for Ben, he wheeled himself through the hall to the downstairs bath. The entire room had been retrofitted, including a widened door to accommodate his wheelchair and a refurbished tub with a lowered platform and aluminum rails along the sides. Ben quietly stepped into the room and helped him remove his bathrobe, then slid his hands under Everett's arms and lifted him with one graceful heave into the tub. As Ben reached for the faucets, Everett waved him off.

"It's all right. I'll do it." A bit of edge crept into his voice.

If Ben noticed, he gave no sign.

"No problem. I'll get you some clothes." He left the room and even though only the two of them were home, shut the door softly behind him.

Everett reached for the faucets and turned them both slowly, taking care to provide an even amount of hot and cold. In the past, he had made the water too warm and, without realizing it, had scalded the skin on his feet and legs. Steam rose around him, making the air thick and humid as a sauna. When the tub was full, Everett cranked off the roaring water, leaving the room silent except for a series of quiet drips.

He sat for a moment, studying his legs, which lay like two white logs on the floor of the tub. How thin they'd become in the past three years. His penis floated up between them, bobbing at the surface like a fish seeking air. Everett leaned back and lifted his hands to his forehead, baptizing himself with sheets of water and wiping the excess off his face. How easy it would be to slide below the surface, to hold his breath until his lungs burst.

How easy.

He reached for the soap, a thin bar that smelled slightly of eucalyptus. Carolyn had bought him a set of three, including shampoo, for his birthday. He had made it last all year, stretching the gift as long as he could. The scent reminded him of the days, just after the accident, when she used to help him bathe. Everett closed his eyes and thought back to the last time she had unwrapped a bar and lathered it against a washcloth. As she began to scrub his back, he had felt her hand on his shoulder, just touching the fringe of hair along his neck. He could feel her breath on his skin as she spoke.

"I'm not strong enough to do this," she'd said.

"What do you mean?"

"It's too much for me. Lifting you and feeding you and trying to get you dressed." The steam caused her hair to curl in upon itself in tight ringlets around her face. "I'm sorry, Everett. I'm really trying, but this is just too difficult." Her voice had become a whisper as she dropped the soapy washcloth into the tub in front of him. White bands of suds, like tiny oil slicks, drifted on the surface toward his belly.

She wiped the sweat off her forehead and then swabbed at her eyes with dripping hands.

"I'm sorry," she'd said, and that was the end of it.

Everett couldn't recall exactly when—a week, maybe two weeks later—they hired Ben. Once he was on board, Carolyn avoided all aspects of Everett's care. He couldn't tell if the real reason was because it had become too painful for her to see him this way or if she had just lost interest. He suspected it was a little of both.

After releasing the stopper and watching the water spiral down the drain, Everett reached for a towel from the rack hanging just above his head. Everything, in this room at least, was within reach. He toweled his arms and then the springy hair on his chest. Almost as if on cue, Ben tapped on the door and opened it. He carried underwear, socks, jeans, and a t-shirt. He spread a dry towel on the seat of the wheelchair and, without saying a word, reached under Everett's arms and lifted him over the edge of the tub and onto the chair. While Ben dried his ankles and feet, Everett tried to make amends.

"I'm sorry if I sounded curt a minute ago. I didn't mean to be short with you."

"You weren't," Ben replied. "And if I'm ever in your way, please tell me."

"You're never in the way." Everett leaned forward as Ben pulled the shirt over his head. He pushed his arms through the sleeves and then rotated his torso to one side so Ben could pull up the right leg of his jeans. "Christ, I couldn't function without you." He leaned the other way while Ben pulled his left pant leg up over his hip and then he snapped his jeans shut himself. He had gotten over the indignity of having to be helped with his clothes years ago. In fact, he'd come to look forward to these mornings as the only shot at intimacy he'd have all day.

"Let me get these on for you," Ben said as he knelt in front of the wheelchair and unfolded the socks. Everett studied the top of his head, noticing the way the sunlight from the bathroom window lit the younger man's hair. If a human being could justify wearing a halo, it would be Ben.

"It threw me this morning," Everett said, watching as Ben eased a sock over his right foot. He suddenly had the urge to scratch that foot and then dismissed it as one of the phantom pains that had plagued him for the last three years. "When she walked in the room and dumped that bag on the counter, I didn't know what to say." He waited for Ben to place the other sock on his left foot. Ben sat back and looked up at him.

"It's over," Everett said. "My marriage is over."

"I know," Ben said. He placed both hands on Everett's feet as if absolving him. "I'm sorry." He rose and moved behind Everett's chair, then wheeled him out of the bathroom and into the office. The model planes stirred slightly as they entered. Ben positioned the chair in front of the tabletop where the crushed pieces of the Huey lay spread across the surface.

"Just be kind when you tell her," Ben said.

"Tell her what?"

"Whatever you've decided to say." Ben thought a moment. "Tell her that you know what's going on, that you want her to stop, or you want her back, or you want her to tell you the truth." He looked at Everett. "Tell her that you want to know why."

"I know why," Everett said.

"Do you?"

Everett sat up straight in his chair. Did anyone know why love ended, he wondered. He could think of a hundred reasons for Carolyn to leave him—his own infidelity, being the first. The loss of their son, another. The accident. Understanding why she didn't love him, he realized, was easy. Could he name one reason she should stay with him? That was the harder thing to articulate.

He looked at Ben, who was leaning against the desk, his hands gripping the edge tightly. Everett could see the veins stand out on his arms.

"Do you know why?" he asked.

Ben hung his head. "I know she's unhappy." He looked up at Everett. "I know that she's seeing someone else." He stopped a moment. "I saw them."

The hard truth of this made Everett's gut clench.

"Was it someone I know?" he asked. He steeled himself, hoping that Ben wouldn't name anyone he considered a friend.

"I don't think so."

Everett let his breath out.

"But, the thing is, Mr. Weedman, she saw me, too," Ben continued. "She knows as much about me as I know about her."

Everett was confused. What was Ben trying to say?

"Are you seeing someone, too?" Everett asked.

"Yes," Ben said. "Well, no." He sighed in exasperation and then gazed directly at Everett. "I have a lover." He looked down at his hands and then up again. "It's not a woman."

"I know," Everett said.

Ben's eyes widened. Everett noticed that they were as clear and gray-green as his favorite cat's eye when he was a child.

"Does that surprise you?" he asked.

"I guess so," Ben said. "It surprised my parents. I decided to share that part of my life with them, and now they want to disown me." He looked down at his fingers, pausing a second to study the tips. "That's why you have to be kind when you talk to Mrs. Weedman." He stepped away from the desk and ran a finger back and forth along the arm of Everett's chair. "Otherwise, saying anything is a mistake."

Everett stared at the window above the desk as Ben quietly stepped out of the room. There was a jangle of keys and then the click of the front door closing. Everett was alone. He sat a moment and then, with a pair of thin tweezers, delicately lifted one of the helicopter wings. Turning it this way and that under the light, he surveyed the damaged parts to determine if there was any hope of putting them back together.

When Delores woke the next morning, she thought she heard the sound of a small bell. It was a single note, pure and high. She listened hard to see if she could capture it again, but there was only a faint echo in the back of her mind. Anything was better than the drumbeats, she decided, although she felt a bit uncertain about this solitary ring. Deciding that its meaning would be revealed to her soon enough, she shrugged her feet into shapeless terrycloth slippers and pulled a cotton shift over her head. Feeling along the edge of the nightstand, she located her glasses, and the world came into focus.

After untying the braids she'd slept in, she let her long hair swing down her back for a moment before twisting it around her hand and then tying it into a bun at the nape of her neck. Stumbling into the kitchen, she stopped and lifted her head. The only sound was the quiet coo of the pair of morning doves that nested outside her back door. She plucked a clump of chamomile from a cracked earthenware jar at the back of the kitchen sink and steeped her morning cup of *kafée* in a stained white mug imprinted with the logo of the Las Vegas Flamingo hotel.

There it was again.

As she carried the cup to the table, she heard the bell sound, this time unmistakably sharp and clear. Where was it coming from? She marched through the tiny kitchen and bedroom, but all was silent. She noticed but saw nothing that could produce the high pinging note. As she headed toward the front door to retrieve her morning copy of the Inland Corridor News, the harsh jangling of the telephone caused her to jump. Finally, a ringing sound she recognized. She hustled back to the kitchen to answer it.

"Yes," she said flatly, making it more a statement than a question. She hoped it would be Roy calling with news about Luke.

"Ms. Washburn?" The woman's voice at the other end sounded young. Thinking it might be a sales person, Delores started to hang up, but the woman's next words stopped her cold. "It's about Luke."

"Who is this?" Delores asked.

"I'm sorry, I should have introduced myself. I'm a friend of Luke's, Nancy Meza. We went to Pala High together."

Delores knew the Mezas and tried to recall which daughter this was. Could it be the youngest one? She had known Nancy's mother when they were at the same school. Renata must be pushing fifty by now, she mused, and then realized that she was only two years younger, which was a disconcerting thought. But this girl knew something about Luke, and that was all that mattered.

"Where is he?" Delores asked. "Have you seen him?"

"Well, no," Nancy sounded disappointed. "That's why I was calling you. I've been trying to reach him for three days, but his dad said he hasn't been home. Mr. Washburn thought you might have heard from him."

Delores felt her shoulders sag.

"No. He hasn't called here."

"Where do you think he is?" Nancy asked.

Delores thought a moment. How well did this girl know Luke? Probably too well, if she was trying to track him down. She sighed and then decided to tell the truth. "I think he's somewhere on the res, hearing voices and trying to figure out what they mean." Delores paused a moment. "Or maybe he's shacking up with some girlfriend from high school. Hell, I don't know." There was silence on the other end. Delores felt a stab of guilt for her last remark.

"Look," she said, "why don't you give me your number? If he shows up I'll have him call you." She rummaged through a junk drawer until she found a chewed pencil stub, then scribbled Nancy's number across the margin of the newspaper, which she'd been clutching under her arm.

"This is serious, isn't it?" Nancy asked.

"Yes, I think it is." As she was about to hang up the receiver, Delores had a sudden vision. "There's an eagle hovering over you," she said.

"That's funny," Nancy replied. "I dreamt about an eagle last night. It had an emerald in its beak." There was a pause. "It circled around me a few times and then dropped the jewel into my hands."

"You have eagle power."

"My mother always said the same thing," Nancy replied. "If it's true, now's the time to call on it, isn't it?"

As she hung up the phone, Delores considered the girl's last words. The image of the bird lingered in her mind, taking her back to a day as a child when she'd found an eagle feather while playing on the res with her cousin, Louis. He was six-years-old at the time, a tubby, brown-skinned child, serious for his age and completely gullible. She'd stuck the feather in her hair and told him it was an *'apúumu*, ceremonial feather, and that she was going to perform *'áʂwuti móknash*, a killing ceremony, on him. He had run home and told her mother, who made her take the feather out of her hair. Later that night, her father told her how in the old days, their Luiseno ancestors had used eagle feathers to commemorate the anniversary of a chief's death.

"The chief's kinfolk would hold a night-long dance," her father had said. "They would kill an eagle and then skin and cremate it."

"What's 'cremate' mean?" Delores had asked.

"It means to burn something until only ashes remain," her father said. "Then they used the eagle's feathers as part of the dance outfit."

"Do they still do that?"

"No," her father answered. "It's against the law to kill an eagle."

"So what do they do now when a tribal chief dies?"

"Nothing," he'd said.

The memory of her father's voice faded away in the back of her mind.

Having suddenly lost the urge to read, she set the newspaper aside and went out to the backyard. The sun was just beginning to beat down on the reservation, not quite in full force. Delores stopped to break off a few stems of lavender by her porch and then stood still. Something was different about her yard. She wandered toward the tomato plants and saw what she was looking for. Two of them, loaded to the ground yesterday, had been stripped of fruit. She rooted through her zucchini and cucumber vines and saw that they, too, had been plundered. Whoever the intruder was had been stealthy about it. She hadn't heard any unusual sounds last night.

A shadow crossed over her.

She shielded her eyes with her hands and gazed up at the sun. A hawk flew in a lazy circle over the northern end of the reservation. Normally the sight would have pleased her, but instead she thought of her conversation with Nancy and knew that it meant something else. Luke had been here. She would have known it without seeing the bird. But the sight of it, wings spread ominously as it cruised the ground in search of prey, confirmed her gut feeling.

As she turned to go back to the house, a slight motion near the fence caught her eye. She walked towards it and reached through the branches of morning glory. It was a piece of newspaper, still slightly damp from the morning dew. Delores set down the bunch of lavender and straightened out the sheet, which was torn from today's edition. The headline read "County environmental director supports plan for landfill in Pala." The author was listed as Nancy Meza, staff writer. So this was why Nancy had been trying to reach Luke.

Delores quickly read the article. Martin Erman, the county director, had decided to support the development despite areas of concern brought up by opponents. "If the Gregory Canyon landfill is not established, the county could run out of space for trash disposal within ten years," Erman's statement read. The article went on to state that other agencies, including the Regional Water Quality Control Board and the Army Corps of Engineers, still had to sign off on the project and issue permits. Robert Quinlan, the project manager for Inland Mining, was also quoted, noting that Erman's finding put the company "one step closer toward approval."

Delores stared at the piece of paper. In Luke's hands, this news would be like touching flame to a stack of dry twigs. She must call a meeting of the council, but first she and Roy would have to find Luke. When she reached for the bouquet of lavender on the ground beside her, she noticed that a dark feather lay next to it. *'apúumu.* Someone was preparing the eagle ceremony. With one quick motion, Delores gathered the flowers and the feather and hurried toward the house.

As she opened the door, she heard it again—the high thin note of a bell ringing. This time she ignored the sound and went inside to telephone her brother.

THE TOVOT SMOKE ROSE IN TWISTING SPIRALS OF BLUE AND GRAY. In the dim light of the painted cave, Luke waved his hands through the swirling clouds as he hummed the *cháatush.*

hmm hmm hmm

He had made the *pisáatush* offering at the sacred site.

hmm hmm

He had gathered the *púumush* feathers.

hmm hmm hmm

He had heeded the call of his ancestors.

In seven days, at the time of the *móyla* moon, the *tó'ma* would begin.

His *pómkilawish* would be fulfilled.

His land would be protected.

His tribe would be avenged.

He raised the *péshlish* bowl and tapped it lightly with the barrel of his grandfather's gun. A clear sweet note reverberated through the cave and rang out over the reservation.

Ngé´´i. Revenge.

Chapter 8

Carolyn adjusted the rear view mirror for the third time, hoping that what she was looking for wouldn't appear. But there it was, the Porsche, in a color so blue it was almost black. She was certain that it had been following her since she passed Temecula. Weaving in and out of traffic, it hung on her tail all the way up Highway 15 until she signaled for the turn off for the Pala reservation. She tried to get a look at the driver as he shot past, but all she could make out was a pair of sunglasses and dark hair.

She cruised down the exit ramp and stopped at the signal. It took a moment to shake off the sensation of being hunted. Taking a deep breath, she turned up Highway 76 toward Roy's house. The cars sat hunkered and silvery in the sunlight as she passed the casino, which towered over the reservation in the afternoon heat. She turned into Roy's driveway and saw that his car wasn't there. It was Thursday afternoon and his classes should be over by now. Deciding it was too warm to wait in her Toyota, Carolyn got out and walked over to the front porch. Feeling around the edge of the trim above the door, she located the key Roy had told her was hidden there and let herself in. She steeled herself for Tóowish to come bounding out at her, but there was no sign of the dog. As she swung the door open, she was greeted only by silence and the still hot air of an empty house in the middle of the day.

Carolyn set her purse on the living room end table and sat on the couch to wait. For what, she wasn't sure. She had come here to tell Roy that their affair was over and that Tóowish's owner wanted her back. But now that she was here, doubts about her original plan began to seep into her mind.

The house felt familiar to her now. Gazing at the faded red cross of the British flag on the wall, the battered coffee table with its piles of student papers neatly stacked on one corner, she realized that she had been here enough times, had whispered secrets and sat barelegged upon this very sofa, that she belonged a little. It was strange to be so at home in a place to which she might never return again.

At her elbow on an end table sat a small gray stone. She picked it up, recognizing it as one of the items she and Roy had gathered when they took their initial walk together in the canyon. She ran her thumb over its smooth face, remembering the first time he had touched her. How powerful and sure his hands had been. He was much stronger than she, Carolyn realized and that, she was sure, was much of the attraction.

She wished she could be more like him. What would a stronger woman have done in her situation, she wondered. Left her husband after telling him the truth? She hung her head. Maybe she wasn't a strong person, but no one would know how much it took to decide to stay with Everett. This decision would be a first step in becoming the person she wanted to be.

Carolyn watched the dust motes swirl in the light streaming through the living room window. If she listened hard, she could make out the steady tick of the clock in the kitchen, patiently tapping out what was left of her time here in a domestic Morse code. Where was Roy? Tired of waiting, she pulled out the notice that was still crumpled in her skirt pocket. She would leave it and come back another time. She surveyed the living room, but the posters of Elizabeth and Henry, along with the photograph of Sonia, stared back at her in judgment. This is not your home, they seemed to say. She decided against setting the paper anywhere out in the open. Roy's bedroom would be the better place.

The floorboards creaked in the quiet as she made her way to the back of the house. The sight of Roy's bed, carefully made so that its brown quilt lay smooth and even, made her clutch the paper to her chest. She paused a moment before laying the notice on one of the pillows, then stood upright at the quick gun of a motorcycle engine.

Luke.

Her heart began to pound in her chest as she realized that it was too late to run. He would have already seen her car in the driveway.

She reached down to retrieve the paper she had left on the bed, then froze as she heard a step behind her.

When she turned, she had to stifle a scream.

Luke stood in the doorway, one arm resting against the frame, the other clutching a plastic shopping bag. His hair, coated in dust, stuck out in matted spikes and he sported a growth of dark stubble across his cheeks. Carolyn stood paralyzed in front of the bed as his sunken eyes bored into hers.

"*Mómngaash pí' wut.*" Luke spoke in a taunting whisper. *White witch.*

Carolyn whimpered in spite of herself. No, she thought, be strong. She tried to sidle past him, but he moved his arm and blocked her path out the door.

"*Michíyk su´ óm monáa?*" He stood so close to her she could feel his breath, hot and moist, against her neck. *Where are you going?*

"Let me by," she said. When Luke didn't move, she tried to step around him, but he blocked her way with his body. The acrid odor of perspiration and smoke rose from his shirt. A small trickle of sweat snaked down her back.

"Please." She crossed her arms and tried to move past him, but he pushed himself against her even more, causing her to step back until she stood with her legs pressed against the mattress on Roy's bed.

"*Lóoviqup o$uwóo´pi,*" he whispered. *Be afraid.*

Carolyn stood still a moment, unable to make a move. Where was Roy, she wondered, as she studied Luke. Attempting to distract him, she shifted her gaze to the bag he still clutched in his one hand. His eyes followed her just enough that she was able to move past him, away from the bed. He reached out for her as she lunged toward the doorframe and caught her by the arm. Spinning her toward him, he shoved her up against the door and pinned her there with one hand against her throat.

"*Tóovit 'anáala.*" He let out a short laugh. *Scared rabbit.* He leaned toward her, his breath hot on her face, and sniffed at her, a wolf inspecting its prey. A look of disgust combed his features, and he tightened his grip on her throat.

"Why did you come here?" His words, the first he'd spoken in English, sounded harsh and guttural.

She answered without thinking. "I wanted to say goodbye."

He pushed her harder against the door.

"Say it," he said.

Carolyn gagged as his hand tightened around her throat.

He pushed her again.

"Say it," he repeated.

"Goodbye," she whispered.

"Again." His hand pressed hard on her throat.

"Goodbye." She barely got the words out. Her heart raced and her head throbbed and just as she was certain she was going to faint, she heard the sound of the front door opening and Roy's voice calling her name.

"In here." She tried to yell but the words came out in a hoarse bleat. Luke released her and disappeared down the hall. She reached up and placed a hand at her throat, then stumbled down the hallway, where she ran directly into Roy. She threw herself against him.

"Are you alright?" He held her tight. She nodded, trying to still the shakiness in her arms and hands.

"Where's Luke?" Roy asked.

"In the back," she said, hearing a slight quaver in her voice.

Roy moved as if to follow his son, but Carolyn held him back with her hand. Pushing herself away, she stood, facing him. After drawing a deep breath, she spoke.

"I came here to tell you something." She paused and put her hand up to his face. "I can't do this anymore." She dropped her hand. "It's time for me to go home."

"What do you mean?" His eyes, soft and brown, moved over her face.

"This—what we've had—it's been wonderful." She touched his cheek again and smiled. "You are wonderful." She wrapped her arms across her chest and squared her shoulders. "But, I don't belong here." She paused and studied him, her eyes sweeping over his cheeks, his lips, his hair, drinking in every aspect of his face. "I won't be coming back."

Roy's body seemed to freeze. She watched as he stood there motionless and hoped that he would not fight, that he would let her go.

"It's Luke, isn't it? He's scared you."

Carolyn thought a moment. Should she tell him what she really thought about Luke—that he was probably schizophrenic? Even worse, that he was manic and dangerous?

"No," she answered. "It's me. I'm not meant to be here. I never was."

"I don't believe that," Roy said. "I don't think you do either."

Was it a matter of belief? She wasn't sure. All she knew is that if she stayed with Roy her marriage would end, and she wasn't ready to let that part of her life slip away.

"It's not a matter of what I believe," she said, "It's something I have to do." She put her hand on his arm. "I'm sorry."

He took her hand in his and brought it to his lips, then reached out and wrapped his arms around her. She let the clean scent of soap and cedar from his hair and shirt envelop her one last time.

"Don't do this," he whispered.

She said nothing, holding him, feeling the faint steady thump of his heart as his chest rested against hers. Finally, she gently stepped back and gave him what she hoped was a brave smile. As she picked up her purse and walked out the door, she prayed she would have the strength not to turn around.

When she stepped off the front porch, there was a slight stirring in the bushes along the fence, and Tóowish's head emerged. The dog came bounding toward her and buried her wet nose in Carolyn's hand. Carolyn thought back to the day of the accident, when this whole crazy dream had begun. She reached down and wrapped her arms around the collie's neck.

"Goodbye," she whispered. She pushed the dog away so it wouldn't follow her and climbed into the car. The interior closed in on her, hot and airless, and the steering wheel seared her hands as she pulled out of the driveway. She backed out slowly, tires crunching on the gravel drive. On the way home, she did her best to avoid the red eyes that glared at her whenever she caught sight of them in the rear view mirror.

ROY STOOD IN THE DIM HALLWAY FEELING AS IF HE HAD JUST BEEN punched in the gut by an enormous fist. *I won't be coming back.* The words hung in the air, reverberating in a dull whisper at the back of his mind. His skin prickled and his eyes, suddenly wet, blinked rapidly. Breathing hard and fast, he leaned against the wall and waited for the adrenaline rush to pass. No, he wouldn't let this happen to him again. Losing Sonia had left him flattened, feeling more unlike himself than he could ever have imagined. . It had taken six years to return to this world, to get back to a place where he could even consider love again. Now that he'd found it, he would not let it defeat him. If Carolyn was afraid, he would dash her fears. If the problem was Luke, he would ensure that his son did not stand in their way.

The blood began to pound in his temples, and he felt a surge of energy as he made his way down the hall to Luke's room. Without knocking, he shoved the door open and then stopped, stunned.

In the center of the floor, Luke sat cross-legged, mumbling quietly to himself. His eyes had a faraway look and a plastic bag sat cradled in his lap. The afternoon sun pushed its way in filtered streams through the curtains, giving the airless room the shaded darkness of a hidden cave.

It wasn't his son's dusty matted hair or the filthy t-shirt that made Roy's blood freeze. Even the dull look in his eyes and the eerie mumbling didn't scare him as much as the hundreds of pieces of paper covering the walls of the room. White sheets, some of them 8 ½ by 11 inches, some bits of newsprint cut into uneven shapes, lay spread edge to edge from every corner, making the hot oppressive room look like the inside of a hellish igloo. Roy could make out enough black type on the pages to see that they were printouts of landfill articles. Even more disturbing were the hieroglyphics, painted in something dark and reddish brown, smeared across each of them. The symbols reminded him of the paintings he'd seen in some of the caves on the reservation.

"Get up," Roy said.

Luke sat, chanting in a low voice, as if his father wasn't there.

"Now." Roy reached out to grab his son by the arm. But the softness and warmth of Luke's skin stopped him cold. He felt the anger begin to seep out of him and dropped his hand. What had become of them? He and Luke, once the central parts of a closely knit family, had slowly spun out into loose, disintegrating fragments since Sonia died. This was the outcome—his son hearing voices and himself unable to connect with anyone. He hung his head and took a deep breath, then reached out and lifted Luke's chin so he had to look at him.

"She's gone, Luke," he said.

Luke stopped chanting and stared defiantly at his father. His eyes seemed to clear, as if he was seeing him for the first time. When he spoke, his voice sounded rusty and rough and the room became suddenly still.

"It's time, father." His nostrils flared and his chin stuck out resolutely. "It's time for us to avenge our people."

"It's not our job to police this reservation. You know that. Besides, nothing good will come of it." Roy looked down at his hands. "I won't do it."

"Why not?" Luke's eyes welled up. "How can you leave this to me to do alone?"

Roy felt his blood pressure rise. "It's not a question of abandoning you or our ancestors. I love our tribe. But I know who I am." He straightened his shoulders and let out another deep breath. "I don't see myself as being only a Luiseno. I'm much more than that." He paused and looked directly at his son. "You're much more than that. When you come to accept this fact, you'll realize your true destiny. And it won't have anything to do with revenge."

"So, you won't join me?" Luke stood as he said this, the bag clutched in his hand.

"I can't," Roy said.

Luke pushed his shoulders back and thrust out his chest. "Then you leave me no choice." He reached into the bag and pulled out a pistol. It gleamed grayish blue in his hand as he raised it to his head and pulled back the hammer with a sharp click.

Without thinking, Roy leapt forward, shouting "No!" and slapping at the Colt in an attempt to move it away from his son's head. Luke pushed back at his father, shoving him aside as he let out a joyless laugh.

"Give me the gun, Luke." Roy saw that his hand was shaking as he extended it toward his son.

"You would save me but do nothing for our people?" Luke hissed the words out, his voice a sneer.

"Give it to me."

Luke backed away, releasing the cocked hammer as he moved toward the door. "Don't worry," he said. "I have better plans for my grandfather's gun."

Roy wanted to shout, to reach out for his son, but Luke was gone in a breath of angry wind, slamming the bedroom door behind him. The pages on the wall suddenly stirred, fluttering in the resulting breeze like a flock of white butterflies. Roy heard the bang of the living room screen as it opened and shut, then the sputtering pops of a motorcycle engine. He stood immobile, his chest heaving, sweat soaking the shirt under his arms, until the shrill cry of the telephone forced him out of his reverie.

EVERETT TOOK ONE MORE STAGGERING STEP BEFORE SITTING DOWN with a thump into his wheelchair. He leaned the braces against the windowsill, then gazed up at a spider dangling in the corner where the walls met above his worktable. The arachnid silently glided along a single thread leading to its web. Weightless and delicate, like an eight-legged ballet dancer, it paused, its long legs tapping tenderly along the translucent white threads. The edges pulsed as the spider busily spun out new layers of gossamer strands along the web's periphery. When it finished, it crawled into the center, waiting, Everett assumed, for its prey to light there. He marveled at the creature's artistry and patience, its ability to construct its home from a substance within its own body. Such a tiny animal, yet it carried its sanctuary within itself.

In contrast to the miracle he'd just witnessed, his own life was slowly unraveling. Carolyn was gone almost every day now, coming home late in the evenings and going straight upstairs to bed without even speaking to him. It had taken awhile to accept the reality of their new lifestyle and the loss of her companionship.

It was even harder hearing Ben say that she had a lover. Even though he suspected it already, the spoken words had shattered his sense of denial. He could no longer pretend that any shred of his marriage remained. The intimacy that he and Carolyn had shared had evaporated into the air like the last few wisps of smoke from an extinguished candle.

Everett stared for a moment at the model helicopter sitting slightly askew on the work surface in front of him. He'd been able to piece most of it together, but the broken fuselage had resisted any attempts to regain its original shape. Although he'd been careful when he glued the pieces, the model still listed to one side, like a wounded animal, hunched over to protect its injury. He ran his finger along the edge of the propeller, trying to recover the excitement that he'd initially felt when he first began building the tiny planes. No emotion surfaced. The events of the past few months had drained any remaining joy out of him, making even the activities he used to treasure now seem empty and routine.

He wheeled his chair out of his office and sat in the hallway, uncertain of which way to turn. His watch said it was five o'clock in the afternoon. It could be hours before Carolyn returned home. But something in him told him to stay there, to wait for her, patiently, and do what he could to make one last stand. If she acknowledged she loved someone else then he would have no choice. They would have to separate. The thought made his stomach clutch and his eyes tear. Who would take care of him, talk to him in the morning, say goodnight at the end of the day? Even though they'd drifted apart this summer, the years of experiences they shared caved in on him, pulling at him to make every attempt to keep their relationship together.

What if she said it wasn't true, that there was no other man in her life? Everett brushed this idea aside with a wave of his hand. Of course there was someone else. Ben had said so and even if he hadn't, Everett knew in his heart that it was true.

He would wait, then. Rolling the wheelchair a bit forward, he positioned himself so that he was within a few feet of both the front door and the entry from the garage. When Carolyn got home she would come in through one of those entrances. She would have no choice but to talk to him. He set the brake on his right wheel and placed his hands in his lap. He would wait.

THE CLICK OF THE FRONT DOOR LATCH AS IT OPENED MADE EVERETT jump. He realized that he must have dozed off, then looked up at the clock to see that it was seven thirty. He turned to face Carolyn as she crept into the hallway, obviously trying her best to remain unheard. She stopped and then froze, reminding Everett of a rabbit suddenly caught in a beam of light. Both of them stayed where they were for a moment, then Carolyn made a motion as if she planned to head for the stairs. Everett moved his wheelchair toward her, forcing her to stay where she was.

He studied her for a brief instant, noticing that her hair looked wild and knotted and her face was pale and drawn. It saddened him to see these changes in her; she had once been as neat and fresh as a summer garden. Now she seemed frazzled and wan. He was about to speak when she turned her head, and he noticed a bluish spot on her neck. The sight of what was clearly a love bite caused an electric surge of anger.

"Isn't it time that you stop trying to sneak past me?" Everett asked, trying to sound calm despite the quaver in his voice.

"I wasn't sneaking." Carolyn gazed down at the ground and put her hand to her throat. The gesture, which Everett took as an attempt to hide the mark on her neck, angered him even more.

"What were you doing then? Coming home to talk to me?"

"There's nothing to talk about." Carolyn tried to brush past him, but Everett reached out and took hold of her forearm.

"I think there is, Carolyn." He stared up at her, noticing the paleness of her skin and the slight odor of sweat. "In fact, I know there is."

Carolyn looked startled at this last statement. Pulling her arm away, she squared herself off in front of him.

"What do you mean by that?"

He realized that she was going to force him to confront her, to say what they both knew but were afraid to verbalize. But something stopped him, made him suddenly afraid to tell the truth.

"I know you're not happy," he heard himself saying. "I probably don't deserve to know what you're doing and with whom, but I just want to know one thing." He paused and looked into her eyes. They were the eyes of a stranger, grayish-green and frightened. "Does he make you happy?" The words came out in a whisper.

"Yes." Her answer was soft and quick.

"Then we're done here, aren't we?" Before he could think his eyes welled up with tears. He placed his hand over his brow and tried to hide, but there was nowhere to go in the full bare light of her indirect confession.

Carolyn stood silent, biting her lower lip, her arms wrapped around her waist.

"I want it to be over," Everett said. He could feel the hot tears crawling slowly down his cheeks. "I want you to be gone from here." After finally reaching up to wipe his eyes, he glanced away. "I don't want to have to face this anymore."

At these words, Carolyn let out a sob, so low and deep that it sounded like a moan.

"No. Please," she whispered. "I'm sorry. I'm so sorry."

Everett couldn't bear to hear any more. Without a word, he wheeled himself past her and into his study. After shutting the door, he put his hands to his face and wept, so hard that he could feel the muscles in his chest straining as he tried to stifle the sound. When his tears subsided, he wiped the wetness from his face with his hands and gazed up at the model planes that hung above him. They twisted gently in the air, a miniature air force ready to defend him at a moment's notice. His glance drifted over each of them in turn, until he noticed the web, swaying slightly in the corner above his worktable. He pushed his chair closer and saw that the spider crouched in the center of the gossamer strands, its spindly legs working at something small and black beneath it. In a moment, the web began to vibrate. Everett watched in solemn sadness as the arachnid feasted quietly on the doomed insect within its grasp.

LUKE RODE HIS MOTORCYCLE ONTO COUSER CANYON ROAD, THE wind buffeting him until he pulled off into one of the turnouts. Killing the engine, he removed his helmet and shook out his hair, then took the bag with his grandfather's gun from the back of the bike. The fast ride and warm wind against his face had cleared his head, pushing the voices into the background.

As he strode across the desert basin, the coarse gravel crunching below his feet, he relived the last few moments at his father's house. Had he really pinned the white woman up against a doorway with his hand? The scene was cloudy and fractured, as if he had dreamt it or had been a spectator, watching some other person attack his father's girlfriend.

Her fear had been as real as the pulse beating against his palm as he held her neck. Carolyn's lips had quivered as he pushed up against her, so close he could smell the sweat on her skin and the soft odor of her hair. The sweet, flower-like fragrance had made him almost dizzy with its familiar scent. It was the same as his mother's hair, before she had gotten sick. The memory of her reserved smile, her long dark locks flashing as she tied them in a knot, almost froze him in his steps.

He pushed the image aside and stepped around clumps of scrub brush and piles of granite rock until he found the opening of the cave where he had been hiding the last few days. Inside the walls were dark and the air smelled of cedar and soot. Setting his bag on the ground, he searched outside for twigs and branches until he found enough to make a fire. He carried them back inside, dumping them in a pile below the section of the wall covered with hieroglyphics and then sat on the ground. The encounters with Carolyn and his father had weakened him. He felt hungry and realized that he had brought no food. When the voices spoke to him, there was no thought of anything practical. At times, he had trouble even remembering where he had been.

They were not here now and their absence made him feel jumpy and alone. He missed his father and felt a quick pang of regret at the way he'd left him this afternoon. Roy's lack of support and understanding made Luke suddenly wrap his arms around his chest. In the years when his mother was alive, he had had her vision and history to fuel his love for his tribe. Since she'd been gone, his father had refused to play that role. Well, it was his loss. There was no way to convince his old man. There was only Aunt Delores, who sometimes understood, and the voices, calling out to him from the past.

The setting sun sent a few last strokes of amber light streaming inside the cave like probing fingers. Luke reached into his pocket and found his book of matches. Tearing one off, he watched the sulfurous tip flare into life and carefully held it under the pile of dried leaves and twigs. The wood smoldered and then finally caught, a few cautious flames licking at the branches. The flickering light made the painted characters on the cave wall dance before him.

Luke recalled being here with Nancy. He hadn't seen her since the night they met on the beach, and he wondered if she would talk to him again. In his other pocket he fumbled until he located his father's cell phone, which he'd grabbed on his way out of the house. He dialed her number and watched as the small fire belched puffs of smoke against the cave wall. The phone buzzed against his ear, and he felt himself slipping away as the whispers formed at the back of his mind.

"*Ngéem pitóo,*" they murmured. *Go now.*

"Hello?" Nancy's voice sounded small and high.

"*Ngé''i,*" the voices hummed, low and reverberating. *Revenge.*

"Who is this?"

"*Yáx pōi'.*" *Tell her.*

"*Máamayu néy,*" Luke whispered. *Help me.*

"Hello? Who's there?"

"*Ngé''i.*"

"Luke? Is that you?"

"*Pitóo,*" the voices thundered. *The time is now.*

"*Wám nóo 'angéey.*" Luke softly spoke the words for goodbye. He wanted to talk to her, to tell her more, but the voices were chanting so loudly that he couldn't think, couldn't speak, couldn't move.

"Luke? I can't hear you? Are you there?"

There was silence and then the line went dead. Luke dropped the phone to the ground and slumped against the wall of the cave, feeling the pressure of the sharp stones against his back.

"*Ngé''i.*" The voices grew louder, urging him on. "*Ngé''i pitóo.*" *Revenge, now.*

The flames of the tiny fire twisted and twirled in the air, throwing spirals of smoke before him. The cave grew dark. Through the opening he watched the Green Corn moon, now on the wane, rise slowly in the sky. It glowed like a celestial warrior's bow, the crescent tips pointing the way to salvation.

Chapter 9

Carolyn stood still long after the office door clicked shut behind her husband. His words had thrown her, lifted her up into the air and spun her into an emotional freefall, like Alice down the rabbit hole. She could hear the Santa Ana winds outside the kitchen window, blowing with such force that the glass thumped against the frame. The panes rattled until her breathing, rapid and shallow, finally subsided. It took awhile, but she finally felt the floor again beneath her feet.

And where was she now? She had told Roy goodbye, and Everett had asked her to leave. She was nowhere and nothing, with no lover, no husband and now, no home. The wind blew a sharp gust against the sliding glass door, snapping Carolyn out of her reverie. Slipping the latch back, she slid the door open and listened to the rustle of the palm fronds as the warm winds whipped through the yard. It was still light, but the dying sun threw dusky shadows while the breeze whistled through the canyon. Change simmered in the air.

Carolyn slid the door shut, closed the latch, and then crept upstairs to her bedroom. The afternoon heat lingered in the corners, causing sweat to break out on her arms and neck the moment she entered. She opened the closet and reached up into the shelves until she located the handle of her suitcase. Pulling it down with both hands, she set it on the bed and sprung the latches open. The faint odor of mildew and something else—a hint of plumeria—rose into the air as she lifted the lid. She had not used this piece of luggage since she and Everett had gone to Hawaii four years before. With a clutch of despair, Carolyn recalled the happiness she felt as Everett placed a thick lei of tuberose and orchids over her head and kissed her, softly, on the cheek. She had worn the flowers home, inhaling the sweet fragrance that rose up every time she stirred. Despite all that had happened since then, it seemed as if it was only a day ago that she had placed the heavy lei in a plastic bag and set it inside the refrigerator. During the days that followed, she would remove it from the bag and drink in its scent until the blossoms had finally curled up, wilted and brown.

Pushing the memory aside, she pulled open the top dresser drawer and lifted out the entire contents. Thin, faded bras and underwear, brown balls of nylon stockings, even silk-covered sachets that no longer held their scent, left a trail on the floor as they tumbled from her hands. After placing it all in the suitcase, she entered the closet and removed sweaters and blouses, their hangers clicking together like quiet castanets. Running her hands over each item like a blind person, she gathered shorts and jeans, tennis shoes and sandals, and her favorite Gap sweatshirt, a gift from Everett on her thirty-ninth birthday. The sleeve edges were worn and frayed, but she folded it up and laid it in the suitcase along with the other clothes.

As she pulled items from the rack, she stopped and reached toward the bag that had brushed her arm. There, tucked away in the corner, hung her wedding dress, swathed in sheer plastic from the dry cleaners. She set down the clothes and reached beneath the covering, fingering the embossed brocade of the fabric. The satiny feel took her back to her wedding day, twenty-five years ago. There was the justice of the peace, a stout elderly woman with steel-gray hair, smiling benevolently as she read their vows. Her parents, still alive then, huddled uncertain and bewildered beside Everett's mother, who glowed in rose-colored taffeta. The faces of their college friends—shaggy, bearded, long haired—swirled before her. How amused they had all seemed. How happy she had felt then.

Now, as she ran her hand along the lacy hem of the dress, she recalled how the rain the week before the wedding had poured in loud sheets off their rooftop, causing them to consider canceling the outdoor event. But their wedding day had dawned sunny and bright and when Everett had held out his hand and asked her "Are you ready?" she'd answered "Yes" and never looked back.

Until recently.

Carolyn dropped the edge of the skirt and smoothed the plastic lining back over it. It would be one of the many things she would leave behind today. She gathered the clothing she'd set on the floor and brought it to the suitcase, mechanically folding and stuffing the shirts and pants until she could snap the suitcase shut.

Where was she to go?

Shoving the suitcase aside, she sat down next to it, toying with the handle. Her parents were both gone, and she rarely spoke to her brother, who lived in Alaska. There were her roommates in college, who she'd not seen since her wedding day twenty-five years ago. And although she was friendly with her neighbors and coworkers, she didn't know any of them well enough to move in with them. The realization that she had no one to turn to made Carolyn feel suddenly dizzy, as if she was once again in emotional freefall. She laid down on the bed next to the suitcase and hugged her arms close to her chest. The dry August wind shook the windowpanes.

When she tried to cry, the tears wouldn't come.

THE WORDS ON THE PAGE DANCED BEFORE HIM, AS IF THEY WERE rows of ants, crawling until they blurred together into an undecipherable trail of black ink. Roy had been staring at the pile of student essays for over two hours, but had hardly read a word. Instead, he replayed in his mind the events of the last twenty-four hours. He heard Carolyn repeating "I can't see you anymore," as if there was a movie reel spinning the same scene over and over. He saw Luke, standing before him, an angry, lost version of Sonia and himself, cradling his grandfather's gun as if it was his only offspring. These images filled him with sadness. He longed to call Carolyn, but feared that she would resent his disrespecting her wish to end the relationship.

And Luke. Should he call the police? His son was emotionally unstable and armed, certainly a lethal combination. Roy shook his head. He knew how Luke would react when he saw the authorities. The loss of face would be unbearable. Worse, Luke would assume that his father had called them and view it as the ultimate betrayal. Besides, Roy wasn't certain where Luke was. Perhaps Delores would know. He decided to call her. But the telephone rang just as he reached for it, causing him to jump, his hand snapping back as if the cord was a coiled snake. He grabbed the receiver on the fourth ring.

"Professor Washburn?"

It sounded like a student. Roy was always surprised when one of them called him at home.

"Who is this?"

"My name is Nancy Meza. I don't know if you remember me; I went to Pala High."

Roy did remember her. She was a small, Cupa girl with short hair who had taken his Tudor/Stuart history class at the college last fall.

"I'm calling about Luke," she continued.

"Have you seen him?" Roy asked. "Do you know where he is?"

"No, but I think he called me last night."

"What made you think it was Luke?"

"Well, he never identified himself, but it sounded like him," Nancy's voice paused a moment. "And then it didn't. It was a strange conversation."

Roy could imagine.

"What did he say exactly?"

"This is going to sound weird, but I'm not sure. He was whispering and speaking in Luiseno."

"Did you understand any of it?"

"Not really," Nancy answered. "My mom spoke Cupa at home, although we heard some Luiseno when my grandparents visited." She paused again. "Mr. Washburn, I'm worried about him. He sounded different—kind of scary, actually."

"Nancy, this is important. Can you remember any of what he said?" Roy held his breath, hoping this girl would give him some clue as to the whereabouts of his son.

"Well, it was hard to hear, but I thought he said the word "help" or "help me.""

"Was there anything else?"

"Not that I could understand. Oh, wait, there was another word. I recognized it but I don't know what it means."

"What is it?" Roy asked.

"I'm not sure, but I think it was "*Ngé''i*.""

Roy's heart skipped a beat.

"I'm sorry I can't be of more help," Nancy said.

"Thanks, Nancy. You've been great." Roy found a pen and wrote down her cell phone number. "Please call me if Luke contacts you again."

"I will." There was a moment of silence before she continued. "Mr. Washburn," she said. "I'm frightened. Do you think he'll be all right?"

"I hope so," Roy answered.

He hung up the phone and sat a moment, trying to calm the beating of his heart. Luke was seeking revenge. And Carolyn would be the target of his son's actions.

He reached again for the telephone and dialed Delores' number. While the line hummed in a deep purr each time her phone rang, he closed his eyes and said a short prayer to Takwic for strength and guidance in the hours to come.

HE'D NEVER BEEN GOOD AT SAYING GOODBYE. EVERETT TRIED TO keep his balance while Charlie thumped him on the back and Tracy stared at him with an almost motherly look on her chiseled features. It had taken him almost an entire hour to drag himself, excruciating step by excruciating step, from the parking lot up to the third floor.

"You're a warrior, man." Charlie gave Everett one last bone-crushing hug and then almost pushed him down when he broke his grip. "You take care, you hear?"

Everett looked down at the floor, his face flushing hot as he fought back the tears that pricked at the corners of his eyes.

"Thanks for everything, Charles."

At the sound of his name, Charlie teared up. He waved at Everett and Tracy, then stumbled across the PT floor, wiping at his eyes with his paw-like hands.

Tracy smiled at Everett and then shook her head.

"What is it with him and the warrior stuff?" she asked.

Everett shrugged. "Maybe he spent too much time watching the Montezuma mascot at SDSU."

"Well, wherever he gets it, he's right when it comes to you." Tracy hugged her clipboard close to her chest and gave Everett another wide grin. "I still can't believe that you actually walked in here on your own. Last week you seemed to be struggling with some of the longer steps, and now you're really moving." She shook her head again. "What caused the breakthrough?"

Everett wasn't sure. But, for some reason, he had awoken this morning feeling energized and alive for the first time in three years. Ben had offered to help him, but he'd struggled into the van on his own, stowing his chair and braces behind the seat. When he reached the Scripps Hospital parking lot, he'd sat a minute and then decided to leave the chair behind. The walk from the parking structure to the PT floor had been slow and painful, but he'd done it, without falling or asking for help.

"I don't know," he answered. "The fact that I've used up all the PT coverage in my insurance might have something to do with it."

"Well, it couldn't have happened at a better time." Tracy put her hand on his arm and gave it a brief squeeze. "We'll miss you, Everett." She scribbled something on a page in her chart, tore off the sheet, and handed it to him. "Be sure to follow up with your primary doctor and let us know how you're doing." Before he could blink, she leaned forward and gave him a quick kiss on the cheek, then spun around and marched off, the tails of her lab coat flapping like a crisp sail behind her.

Everett felt his face flush again, then shook his head and chuckled. If he didn't know that Tracy was gay and had a live-in partner, he would have sworn that she was sweet on him. He would miss her and Charlie. They had been his own private cheerleading squad, urging him on when the days seemed the darkest. Now that he had found his feet again, he was on his own. It felt strange and wonderful at the same time.

After a thirty-minute struggle to get back to the elevator and down to the parking structure, the wonder had worn off. The heat seemed to rise from the pavement in visible waves and the smell of exhaust and motor oil made Everett feel dizzy. He leaned against the door of the van, sweat pouring down his neck and soaking his shirt on both sides. After popping open the door and placing the braces behind the seat, he started the car, his back and stomach muscles screaming with pain from dragging his feet forward for so many steps. He leaned out the window to pay the attendant the requisite two-dollar parking fee and then, for the first time that day, thought about Carolyn. She hadn't come downstairs that morning, at least not before he left for his appointment at the clinic. She was supposed to be at work today, but Everett wondered if she had called in sick. For a moment, he relived the scene from the night before. He had laid in wait for her; she had admitted her guilt. The memory of her face—looking crumpled and small as he asked her to leave—made his extraordinary achievement today suddenly seem small and unimportant.

The Highway 52 off-ramp loomed before him. He took it and fought down a wave of vertigo as he crested the overpass. While the van's wheels hummed over the road, he drummed his fingers on the steering wheel and tried to decide what to do now that his marriage was essentially over. Would Carolyn decide to leave? Everett moved the van toward the exit for Hwy 15 then stared at the flat brown fields of Miramar Air Station as they flashed by.

Perhaps he should be the one to go. The thought of selling their house and leaving his yard and canyon view saddened him as much as the thought of being alone. Did he really want her gone? Everett struggled with this thought. He'd been betrayed and yet, Carolyn was his one true love. Of that, he was certain. There would be no one else for him.

The orange "MAINT REQ'D" light flashed on the dashboard. At the same time, Everett heard the warning ping as the tiny gasoline can icon lit up on the dash. Luckily, he was almost home and close to his favorite service station. He pulled up to the first row of pumps and killed the engine, then sat a moment trying to decide what to do. He had the wheelchair in the back seat and could easily pull it out, just as he'd always done the last three years. But there were the braces, laying like the graceful legs of a stork across the back seat. As exhausted as he was, Everett reached back for them and pulled them forward. He would walk from now on, no matter how tired he felt.

He heaved himself out of the van, placing first one brace and then the other before him. After swiping his credit card, he placed the nozzle into the tank opening and gazed at the horizon as he squeezed the pump. While the handle kicked against his palm, he noticed that the sky was tinged with brown. Above the fumes leaking from the tank, he caught the scent of burning wood in the warm breeze. Fire season was starting.

After shaking off the nozzle and replacing it, he stowed his braces in the back seat. He didn't know what he would find when he got to the house. Part of him hoped Carolyn would be there; another part of him wished she wouldn't.

He raced his heart home to see which answer awaited him behind his front door.

CAROLYN CRACKED OPEN THE BINDING OF ANOTHER BOOK AND SLID a date card in the inside pocket. After taking one look at her swollen eyes and red nose, Mary had sent her to the back office to do repair and updates, rather than man the front desk. Carolyn was grateful for the reprieve from dealing with the public. She had woken this morning sweaty and cramped, one arm wrapped along the edge of the suitcase on top of the bed. After showering and changing, she'd thrown the luggage in the car and gone to work, noting that Everett had already left. During the short drive to the library, she'd turned off the radio and driven in numb silence, too drained to think about her future.

She thought about it now, though. Everett had made it clear that he didn't want her at home any more. The question was where to go? Having no real answer, she sighed and turned back to the stack of texts beside her. As she picked up a heavy volume on parapsychology, the door swung open and Mary's head appeared.

"You okay?"

Carolyn nodded and forced herself to smile.

Mary's chubby fingers drummed a moment on the doorframe.

"Hey, you got some time this afternoon?" she asked.

"I have all the time in the world," Carolyn answered.

"Good. Come with me."

They left the library, after Mary gave Sheryl instructions to cover the front desk while they were gone. Carolyn followed Mary outside to a faded VW van that had once been red. A peeling "No Bozos" sticker clung to the back bumper. Shoving aside a pile of fast food wrappers and newspapers, Carolyn climbed in the front seat, then held her breath at the doggy odor that rose above the smell of cigarettes. She rolled down her window as Mary revved the engine and careened out of the parking lot.

"Where're we going?" Carolyn asked.

"Stables."

Mary cranked up the stereo and hummed along to some country tune that Carolyn didn't recognize. They drove a few miles and then pulled into the entrance to the stables across the street from the Penasquitos canyon preserve. Hazy clouds of dust rose in their wake as they parked the van next to the iron railing of a large corral. Mary led her to a covered stall where two horses, one brown and one a soft black, eyed them with relaxed curiosity.

"This one here is Shedaisy," Mary said, stroking the brown horse across the nose. "And this is Licorice."

Carolyn eyed the black horse for a moment before reaching out and touching his flank. The stiff hair felt course and smooth at the same time. Licorice stirred and snorted, then stamped his hoof. Carolyn took a step back.

"It's alright," Mary said. "They're both good babies." She patted each of them on the rump.

"They're beautiful," Carolyn said.

"They're expensive and spoiled and Shedaisy's feisty as hell, but I love 'em anyway." Mary reached for the halters hanging on a hook on the back wall of the stall. "Thought we could go for a ride." Without turning around, she added. "It might take your mind off things."

"You know how I feel about riding horses," Carolyn said. "I'm not really comfortable around them."

Mary slid a halter over Licorice's head, then turned and squinted at Carolyn.

"I know. But Licorice is pretty gentle." She walked over to the corner of the stall and picked up a saddle. "And a ride might do you some good."

Carolyn didn't reply. She watched Mary dress the horses, then held her breath as Mary handed her Licorice's reins.

"I'll help you up."

She cupped her hand next to the stirrup. Carolyn stepped on her palm and let Mary push her up and over the horse's back. Licorice danced a bit as Carolyn gripped the saddle horn and tried to find the stirrup with her foot.

"There, you've got it."

Mary heaved herself onto Shedaisy's back and then clicked her tongue. Both horses broke into a slow trot. Carolyn leaned forward, squeezing the reins in her hands. They stopped at the street corner across from the canyon entrance.

"Relax," Mary said. "Sit up straight and let yourself move with the horse. Don't fight him. If you want him to stop, say 'whoa' and pull up on the reins."

They took off toward the canyon entrance and then found the trail at the end of the parking lot. Mary and Shedaisy led the way at a leisurely pace, with Licorice and Carolyn following close behind. The late afternoon sun bore down on Carolyn's back and a stiff breeze blew warm wind on her arms as they wound their way down the trail. She studied the rows of houses that dotted the rise across the canyon and thought she spotted her own back yard through the cluster of trees lining the streambed. At one point, a large hawk circled above them. Carolyn heard the hiss of a rattlesnake and saw Licorice prick his ears up at the sound.

They stopped at a small clearing near the streambed to water the horses. Carolyn dismounted stiffly and sat next to Mary on the knobby surface of a fallen log. Mary pulled a pack of Pall Malls from her jeans pocket and shook out the match after lighting a cigarette. Carolyn watched as Mary exhaled a cloud of white smoke. It was fire season, and the thought of anything lit in the canyon made her nervous. Mary finally spoke.

"So, what's going on with that Indian friend of yours?"

"Nothing," Carolyn answered. "I told him I didn't want to see him anymore."

"Why not?"

"I don't know." Carolyn raked the toe of her tennis shoe back and forth across the sandy ground in front of her. "Our worlds were too different." She thought a moment. "I didn't want it all to happen in the first place. Then it did, and it was okay for awhile." She stopped. "Then it just got scary."

"Moving too fast for you?" Mary blew a thick puff into the air with each word.

"No, it wasn't that." Carolyn answered. "It just didn't feel right." She picked at the bark next to her. "I don't belong with him. I never did."

"What does your husband think of all this?"

"He's pretty angry. Yesterday he told me to leave."

"Men." Mary snorted and shook her head. "Well, I guess he had a right to say that." She took one last puff, then dropped the cigarette stub on the ground and rubbed it out with her foot. "Even so, you two seemed pretty happy until his accident a few years ago." She stood up and readjusted the waistline of her jeans. "Maybe you should try to rediscover whatever you had going for you in the first place."

She walked over to Shedaisy and grabbed the reins, then turned to look at Carolyn.

"Ready to go back?"

Carolyn felt as if she was being asked more than one question. She nodded her head, then reached for Licorice's saddle.

"Think you can get up by yourself?"

Without answering, Carolyn put her foot in the stirrup and swung herself over the horse's back. It wasn't beautiful, but she felt a pleasant flush to her face as she straightened herself in the saddle.

They marched the horses back along the trail the same way they'd come in, this time with Carolyn leading. Halfway back, Licorice lifted his head and snorted, then pulled his neck back and shied nervously.

Carolyn pulled back on the reins to settle the horse then looked around. She thought she caught the scent of something burning.

"Smells like fire," Mary said. "Looks like it's coming from up north."

Gazing past the homes in the distance, Carolyn could see the first few streaks of brown haze stretching across the horizon.

"Is that what's spooking the horses?"

She had just spoken the words, when Licorice took a sudden leap forward and began to gallop down the trail. Carolyn felt her throat constricting as she fought to keep her seat on the saddle. The horse pounded forward. Mary shouted behind her to pull up on the reins. Carolyn screamed "Whoa, whoa!" as they thundered down the trail. Clinging to the saddle horn with one hand, she jolted up and down in the leather seat and pulled helplessly at the reins with the other. When they reached the edge of the parking lot, Licorice reared up and skidded to a stop.

Carolyn felt herself catapult out of the saddle. She remembered seeing first the sky and then the dirt rising up to meet her before everything went black.

DELORES HUNG UP THE RECEIVER AND WIPED THE SWEAT FROM HER brow. Roy was her older brother, yet he continually called on her come to his rescue. This time she didn't know if she could help him. She had not seen Luke for days, although she guessed that her nephew was somewhere in the canyon. At least that's what she told her brother.

The signs told her otherwise. The eagle had circled her garden three times and then dropped a feather. Luke was preparing for war. In the night sky, the moon pointed the warrior's bow toward the south. His enemy would be found there. And the drumbeats in her head had grown louder, telling her that the time was near. Whatever Luke was planning, he would take action soon.

In the kitchen, the teakettle screamed. Delores removed it from the stove, then poured the steaming water into a cup that held a spoonful of chamomile leaves. Once the tea was steeped, she decided that it was too warm outside to be drinking anything hot. She cracked a few ice cubes from a tray in the freezer and placed them in a tall thick glass, then poured the tea over the cubes. The ice cracked as it met the steaming liquid.

Delores carried the drink to her tiny table and shoved aside piles of drying French lavender. Reaching inside a leather pouch she wore on the inside of her skirt, she pulled out a clove cigarette. After lighting the end, she took two quick, deep drags and watched as the smoke circled above her head when she exhaled. The sun set orange and red outside her window and the Santa Ana winds rattled the panes.

Delores studied the images that danced in the vapor before her. As the herbs relaxed her nerves, she imagined tall tongues of flame licking at the edges of the canyon. She took another drag and then exhaled. In the swirling drifts, she saw Luke load a pistol. The moon rose above her nephew as the darkness gathered. In her mind's eye she pictured him leaning his head back and howling at the moon, an anguished, bitter cry that echoed in her thoughts long after the image had faded.

When the cigarette was finally nothing but a stub, she set it in an ashtray and took a sip of tea. Luke would avenge their people, and there was nothing she or his father could do about it. Unless they could find him first.

She poured the last of the tea down the kitchen sink, the ice now melted to slivers of white. The windowpanes rattled in the wind. As she latched them shut, Delores caught the strong odor of burning wood. There would be fire in the canyon tonight. She gathered her purse and keys, then headed out to her ancient Chevy to pick up her brother and, hopefully, find Luke before it was too late.

As she opened the car door, the wind blew hard in warm gusts and the smell of smoke got stronger. In the distance, a coyote yipped, its mournful plea urging her on her way.

Chapter 10

Everett dropped the receiver into the cradle and scooped up his car keys. He'd just received a call from the Scripps Urgent Care office in Rancho Bernardo.

"Your wife has been in an accident."

His wife.

He maneuvered through Friday afternoon traffic, pulling up on the brake handle each time a motorist cut him off, his heart beating hard against his chest. The last time he'd received a phone call like this one was when his father, a foreman for a construction firm, had been in an accident. A concrete pipe had gotten away from a crane operator and crushed his dad's right leg. Home alone at thirteen, he had finally located his mother and found a neighbor willing to give him a ride to the hospital. His father had survived, although the leg was never right. He died at sixty-two, a year before Everett and Carolyn were married.

His wife.

After pulling into the Scripps Clinic parking lot, he took a deep breath and tried to calm his jumpy pulse. There had been so many accidents in his life—his father's, his own, and now Carolyn's. Worst of all had been the stillborn death of his son. The memory of losing the baby, so soon after birth, was like a punch to the gut, causing a sudden, painful stricture of his chest and throat muscles.

Each time these incidents had occurred, he'd experienced the same sensation, as if he was perched on the edge of a cliff, looking down into an enormous chasm to which there was no bottom. His psychologist, Leo Osterman, tried to convince him that this image had to do with the fear of losing someone dear. While such occurrences were normal, Osterman argued, it was important to let go of the feelings as soon as they started. Losing friends, pets, jobs, in fact, anything that was loved, he said, was a part of living. Of course, Osterman looked as if he'd never lost anything in his life. He was a hale, iron-pumping jock with a thick shock of dark hair and a receptionist, Heidi, who was blonde, twenty-something, and so roundly ripe that Everett found himself tongue tied whenever he came into the office.

"All loss is relative, Everett," Osterman had told him one April afternoon, as they sat in the doctor's Del Mar office, watching the rain tap in fat gray drops against the windowpane. "It's what you have left that matters."

Everett didn't know if he agreed. Sometimes what was left wasn't enough.

He pulled into the blue-lined handicap space next to the entrance and reached for his chair. There were no empty seats in the waiting room. Everett steered past two coughing children and a teenager with his hand wrapped in a bag of ice to tell the receptionist he was here to see his wife.

His wife.

The woman behind the counter buzzed him into another reception area with a nurse's station and two curtained off hospital beds.

"She's in room three," an orderly told him.

She was lying still and pale atop a paper-covered examination table. Her arm, wrapped in a gauze sling and bent up against her chest, reminded him of a broken bird's wing. The sight of it made him want to weep. She turned when he entered and gazed at him with red-rimmed eyes, her hair mussed and lines of dirt streaked across the side of her face.

He reached for her.

"I'm sorry. So sorry," she murmured. "Mary took me riding after work and the horse bolted. I don't remember much about what happened after that." She looked up at Everett. "I think Mary stayed with the horses and the paramedics brought me here."

"Shh," he said. "It's all right." He stroked the hair back from her forehead.

The x-rays were negative. She had a bruised collarbone and a minor concussion. The doctor warned Carolyn to watch for dizziness. It would take six weeks or more for the inner ear to heal from the jolt her head had received.

On the way home, they talked about stopping to get Carolyn's car, which was still at the library. He urged her to wait until tomorrow, until she'd had some time to rest.

They held hands while he drove, letting go only when Everett had to use the brake.

When they got home, Carolyn gingerly climbed out of the front seat and walked with halting steps into the house. Everett pressed the switch to close the garage door behind him, then stopped a moment before tackling the ramp leading into the hallway. He promised himself that when he crossed the threshold this time, everything would be different. He would be more present. He would confess to Carolyn that he could walk, and he would make every effort to do so, no matter how painful.

He pushed his chair inside and noticed that the house was stifling in the late afternoon heat. Rolling past his wife, who had lain down on the couch in the family room, he cracked open the sliding glass door to the backyard and paused a moment to gaze at the sunset. Brilliant strokes of orange and red raked the horizon while the sun sank into the edge of the canyon. The palm leaves rustled in the Santa Ana breeze. For the first time in weeks, Everett felt a sense of peace.

Then he noticed the scent of smoke in the air. It was a fire, somewhere to the north of them. He was about to comment on this to Carolyn when the telephone rang, causing him to jump in his seat.

He picked up the receiver on the second ring.

"Mr. Weedman?" Everett relaxed at the sound of Ben's voice, then told him what had happened to Carolyn.

"Geez," Ben said. "Is she all right?"

"Yes, she'll be fine. She has a slight concussion and a bruised collarbone. We were lucky it wasn't more serious."

"Thank God." There was a pause. "I was calling to see if I could stop by tonight," Ben said. "I have something important to tell you both."

"Sure. We'll be here. Take your time and drive carefully," Everett warned before hanging up.

"Who was it?" Carolyn asked.

"Ben," Everett replied. "He's coming over in a little while."

The shadows deepened as night began to fall. Everett flipped on the kitchen lights and then sat by Carolyn, an unread newspaper in his lap.

Outside, the crickets creaked out a song of innocence, blind to any intruder who might join them in the grass.

ROY HADN'T HUGGED HIS SISTER IN YEARS. ALTHOUGH SHE WOULD give him a peck on the cheek on occasion, hugging was not something they did much, even at holidays. But when he saw Delores standing outside his screen door, he let her in and then, without saying a word, wrapped his arms around her. Her shoulders felt thin and bony; her hair smelled of sage. As they held each other, he glanced out the window and noticed an odd sight. Perched on the empty clothesline in the front yard sat a large group of crows. At least twenty of them clung to the thin wires, huddled together as if holding a conference beneath the darkening sky, which had turned the color of rust.

"We'll find him," Delores said. She gently disengaged herself from her brother's embrace and readjusted her thick glasses. Tóowish sat at their feet, tongue out and tail thumping on the floor.

"Luke talks to you," Roy said. "Has he given any clues about where he might be hiding?" He glanced one last time at the birds in the yard as he shut the front door. None of them had moved.

"No," she answered. "But if he's anywhere near Medicine Rock, we'll never get there. The roads are all backed up because of the fires near Couser Canyon."

"The canyon's on fire?"

Before Delores could answer, Roy reached for the remote and turned on the television set. A local news reporter in foul weather gear stood on the shoulder of Hwy 76, just outside the turnoff for the reservation. Dark smoke billowed as orange flames licked the hillside in the background behind him.

"The fire has spread along the eastern side of the reservation between King and Couser Canyon roads," the reporter said. "The police are setting up road blocks and telling us that residents north of Highway 76 may be asked to evacuate. We'll have a briefing from the fire chief at seven thirty this evening."

Roy turned toward the living room window, where the late afternoon sky rolled on above them in a blanket of brown haze. His homeland was on fire, and his son was out there somewhere, armed and hearing voices. Roy glanced at the contents of the tiny living room. The British posters tacked to the wall, the stacks of papers on the table, the small piles of stones and rocks collected on walks through the canyon. He could bear to leave all of it, but he couldn't bear to lose Luke, the last hard connection to his life with Sonia. He could not fail her now by allowing Luke to be consumed in this latest episode of mental illness.

He turned to his sister.

"Luke's out there," he said. "I have to find him."

Delores reached for a duffel bag on the floor next to the couch. "Why don't you gather a few of your things, in case we can't get back."

Roy rummaged through the small filing cabinet in the back corner of his bedroom. He pulled out a copy of the deed to the house, Luke's and his birth certificates, his college diplomas, and a copy of his teaching credential. As he was about to shut the drawer, he noticed that a piece of pale brown parchment was protruding from one of the folders. He pulled it out and then stood a moment, running his finger along the edge of the paper. It was his marriage license. He stared at the two signatures at the bottom of the page. His lay small and neat, each letter clearly and completely defined, while Sonia's sprawled out beside it in bold loops and generous swirls. He didn't really need this piece of paper anymore, but his chest suddenly grew tight at the thought of leaving it. He placed it with the others in his hand and slammed the drawer shut.

After adding a few photographs and a couple of jackets to the duffel bag, Roy and Delores climbed into his truck, the dog jumping behind the passenger's seat. As Roy backed the old Chevy out of the driveway, he noticed that the crows were gone, the clothesline wires swaying weakly in the wind. He and Delores headed out along Mission Avenue toward the highway. The air was thick with soot and burned cinders.

"He goes to the painted caves," she said. "I'm just not sure which ones."

"It doesn't matter," Roy answered, slowing the truck. Before them brake lights glowed like a string of rubies along the highway. "They must have the roads blocked off."

Roy felt helpless behind the wheel, unable to move in the stopped traffic. To his left sat the Pala Casino, looking strangely vulnerable below the growing mushroom cloud of smoke that loomed above its roof.

"What if he's not on the res?" Delores asked.

"What do you mean?"

"What if he's somewhere else?" She turned to look at him, her eyes large and swimming behind the lenses of her glasses.

Roy realized that she was right. Luke wouldn't be in the canyon. He would be looking for Carolyn and her husband. Roy had her work telephone number, but he'd never called her at home. He didn't even know where in Rancho Penasquitos she lived.

A large flake of white ash floated by on the breeze, reminding Roy of the pages plastered to the wall in his son's room.

"I think I know where he might be," Roy said. He waved at the driver behind him, then put the truck in reverse and maneuvered it until he could turn back onto the highway leading toward his house. Once he was clear of the stopped traffic, he stepped on the gas pedal. The truck sped toward the mission.

"Where are we going?" Delores asked, her hand gripping the dashboard.

"Back home," Roy answered. "If Luke is trying to find Carolyn, he'd have to have her address. Maybe he left something behind that will tell us where he thinks she is."

Delores reached into her purse, which was slung over one shoulder. She pulled out a cell phone.

"What's her name again?" she asked.

"Weedman. Carolyn Weedman."

She dialed 411, then held the phone to her ear.

"Rancho Penasquitos," she said. "Carolyn Weedman." She waited a moment. "Okay. Thank you."

She turned to her brother. "No listing."

"Then we've got to get back to the house," Roy said.

"How will we get there?" Delores asked. "They're evacuating everyone. We won't be able to get through."

Roy thought a moment. His sister was right. With the fires this close to his home, the local authorities would not allow them near his neighborhood.

"We've got to try," he said.

They headed toward the turnoff for Ortega Street, the only sound the drum of the tires against pavement. As they neared his neighborhood, Roy summoned the courage to ask a question that had been at the back of his mind all evening.

"Do you think I did the right thing, not taking him to a doctor all those years?"

Delores sat still, her head bent as if in deep thought.

"I don't know," she answered. "There were times when I thought he had *téngalpi*—healing powers. Other times, I thought he just needed time to grow up, to get over losing Sonia." She stopped and smoothed her hands over her lap. "But no matter what, I think you did the best you could, Brother." She turned her head toward the window. "We all did the best we could."

They reached the corner of Ortega Street, where a police car and two officers standing in the intersection. One of them raised his hand and waved for Roy to pull over.

"Good evening, sir." The policeman leaned toward the window. Roy recognized the hazel eyes and thin band of hair on the young man's upper lip. It was Jonathan Cabrillo, one of his son's friends.

"Hello, Jon. Do you remember me?" Roy asked. "I'm Luke Washburn's dad."

The officer's face went blank for a moment, then a slow smile spread below his moustache.

"Sure I do. It's Professor Washburn, right?" He paused a moment, then leaned closer to the car window. "I'm sorry, Professor. No motorists are allowed in this area. We're evacuating the residents. "

"I've got to get back to my house," Roy said. "Luke is missing."

"Hang on a minute." Jonathan straightened up from the window and jogged back to the other officer. They conferred a moment, their heads ducked so low together that they seemed to be touching foreheads. Then the young officer trotted over to Roy and Delores.

"I'm sorry. Strict orders. No one can go through." Jonathan spoke in a raised voice, so that he could be heard beyond the truck. Then he leaned down and whispered so only Roy could hear. "They won't let any cars through, but there's no one posted near your house. If you come back on foot along the back fence, no one will see you." He suddenly stood tall and waved his arm toward the intersection. "Please turn your vehicle around and exit back toward the highway."

Roy gave Jonathan a quick nod, then turned the truck around and headed out, his hands tight on the steering wheel. They pulled up behind the long lines of traffic waiting to leave the area.

He turned toward Delores.

"I'll need your help," he said.

A moment later, his sister slid into his place behind the wheel. Roy struck out on foot, cutting back through the yards on Mission Avenue toward his house on Ortega Street. High above him, a flock of crows glided forward in stealth formation, cawing loudly as they flapped their wings along the crimson horizon.

THERE WAS SOMETHING MOVING OUT IN THE YARD.

Carolyn peered through the reflective glass of the kitchen window at the darkness outside. It might be a coyote or even a deer, but as the evening turned to night, the diminishing Santa Anas left behind only a thick, velvety blackness.

Massaging her sore shoulder, she stood a moment at the sink, trying to drum up the energy to go through the cupboards to find something to eat. It had taken all her strength to push herself up from the couch this evening, and she walked with careful steps so as not to exacerbate the ache in her tailbone from the horseback ride. A cool gust blew down on her from the vent above the refrigerator. Everett must have turned on the air conditioner. The cold air made her skin prickle, giving her the sensation that was the beginning of winter and not the end of August.

She opened one of the cabinet doors and shuffled through the stacked items until she found a can of chicken soup. After locating an opener and a small saucepan, she dumped the soup into the pan and lit the stove beneath it. As she stirred the noodles, limp and pale in the murky broth, the door leading to the garage opened. Everett rolled in in his wheelchair, his leg braces lying across his lap. Carolyn hadn't seen him bring them out in awhile; at least not since early after the accident when his first attempts to use them had been disastrous. He propped the braces against the wall.

"Are you going to give those a try again?" she asked.

"I'm thinking about it." He steadied them one last time and then joined her at the stove.

"Soup?"

"I'm sorry," she replied. "It's not much, but it's all I can seem to handle this evening."

"It's fine," he said. "In fact, you should let me do that. You go and rest."

"I'm all right." Carolyn gave him what she hoped was a convincing smile and turned back to the stove. While Everett gathered spoons and napkins and set the table, she pondered their sudden domestic turn. She hadn't cooked anything in weeks, yet it felt right to be fixing dinner again. It was as if she'd been gone far away and was now back home, like Dorothy at the end of the Wizard of Oz.

They watched television as they ate, flipping between two local news stations for updates on the fires that still raged along Highway 76.

Carolyn set down her spoon and looked up at the sliding glass door.

"What is it?" Everett asked.

"I don't know," she answered. "I keep imagining I see something, but whenever I check, there's nothing there." She turned and gazed at him. "It's almost as if we're being watched."

Everett put down his napkin and rolled his wheelchair to the sliding glass door. He turned the latch and pulled it open, then peered outside into the deepening night. Carolyn felt a blast of warm air as the glass slid wide. She could hear crickets chirping, their creaky song sounding sleepy and far away. He stayed there a moment, then sat back in the chair and closed the door.

"I can't see anything," he said. "But that doesn't mean there's nothing there. Do you want me to take a look outside?"

"No, don't bother." She stacked the plates and silverware and carried them to the kitchen with her left hand, taking care not to jolt herself too much as she took each step. Just as she went to put them in the sink the doorbell rang, pealing a bit loudly over the drone of the television set. The sound startled her so that the dishes tumbled forward with a loud clatter. Luckily, nothing was broken.

Everett seemed to study her a moment.

"I'll get it," he said.

As he wheeled himself out of the room, she put a shaky hand to her head. This day, the past few weeks, the entire summer, in fact, had been too much. She felt the urge to run away and hide, to be alone so she could sort out her feelings. Would it be possible to forgive herself? She thought not. If so, her marriage, so fractured and broken apart, would never be the same.

The murmur of Ben and Everett's voices in the front hall interrupted her thoughts of escape. Ben had mentioned that he wanted to speak to them this evening and she wondered what he had to say. The two men conferred awhile in the other room, their voices pitched just low enough that she couldn't quite make out their words. Then they joined her, Ben pushing Everett's wheelchair into the dining area near the kitchen. Carolyn focused on Ben's hands resting on the handlebars. She studied the square sturdiness of his knuckles and fingers as if seeing them for the first time, although she sensed from the set look on Ben's face that this might be the last.

THE MOON ROSE HIGH ABOVE LUKE'S SHOULDER, A SLIVER OF molten lead. He crouched low in the shadows along the back fence, the gun in his right hand. He had parked his motorcycle at the lot near the park two blocks away and walked here, taking care to stay in the shadows as he passed the tract homes in the Weedmans' neighborhood.

"*Ngé´´i.*"

The voices of his ancestors swirled around him, whispering in their collective voices, urging him on in a breath of warm summer wind.

Through the glass door he could see the white woman and an older man sitting in a wheelchair. Another man, this one younger and wearing khaki shorts, stood next to them, appearing serious and gesturing with his hands as he spoke. For a moment, Luke wasn't certain which was Carolyn's husband. In the photographs, the husband had not seemed as old as the man in the chair.

He crept closer to the ramp leading to the door and listened. All he could hear were his ancestors' voices, growing louder and more insistent, until the words, his breath, the loud creak of the crickets in the grass, cried out in unison with the beating of his heart.

Ngé´´i. "*Ngé´´i. Ngé´´i.*

He raised his gun and pointed.

"I DON'T UNDERSTAND," CAROLYN SAID. "THEY JUST TOLD YOU TO leave?"

Ben looked down at the floor, his face pale.

"It was bound to happen," he said. "My parents have never accepted the fact that I'm gay." He shrugged his shoulders. "When I told them I wanted them to meet Michael, they panicked. Said things they shouldn't have, I guess." He tried to smile, but the effect was weak. "They've made it clear that I can't stay."

"So what will you do?" Everett's voice was soft, concerned.

"Michael has a cousin in Vancouver who runs a print shop. They need help. We told them we'd move up there and give them a hand for awhile."

"But what about your degree? You would have graduated this year." Carolyn tried to keep her voice even. "What about your plans for medical school?"

"There's a university up there. I haven't looked into it yet, but figure I can transfer once we're settled." He shrugged. "I've been thinking about traveling a little before I apply for med school. The time off will be a good thing. Give me time to think."

Carolyn glanced at Everett to see how he was taking this. He appeared as shaken and surprised as she was. It wasn't just that they were losing Ben's help, she realized. The bigger blow was that they were losing someone who was like a son to them.

Carolyn felt suddenly as if the floor was moving away from her. She reached out for the handle on Everett's wheelchair to steady herself, but he intercepted her hand and grasped it in his.

"I have a revelation of my own to share with you," he said.

Carolyn and Ben looked at each other. She wondered if Ben knew what Everett was about to say.

"Ben," Everett said, "would you please hand me those braces over there?"

Ben reached for the braces and brought them to Everett. It surprised Carolyn to see Everett holding them again. When they had first learned that his spinal cord injury was a partial, the doctors had told them that there was a slight possibility that he could regain the ability to use his legs. He had tried, though, and it had been so difficult for him that he'd given up. She had assumed that he would never walk again. Now she gazed in amazement as her husband placed his biceps in the armbands and pushed himself up from his chair.

"Watch," he said.

He struggled a bit on the first step. Carolyn had to stop herself from reaching out to help him and noticed that Ben seemed poised to do the same thing. The two of them watched as Everett slid his feet forward in two shuffling steps, then turned toward them and beamed.

"What do you think?" he asked.

"Awesome," Ben replied. He clapped Everett on the back.

"I can't believe it," Carolyn murmured. "It's a miracle." She stood frozen, as if a pair of hands had broken through the floor and held her anchored to the ground.

"Guess you won't be needing me anymore after all," Ben said. "Or this chair." He folded his long legs and sat down in it, rolling a bit back and forth to test the wheels. "What do think Mrs. Weedman? Want to give me a push?"

Carolyn reached for the handles but something made her turn toward the sliding door. At first all she saw was the reflection of the three of them, like a tableau from a Rockwell painting—Everett leaning against his braces, Ben in the wheel chair, and herself, looking at first small and surprised and then horrified as she saw past the reflection. Silhouetted against the fire-streaked sky was a man pointing a gun at them.

In the next instant, she heard the crack and the bursting of glass, saw the gigantic orange flower of gunfire light up the room, and smelled a sulfurous odor, like the fireworks on the fourth of July. Her last recollection before hitting the floor was the image of Ben, slumped over in the chair as if he was sleeping, a bright burst of blood like a red rose behind his ear.

AT THE SOUND OF THE GUNSHOT, THE HUNTER IN EVERETT TOOK over. He hit the floor, braces scattering, the floor glistening with shards of glass as if someone had tossed a bag of diamonds into the room. Without thinking, he pulled himself across the tile, the sharp pieces of the door cutting into his forearms and elbows as he scrambled on his belly like a giant lizard toward the gun rack. In seconds, he pulled down his rifle, opened the lock and without even looking, pointed through the gaping hole that was once the sliding glass door. He fired toward the shadows that rustled near the fence. He fired again, and a third time, and then once more before dropping the gun. After the last shot, he thought he heard a yip, like the sound an injured dog makes, but he didn't stop to look. Instead, he twisted his body around and crawled across the floor to his wife, who lay crumpled and white like a discarded doll. He reached for her head and turned her face toward him. She was breathing. He felt an odd release at that moment, as if someone had pulled a plug and let the adrenaline leak out of him.

Then he turned toward Ben and saw him leaning against the right arm of the chair. Everett was about to call out to him when he noticed the bright pool of red beneath the right wheel, as if someone had tipped over one of the jars of paint for his model airplanes. At the same moment, the telephone rang, and Everett heard the brief blare of police sirens as they pulled up outside his house. He lay back against the tile, his arms around his wife, swallowing back the familiar taste of metal as he waited for help to arrive.

THEY WERE TOO LATE. ROY KNEW, BY THE TIME HE'D RUMMAGED through Luke's room and found the sheet with Carolyn's address circled, that they would not get there in time. Delores had pulled up on Mission Avenue to pick him up, and they sat frozen in the lines of traffic backed up behind the Highway 15 off ramp. Hundreds of Pala residents crawled forward like an army of burdened elephants, their cars packed full with family members and important belongings. As the evening sky turned dark and the moon rose up above them, Roy breathed in sooty air from the raging fires and felt an inescapable sense of doom.

When they finally made it to the freeway, he sped toward the Ted Williams Parkway exit. They took the off ramp at eighty miles per hour and then flew up Village Parkway toward Carolyn's neighborhood.

As they turned the corner onto her street, they were met with the glare of flashing red lights above a battery of police cars. Roy left the truck, engine still running, and raced toward the house, but stopped at a cluster of neighbors and police officers near the driveway. They were gathered around a body lying on the ground, a circle of red like a wine stain on the back of the victim's t-shirt. He felt his blood start to pound in his head and then shoved his way through the throng.

"Hey, wait right there." A large man in an officer's uniform grabbed Roy across the chest and pushed him back.

"Luke!" Roy heard his own voice as if from far away. He crashed through the arms that held him back, then knelt next to Luke's body, reaching with a shaking hand for his son's shoulder.

"Are you a family member, sir?" A tall woman in a police uniform crouched next to him.

For a moment, Roy couldn't answer.

"No-káamay," he whispered. He began to rock back and forth. "No-káamay."

"Sir? Are you related to the victim?"

Roy turned and looked at the woman. She had a high forehead, and her eyes were dark and luminous in the moonlight. Behind him he heard a scream and then the words "No, no!" followed by broken sobbing. It was Delores.

"Yes," he answered. "This is my son."

Somewhere back in the canyon preserve, he heard a coyote lift its voice to the night sky in a mournful, howling salute.

Chapter 11

The knock on the door matched the throbbing in Everett's head. He set down the newspaper and looked up at the clock. Six a.m. Fuck whoever was out there.

He and Carolyn had been up until four o'clock in the morning, filling out forms and answering questions for the police. The detective assigned to their case was a tall man with pale skin and gelled hair. He'd written notes with a jerky, left-handed motion, stabbing the pen hard against the paper as he took their statements. Each time he swept his arm across his notepad, he'd given off the woodsy scent of expensive aftershave. He said that the incident would be considered a home invasion and Ben's death a homicide. Since Everett's rifle was registered, and the killing of the Indian boy was in self-defense, no charges would be filed.

Even so, the sequence of events had left Everett feeling stunned and sore, his knees and elbows still raw with cuts from the bits of glass on the floor. After the police and newsmen had left, he'd gone to his room and closed the door. With the adrenaline still pumping in his system, he lay awake for over an hour, then came out to the kitchen to read the paper. Instead, he'd sat in a kind of suspended reverie, staring at the pinkish gray streaks of sky as the sun rose through the tiny window over the sink.

The pounding outside continued. Exasperated, he pulled his leg braces from the chair they leaned against and hobbled to the front door. He yanked it open.

"What is it?"

Standing before him was a young woman with dark hair and eyes. She looked Native American, which made Everett wonder if she was a family member of his shooting victim. From the startled look in her eyes, he realized that his appearance must be frightening—squeaking leg braces, uncombed hair, and crumpled t-shirt.

"I'm sorry to disturb you. My name is Nancy Meza. I'm a reporter for the *Corridor Times*. I wondered if I could talk to you about last night."

"We've already had reporters here," Everett said. "I'll tell you what I told them—no comment." He began to close the door, but she raised her hand to stop it.

"Please," she said. "Luke Washburn was a friend of mine. We went to high school together." She stopped a moment. Everett noticed that there were dark circles under her eyes. "It'll be off the record. I just have to know what happened."

The plaintive tone of her voice drained the anger out of Everett. What would it hurt? Maybe explaining it again would make him feel better.

He paused a moment. "All right. Come in."

He limped ahead of her into the living room, stopping to twist open the blinds covering the front window. They sat across from each other, Everett in a large armchair, the girl looking small in the middle of the sofa. He studied her a moment, noticing that she wore a tiny cross of silver and dark blue lapis at her throat. Her white blouse and khaki pants looked pressed and clean. She seemed fresh and sophisticated, like someone who would work in an ad agency or an office somewhere. He wondered if she lived on the reservation.

"Would you like something to drink? Coffee or tea?"

"No thanks." She waved his offer aside with a small brown hand.

"What do you want to know?" he asked.

She started to speak, but then stopped and put her hand to her mouth, her eyes welling up with tears. "I'm sorry," she said. "I already know what happened. I just wanted to see where Luke died." She wiped at her face with the back of her hand. "I thought it might give me a chance to feel close to him one last time."

"Excuse me." Everett pulled himself up with his braces and staggered to the bathroom, grabbing a box of Kleenex. He came back into the living room and set the box on the couch next to Nancy. She reached for a tissue and blew her nose.

"Not very professional of me." She sniffed as she wiped at her eyes. "I'm supposed to be the reporter, but this story—" Her voice trailed off. "I'm not sure I can cover it."

"Was he a close friend of yours?" Everett asked.

"We were good friends. Not so much when we were in high school, but more so afterwards." She pressed her hands into her lap. "We were working together on a story about the Pala landfill. Do you know about that?"

"Yes," Everett answered. He shifted a bit in his seat.

"Luke was so passionate about it. He wanted me to cover it for my paper, but the last time I saw him, he wasn't making much sense." She glanced up at Everett. "I think he was starting to lose it a little."

Everett said nothing.

"Did he say anything before he died?" she asked.

"I don't know. I never saw him." He remembered firing the rifle and falling onto the floor, but he didn't even know that he'd hit anyone until the officers told him.

A sudden wave of exhaustion washed over him. The girl looked at him expectantly, as if what he had to say would somehow save her.

"I'm sorry; it was all a blur. We—that is, my wife and a friend and I—were in our kitchen when someone fired a shot through the sliding glass door. I got my rifle and fired, and then I kind of passed out." What came next? "I remember an ambulance coming and a crowd of paramedics. There were police and reporters. All our neighbors were there, too." He ran a weary hand over his brow, an image coming clear in his mind. "There was a man wearing a white shirt with your friend."

Everett stopped as he recalled finding Carolyn at the living room window, staring at the paramedics load a body onto a stretcher. She was watching the man with the long black hair. Everett had learned later that he was the person she had been seeing; it was the man's son who had shot Ben. He remembered the ambulance lights pulsing, casting a harsh red aura around his wife as she stood at the window. She'd remained there as if hypnotized, until he reached out and gently pulled her away.

"That was Professor Washburn," Nancy said. "Luke's dad." She looked down at her fingers. "I tried to call him this morning, but he didn't answer."

Everett was surprised; the police hadn't said that the boy's father was a professor.

"Well," she said. "I shouldn't keep you. You must be exhausted from … all that's happened." She stood up and gave Everett her hand. "I'm sorry about your friend."

Everett was startled by the reference to Ben. He reached for her hand and touched it briefly.

"My condolences to you and your wife." She drew back her hand. "I hope you won't think badly of Luke. He had a lot of problems. There were a number of us who tried to help him, but we couldn't." She paused, wiping at her nose. "He wasn't a bad person." Her eyes were swollen and dark. "I hope you can someday forgive him."

She turned and walked out, closing the front door softly behind her.

Everett fell back into his chair, watching through the window as Nancy's small silver car pulled out of the driveway. Her last words echoed in his head. He didn't think he could ever pardon Luke. And forgiving Carolyn and himself would be even tougher.

As he gathered his braces and struggled to his feet, a stream of local news vans pulled up to the curb outside the house. He twisted the lever on the front window blinds to close them and headed off to his room. He knew Carolyn wouldn't answer the door this early, so he ignored the persistent banging until the reporters gave up and went away.

WHEN CAROLYN AWOKE THE NEXT MORNING, HER MOUTH TASTED as if she'd swallowed ashes and her injured arm ached. Sunlight streamed through the window, throwing bright yellow arcs across her pillow. The room felt stuffy and hot. Turning back the covers, she glanced at the alarm clock and, at first, thought something must be wrong. It said twelve o'clock. Then she remembered the night before. She and Everett were up until four in the morning, the ambulance drivers and police detectives lingering until she'd felt herself weaving back and forth on her feet, dizzy with exhaustion.

She'd dreamed that she, Ben, and Roy were in a boat floating along on a river. Up ahead was an enormous waterfall, the currents rushing over the edge in a loud roar. In slow motion certainty, she'd stood up and leapt from the bow, hitting the cold water in a smooth dive just before the boat tipped over the edge and fell away.

It seemed so real that she'd gasped herself awake. Her body was soaked with sticky sweat and she shivered under the comforter, even though the night was warm. She thought she heard people talking downstairs, but was too tired to investigate and fell back asleep.

Now, the house was still.

After wrapping herself in her summer robe, she cradled her sore arm as she limped downstairs. The only sound was the steady tick of the clock in the kitchen. She took a few steps past the table and stopped in front of what had once been the sliding glass door. It was now an empty frame, strung with crisscrossed strips of yellow tape, a few bits of jagged glass clinging to the edges like jewels lining a mirror. Through the missing door she could see the backyard lawn, manicured and strangely normal in the noonday sun.

Wondering where Everett was, she checked his bedroom and then the garage. His van was gone. She made a cup of coffee and sat at the kitchen table, watching the steam twist into the air before her. The black brew tasted hot and bitter, but she sipped at it anyway images from the night before flying at her like startled birds: Everett standing with his braces, Ben telling them he was leaving, gunshots and the wail of police sirens, and then a woman in blue helping her to her feet.

She'd walked to the living room window and there was Roy next to an ambulance, the red lights flashing. He looked up at her and raised his hand, almost as if he were reaching for her. She was so stunned to see him standing in her driveway that she stood frozen at the window, a helpless statue, unable to move until someone had pulled her away.

When the police told her that Ben was dead, she gasped and felt the room spin. She remembered Everett's face turning a ghastly putty color, as if all the blood had drained out of him.

He hadn't spoken a word after the detective left. He went into his room and closed the door and right then she had felt the totality of his censure and heartache over her involvement with Roy.

She shook her head to send the images away and poured her coffee into the sink, watching the brown liquid swirl down the drain. After a quick shower, she combed out her wet hair, trying to decide what to do. She didn't have to work today and she wasn't up to the silence and brooding when Everett returned. Instead, she decided to go for a walk around Miramar Lake. Then she remembered seeing Ben the last time she was there. The thought of him, so kind and understanding that day, made her stomach muscles clench. She had to stop and hold onto the edge of the bathroom counter and take deep breaths before she could go downstairs.

Before leaving the house, she pushed the tape aside and stepped carefully through the empty doorframe into the yard. She picked a few day lilies, along with a handful of larkspur and carnations. The leaves tickled her hands as she pinched off the green stems and the sun felt hot on her arms. She wrapped the flowers in a damp paper towel and carried them to the car, holding the bundle in the crook of her arm like an infant. She'd planned to scatter them over the water at the lake, but when she got to Mira Mesa Boulevard, instead of turning left toward Miramar, she made a right and followed the road to the 805 freeway. At Scranton Road, she turned left and then found herself passing through the white arched gates of El Camino Memorial Park.

She followed the road past the pink mausoleum, the cutouts for the internment slots looking like prison windows, until she came to the Madonna memorial. She turned up Vista Del Sol and then parked the car at the Y-intersection, sitting a moment to take in the wide green lawns and the tiny headstones that dotted them. On the right, was the Garden of Innocents, where the graves of abandoned children lay shrouded in the dense cover of pine trees and heather. To her left sat a different plot of children's graves. There, the grass was festooned with colored stuffed animals and spinning pinwheels.

It was a Friday afternoon, and there seemed to be few visitors. Carolyn could hear the distant drone of lawn mowers and weed whackers. As she stepped out of the car, she caught the scent of newly mown grass, reminding her of the days that she and her brother sat and watched while her father pushed their old hand mower, its rusted blades making a grinding noise as it chopped at their tiny lawn.

She locked the car, clutching against her breast the flowers that she'd originally picked for Ben, and wandered over to the row of small tombstones that rested below a large magnolia tree. In the center lay a marker made of red marble, etched lilies and vines curled along its edges. She placed the flowers over the carved letters "Jesse Alan Weedman, July 27, 1988," then sat down in the grass.

The sun warmed the top of her head and a slight breeze twirled the pinwheels on the other graves at a crisp speed. In the trees hung mementos left by family members: a pink and yellow banner with silver tassels, a bird house, a set of tiny wind chimes, the clinking silver tubes sounding delicate and sweet, like miniature bells. In the tree near Jesse's marker someone had hung an orange monkey and a small gray airplane, its thin propeller making weak, jerky dance movements in the breeze. It looked familiar. She recalled other items from past visits, some new and shiny, some wet and withered after a winter rainstorm.

She and Everett had come to this spot for ten years after Jesse's death. They never said much when they visited. Instead, they spent the time picking the headstone free of stray weeds and quietly thinking their own thoughts. Carolyn always felt a strange comfort there. It was as if they were, for those brief moments, a family. Once Everett had his accident, she had come a few times by herself. But instead of comforting her, as they had when she and Everett came together, the trips she made alone left her feeling sad and lost. She'd stopped coming altogether.

What made her steer the car here today? Perhaps it was fear of being overwhelmed by guilt. Or maybe her love for Ben had reminded her of the feelings she'd had for her son. Whatever the reason, it seemed too hard to face the lake right now. Easier to face her own child, whom she had never known.

She heard the sound of a motor running and turned to find one of the grounds crew, a man in dark pants and a light blue work shirt, shutting off the engine of his golf cart. He strode toward her, all red hair and freckles, an apologetic smile on his face.

"Ma'am, do you expect to stay here much longer?"

Carolyn put her hand up to her forehead to ward off the sun and gazed up at him.

"I don't know. Why?"

"There are three sets of sprinklers set to go off here soon. The first one, over here, will start in about five minutes." He pointed toward the copse of trees lining the west end of the gravesite. "There's one up ahead and another to the left there that will follow in about ten minutes."

Carolyn looked where he was pointing.

"I'm really sorry about the timing." He smiled at her again. "Just wanted to let you know so you wouldn't get wet."

"Thank you," Carolyn said, as she struggled to her feet. "I was just leaving anyway."

"It's all right," he said. "You have a few more minutes if you'd like to stay." He glanced down at the tombstone where her flowers lay.

"No, I'll get moving," Carolyn said, brushing at the grass stuck to the back of her shorts.

"Are you a relative of the Weedmans?" he asked

The question sounded innocent, but it made Carolyn pause a moment, embarrassed that she didn't come often enough that he'd know who she was. She wanted to shout at him, *"You idiot, this is my son!"* but the words stuck in her throat. All she could come up with was a meek-sounding "Yes."

"I just wondered," he said, wiping at the sweat on his brow with a freckled arm. "I see Jesse's father, Mr. Weedman, here all the time. I usually try to stop by and say hello whenever I spot him. Sometimes I help him get his chair over the grass there." The man gestured toward the magnolia tree. "He's brought some great models to hang in the trees. We always save them for him when we do decoration removals."

Carolyn froze. After all these years, she finally understood why Everett built model airplanes. It was his way of paying tribute to their son. She gazed at the grounds keeper, realizing that this stranger might know her husband better than she did. She hung her head and wondered if she really knew Everett at all. The warm and generous man she'd married, who believed in his principles and what he stood for, had slowly disappeared during the past three years. In his place, was a quiet, withdrawn invalid with silver hair, who seemed only interested in his models and his air rifles. She had attributed the changes in him to the accident, which had come so suddenly and at such a low point in their marriage, washing over them like a harsh wave and tossing them apart like empty, bleached-out shells. Now she knew it might have more to do with losing Jesse.

The man was staring at her, waiting for an answer.

"Thanks for the warning," she said. She turned toward her car. "It would have been quite a shock to have the water come on while I was sitting here."

He waved goodbye as she fumbled for her keys in her pocket and climbed into the front seat. The interior was hot, so she turned on the air conditioner, positioning the vents so that the cold air pumped directly onto her arms. She stared at the intersection of the two roads and remembered the first time she and Everett had come up here, following the mortuary hearse to this same corner. There had been a covered awning and four rows of chairs and a piece of green cloth covering the tiny hole dug in the ground. She remembered leaning on Everett the whole time, unable to stand on her own feet. Even when they sat, while the priest spoke words she hardly heard, she'd clung to her husband's sleeve, not letting go until they stood up to say their final goodbye.

Everett had placed his hand on the tiny coffin, his chest heaving and tears streaming down his face. Her heart ached at the sight of his grief. Somehow, it seemed more terrible then her own. She had reached into her purse and pulled out a tissue and wiped her husband's face as if he were a child. After numbly thanking those who'd attended the service, they'd driven home silent as corpses, then climbed the stairs to their bedroom where they both lay down and slept straight through until the next day.

The air began to cool, causing the hair to rise on her forearms. She turned down the thermostat and then wrapped her arms around herself and let her chin sink to her chest. Breathing softly for a moment, she remembered the quiet murmuring of the priest that morning so many years ago, when they'd lain her son to rest. She tried to recall the words, but they'd been lost in the years of silence and grief.

Instead, she closed her eyes and tried to imagine what Jesse would look like now, at fourteen years of age. She conjured an image of a smiling teenage boy with brown hair and light eyes but the features faded and twisted until all she could see was Ben.

She laid her head in her hands, the tears that dripped down her cheeks tasting salty and warm. The events of the past few weeks seemed almost unreal, as if they had happened to someone else. Her feelings for Roy had sprung out of nowhere, from somewhere deep within herself that she didn't know even existed. Sadly, it was a place to which she could never return.

And where did that leave her now? She wasn't certain Everett would ever forgive her. She didn't know if she was capable of forgiving herself.

There was a sudden fizzing sound as the pop-up sprinklers shot up along the edge of the grass outside the car. Carolyn lifted her head and watched as arcs of water sprayed out onto the ground below like small, shimmering waterfalls. A few drops hit the windshield and glistened in the summer sun. She studied them as they slowly dripped down the dusty glass, leaving clear, clean trails behind them.

Without signaling, she pulled out into the intersection and headed back home.

DURING THE PAST FEW YEARS, ROY HADN'T SPENT MUCH TIME IN his son's room, other than to stick his head inside to wake Luke up or tell him to clean it before company came. Today he sat on the bed, ignoring the sunlight that streamed through the window and threw tiny yellow halos across the dresser. Rubbing his hands together, he rocked himself back and forth, trying to fight the crushing sense of loss that washed over him in wave after wave.

The room was as Luke had left it the night of his death—the white pages hanging like limp butterflies on the wall, the tangle of sheets and blankets on the bed, the landfill articles scattered below the desk like giant flakes of snow.

A shadow appeared across the floor. Delores stood in the doorway.

"You sure you don't want me to do it?" she asked.

"No, no. I'll pick something out."

She gave him a weak smile as she left. Her blouse and pants hung on her thin frame even more than usual. Neither of them had eaten or slept much since Luke's death three days earlier. When the funeral parlor director had asked for some clothing for Luke, Roy insisted on choosing the items himself, even though Delores argued with him about it.

Now it was up to him to pick out clothes for his son one last time, just as he had for his wife eight years ago. The horror of having to do this again struck him as he sat in the middle of the room, paralyzed from the anguish of the past few days. To his left, the words on Luke's computer monitor—*churó''i 'otéelay*—scrolled rhythmically across the screen. Keep your promise. Was the message for him? Roy wondered. Had Luke planned this moment all along?

Roy looked down at the palm of his hand and rubbed it with his thumb. He tried to remember the last conversation he'd had with Luke. Something about avenging their people. He shook his head. His son's passion had always tormented him and yet, it reminded him of Sonia, who had been so determined and strong. Luke was the same in his love for the Pala culture. In a way, it was the one connection that their son still maintained with his mother, even after her death.

Roy stood and began straightening the rumpled sheets and pillows. It wasn't what he came here to do, but he wanted to make the room as neat as possible before any relatives descended on the house. As he spread the rough blanket across the mattress, he felt as if Luke was still alive and would walk into the room again at any moment.

Roy fought back tears and thought about Sonia again as he wiped his eyes. He was glad that she was spared having to go through this. Yet, there was a part of him that wished she were here to guide him through the next few days. What would she have thought about Luke's demand for vengeance? Roy could imagine her answer, as if she was standing right before him, speaking.

If you've made a promise, then you need to keep it, she'd say.

"But I never said I would do anything." He spoke the words softly, aloud.

Our son is asking. If you won't honor his request, who will?

He could almost hear her voice, low and smooth as brushed cotton. He reached out before him, as if he could conjure her with his bare hands. He would give anything for one more chance to ask for her help, to share his grief.

"It's for you."

Roy turned, startled. Delores stood before him, holding the cordless phone in front of her with her hand over the receiver with a worried expression on her face. He hadn't heard the telephone ring.

"Who is it?" he asked.

"It's that white woman." Her eyes were watery and tired behind the thick frames of her glasses.

His heart began to race. Three nights ago, he had seen Carolyn standing behind the living room window inside her home. She had watched as they loaded Luke's body into an ambulance, a frightened expression on her face. Roy remembered raising his hand toward her, but she had done nothing, remaining frozen at the window like a startled deer, until someone on crutches hobbled up and pulled her away.

"Tell her I'm not here," he said.

Delores raised the telephone to her ear. "He's not in right now. Is there a message for him?" She listened a minute, then covered the mouthpiece with her hand.

"She wants to know if there's going to be a funeral. She wants to come."

Roy considered this request. He knew that no white people, unless they were blood relatives, were invited to Pala ceremonies. If things had been different, he might have considered bringing her with him. But there was nothing left between them now.

He shook his head.

"I'm sorry. That won't be possible. Goodbye." Delores pressed the talk button on the phone to turn it off, then held it to her chest.

"You did good, Brother," she said.

There was a moment of silence, then Roy looked at his sister.

"When is our next council meeting?" he asked

Delores frowned. "Tuesday. Why?"

"I want to be there."

"To talk about Luke?"

"No," he answered. "To take his place."

At first, Delores didn't react to the statement at all. Then, she placed her hand on his arm and gave it a brief squeeze before walking quietly out the door.

Roy turned his head away as she left the room. Reaching for the blanket on Luke's bed, he pulled it up toward his shoulders. After wrapping it across himself, he lay back down on the bed, his knees curled up toward his chest. The faint smoky smell of his son's pillow brought back the memory of Luke as a small boy, lifting his arms up in a victory whoop as he rode past him on his first bicycle. Roy lay on the stiff mattress, trying to hold that image in his mind, until the sunlight disappeared from the window and the deepening darkness enveloped him in sleep.

CAROLYN AND EVERETT SAT AT THE BACK OF THE TINY CHURCH. Before them lay Ben's coffin, polished to a silver sheen and draped with an enormous arrangement of red roses. Hovering above the altar was a giant mosaic of the Virgin Mary, her blue robes seeming to float in a sea of yellow tile, her arms raised in a gesture of unconditional mercy. Carolyn wondered if there was a statute of limitations on the holy Mother's capacity to forgive. Although raised a Catholic, it had been twenty years or more since Carolyn had practiced her faith. She wondered where it had gone. At one time, the faint scent of candles and incense, coupled with the echoing sounds of the mourners' heels on the parquet tiles, would have put her into a religious reverie, making her feel safe and included in the arms of the church. Now the smells and sounds made her nervous. She felt like an interloper, someone who required forgiveness, but was no longer worthy of it.

In the dim light, she could make out the flickering glow of benediction candles near the sacristy. Hymnals fluttered back and forth like white moths as the attendees, most of them well-dressed cronies of Ben's parents, fanned themselves with the small booklets. Carolyn could feel sweat soaking through the armpits of her silk blouse. Long-sleeved and heavy, it wasn't right for the hot summer weather, but it was the only black item of clothing that she owned. With her left arm still strapped across her breast in a cotton sling, she was certain she looked like a refugee from some forgotten battlefield.

There had been a memorial for Ben the night before, but she and Everett had not received an invitation. Carolyn had heard about it through Ben's friend, Michael, who had called to tell them about the funeral. He hadn't been invited either, he told her. Ben's parents had made it clear when he called them that they wanted nothing to do with him or his part in their son's life. His voice had quavered when he told her this on the telephone. She was so touched at the depth of his affection that she broke down and confided in him.

"I saw you and Ben once," she said. "You were with him at the lake."

"I remember that," Michael answered. "You were feeding the fish at the pier." He paused a moment. "Ben worshiped you and your husband, you know. He told me you treated him more like family than his parents."

"We loved him very much," she said.

"Then he was lucky, I guess." Michael's voice had trailed off, and they'd said their goodbyes after he provided directions to the funeral service.

She could see Michael now, sitting with three other men in a pew about halfway to the front of the church. One of the men had his arm around Michael, who sat with head bowed. It was a comforting gesture, but Carolyn wondered what some of the people sitting near them thought of the tableau the two men created.

There was a flurry of commotion when Ben's parents entered the church. His mother was slim and elegant in an ebony colored suit. She wore her taffy colored hair swept up under a large black straw hat; his father was slightly bald and had Ben's height and round, open face. They stopped for a moment when they reached Ben's coffin. Neither of them cried. After a moment, Mr. Miller put his arm around his wife and guided her to their seats.

The priest and altar boys entered, and there was a loud shuffling as everyone stood. At the first "Let us pray," Carolyn turned and looked at Everett, who had remained seated. His face was grim and pale above the slate necktie he wore. The past few days had taken their toll on her husband. After being interrogated by both the police and homicide detectives, they'd been subjected to a relentless onslaught of television and newspaper reporters. The journalists laid in wait outside in the street, shouting questions about her relationship to Luke, who had managed to crawl to their driveway before expiring, a tiny piece of lead from Everett's rifle lodged in his heart. Each time they appeared, her husband patiently asked them to leave. Last night he'd gotten into a shouting match with a persistent reporter, who banged on the door until Everett yanked it open. A cameraman crouched nearby in the flowerbed. Carolyn saw Everett flinch when the reporter mentioned Roy's name, then watched as her husband shoved the man to the end of the porch with one push. After slamming the door shut, Everett reached for his leg braces and limped to his room. The click of the bedroom door closing had sounded like the clang of a prison gate.

The entire congregation except Everett rose as the priest began a reading from the New Testament.

"Ecclesiastes, chapter 3, verse 1. Let us pray." There was a pause as those present fumbled for their prayer books. "There is an appointed time for everything, and a time for every affair under the heavens." The priest's voice rang out strong and clear. "A time to be born, and a time to die; a time to plant and a time to uproot the plant. A time to kill, and a time to heal; a time to tear down, and a time to build."

Carolyn closed her eyes and tried to straighten her shoulders, her body swaying slightly in the heat. What was Roy doing now, she wondered? She'd tried to reach him by telephone yesterday, but his sister had coldly told her that he wasn't available. Carolyn learned from the police that he had ridden along with Luke in the ambulance. They told her that on the way he had spoken only in Luiseno and that he had turned and walked out without uttering a word when they'd finally pronounced Luke dead at the emergency room.

"A time to weep, and a time to laugh; a time to mourn, and a time to dance. A time to scatter stones, and a time to gather them; a time to embrace, and a time to be far from embraces."

Carolyn glanced over at Everett. He sat with his head bowed, his face unreadable.

"A time to seek, and a time to lose; a time to keep, and a time to cast away."

Carolyn stared at Ben's casket, trying to remember him before his death, when he was whole and tall and his kind, gentle self. She felt her eyes burn and lowered her head. He had died because of her. She wasn't sure how she would ever overcome this fact.

"A time to love, and a time to hate; a time of war, and a time of peace."

The rest of the reading was undecipherable to Carolyn. She stood and sat with the rest of the congregation, but didn't hear anything that was spoken until the end of the service, when the priest invited anyone who wished to pay his or her respects before the coffin was taken to the cemetery. Some of the assembly exited to the front courtyard. Others lined up along the aisle leading up to the casket to say their final goodbyes.

Everett struggled to his feet.

"I think I'm going to wait outside," he said, his voice soft and shaky.

"I'll just be a moment." Carolyn helped her husband exit the pew toward the front door. She placed her purse over her good shoulder and joined the slow queue leading toward Ben's casket.

When she finally reached the coffin, she placed her fingers on the corner, the bluish steel feeling surprisingly cool under her hand. She closed her eyes a moment, remembering Ben the first time he had come to their front door, tall and lanky, a shy smile on his face. It did not seem possible that someone as youthful and warm as he had been could be lying in this cold metal box.

Carolyn glanced up and found herself facing Ben's mother across the pile of roses. Carolyn noticed the set appearance of the other woman's jaw, the tired wrinkles around her eyes. They were Ben's eyes, a blue so deep they were almost violet. His mother stared at the coffin, her mouth working as if she were speaking without sound. After a moment, she glanced up at Carolyn, who felt suddenly awash in guilt at the sight of the lost expression on the woman's face. They stared at each other and, for just a moment, Carolyn thought she saw a brief glimmer of recognition and then a hint of a smile. She was about to speak, to tell her how sorry she was, when Ben's father, who had been standing at his wife's side, suddenly reached for her shoulder and led her out of the church.

Carolyn froze, feeling as if the others gathered around Ben's coffin were all looking at her with censure in their eyes. Her first instinct was to run away and hide. She breathed in a moment to calm herself and then decided to face her guilt. She followed Ben's father and caught up with him just inside the door.

"Excuse me."

Mr. Miller turned a moment, then continued walking. Carolyn followed, hurrying to keep up with him. As they stepped through the church doors, she reached out and touched his arm.

"Please," she said. "I'm Carolyn Weedman."

He stopped, his body erect with shoulders squared. The noonday sun played across his face and his thinning hair.

"I know who you are," he said.

Carolyn forced herself to continue. "I just wanted to tell you how sorry we are about Ben. My husband and I--," she paused a moment. "We loved him very much. We feel horribly about what happened."

"You should," Miller said. "My son would be alive right now if not for you."

For a moment, they stared at each other. Carolyn could feel the hot sun on her forehead and the sweat dripping down her arm. He turned as if to walk away and Carolyn reached out for his sleeve once more.

"I know I'm responsible for what happened. I accept that." She struggled to find the words to explain how she felt. "If it was possible, I would do anything to bring your son back."

"Well, that isn't possible is it?" he said, a sardonic smile suddenly turning his lips into a grimace of pain. "I guess we'll all just have to live with it, won't we?" He bit off these words as if they were distasteful, then turned and walked toward the street, where the ushers were loading Ben's coffin into a black limousine. Carolyn felt the world crushing in on her. She watched as they loaded the casket into the back of the car and then suddenly flashed back on her own son's funeral. The small white coffin had looked so tiny, like a box for a large doll. A wave of grief washed over her and she suddenly had to act.

"Wait!" she cried.

Ben's father and mother were standing at the limo door, ready to step inside. They turned as she approached.

"I had a son, too," she said. "He was buried three days after he was born." She struggled to find more words, but couldn't. Her mutual grief was all she had to offer.

Mrs. Miller stared at her a moment, her blue eyes appearing clouded over as if they were seeing something far away. Then she extended her hand, which Carolyn reached out and grasped in her own. The warmth of the smooth papery skin comforted her, in a way that no words could. Mrs. Miller gave Carolyn's hand a squeeze and, without saying a word, turned and climbed into the car.

Ben's father stood a moment, looking down at the ground. He lifted his gaze toward Carolyn, his face solemn when he spoke.

"Well, then, there's no hope for any of us, is there?"

He ducked into the car and slammed the door shut. The limo pulled slowly out onto the street as Everett, his braces creaking, came up behind her.

"Let's go home," he said.

Chapter 12

Everett kept Carolyn company as she planted bulbs and a few annuals near the edge of the backyard fence-line. Even though it was the end of summer and not really the time to be planting color, she'd come home that morning with a few pony packs of pansies and impatiens, along with some tulip and freesia bulbs that she'd found on sale at a local nursery. She crouched over them now, the small bunches of yellow, purple, and pink surrounding her like bouquets, her bare arms starting to redden where the sun hit them.

The sun singed his arms, but he wasn't moving from his yard chair, keeping an eye out for wildlife in the late afternoon heat and breathing in the warm outdoors. A slight breeze from the east brought a hint of cedar and, occasionally, eucalyptus. Everett listened to the sounds of the palm fronds rustling slightly overhead and Carolyn's trowel scraping the dirt.

It had been a week since Ben's funeral, and the tension between them had dissolved into a strangely comfortable silence. After the chaos of fighting off the press and reassuring neighbors that they were all right, they were both happy to settle into the quiet anonymity of their own world. Everett noticed that today Carolyn had removed the sling she'd been wearing, so he assumed her arm felt better. She still seemed to favor it, holding it close against her chest as she leaned over the flowerbed.

He wondered what was going through her mind as she pushed her shovel into the ground and spooned the broken earth into small, even piles. They had not spoken about the shooting at all, even though Ben's absence left an almost palpable hole in their daily life. The silence made Everett uncomfortable. He needed to know that her affair was over; he also wanted to hear that she forgave him for his part in the shootings last week. But how to begin a conversation? He knew that the questions would be as painful for her to answer as they were for him to speak. He hated feeling so tongue-tied and impotent and swatted impatiently at a moth that fluttered near his head.

He was about to ask if she wanted something to drink, just to have something to say, when she suddenly turned toward him with her hand outstretched.

"Look," she said.

Everett struggled up from his chair and pushed his arms in his braces, then staggered over to where she sat. Nestled in the palm of her green gardening glove, its surface crusted over with dried mud, was the compass he used to carry in his pocket years ago. It had been a gift from Carolyn. He had always kept it with him and then suddenly lost it when they moved to Rancho Penasquitos.

"It's your compass, the one I gave you."

He heard a note of sadness in her voice, as if the memory were bittersweet.

"I must have dropped it when we were landscaping the yard." He bent over to take it from her and wiped away the dirt on the glass face. It was an unlidded military pocket model, with a simple black background and white lettering. Its unprotected bezel appeared unharmed. The needle in the center jumped up and down as he cleaned the grit from the surface.

"How about that?" Everett said. "I can't believe it's working after all these years." He pointed the face toward her so she could see that it was still operating, then turned and walked back to his chair. He held the compass still, watching as the red portion of the needle settled in the direction of his chest, its shaky red tip aimed at his heart. It had been Carolyn's gift to him on their first anniversary, twenty-four years ago. He'd opened first the small box and then the aluminum case it came in. Carolyn had watched him expectantly as he lifted the compass out of the case and weighed it in his hand. He'd been lusting after a different model, one with a mirrored sight for hunting, but was taken by the simplicity of the one she'd picked. As he looked at it now, still functioning after years of being lost in the dirt, he realized that she'd chosen wisely.

"Whoa!" Carolyn yelped suddenly, standing up so quickly that Everett jumped a bit in his chair.

"What is it?" he asked.

"I don't know. Something moved in there." Her voice quivered a little as she pulled at her gardening gloves. "It didn't have ears or a tail, but it had fur."

"Maybe it was a gopher or a mole." Everett tried to reassure her. "A few of them come up from the canyon every now and then."

"Whatever it was, it sure startled me." She pulled her injured arm tight against her chest.

Everett watched as she cautiously knelt back down on her gardening pad. She'd seemed so vulnerable when she'd jumped up a moment ago. The look on her face reminded him of her in their younger days, her long curly hair shining brightly in the sun, her eyes innocent and wild and ready to defend the world. That's what she had been to him then, his young warrior, his Joan of Arc, so pure in her convictions, so ready to take on the unrighteous and unkind.

What gave him the right to question her, he wondered. He'd had his own secrets, his own dalliances with other women. She had never questioned him about them and, in a way, had answered him in kind.

A pair of mourning doves flew overhead, flapping their wings like brushes against the sky. No, he thought, he had no right to question her.

The compass needle quivered as it pointed due north. He curled his fingers protectively over the cover. If he waited long enough, perhaps the love they once shared would come back to them.

At that moment, Carolyn sat back and tossed her shovel to the ground, then stood and gazed at the newly planted flowers, their bright colored faces pointing up at the sun. She turned to look at

Everett. He gave her what he hoped was a brave smile, but the young woman he'd glimpsed a few moments ago was gone. Instead a small, middle-aged woman in cut-off jeans glanced away as she wiped at her brow with a gloved hand, a dark half-moon of sweat under her arm.

It would take time.

Chapter 13

The rain tapped against the glass outside the library entrance as Carolyn ripped the page from the desk calendar that sat next to her computer. It was the first day of November, two full months since Ben's funeral. Her heart felt as cold and dreary as the weather outside. Normally she loved the rain. It came so rarely to San Diego that when there finally was some moisture in the air, she usually reveled in it. Today, though, she felt an extra heaviness inside. Since the ending of her relationship with Roy, a part of her had been missing. She couldn't identify exactly where the feeling was located, but she moved through each day with the sensation of an amputee who experiences phantom pain in an absent limb.

Her relationship with Everett was a different matter. Bit by bit they were rebuilding their life together, at first circling warily around each other like wolves sniffing out a new member of the pack. He had confessed that he didn't want to lose her; she admitted that she didn't want to leave. She acknowledged how difficult it was for him to walk. The braces were awkward and the most he could muster was a slow shuffling gait that often seemed to cause him pain.

Having recognized his effort, she made an effort to talk to him rather than avoid conversation, to be more present, to recall what she'd once loved about him. It required almost as much willpower on her part. At times she felt as if she was pushing through a wall that had taken years to build. Sometimes it was harder to break through; at other times, the barrier crumbled easily. She'd locate a chink in his emotional armor or in hers and enough of the old feeling drifted in, allowing them to reconnect.

Today, though, she just felt empty and washed out, adrift in the emotional wake of losing Roy and Ben. She logged onto the computer and typed in her password and then looked up into the soft hazel eyes of Mrs. Arman. The elderly woman's white hair glistened with raindrops, and there were watermarks scattered across her brown sweater and dark skirt. The black handle of an umbrella was draped over one thin arm.

"Mrs. Weedman? I don't know if you remember me," she said. "I'm Mrs. Arman. I brought in a notice a few months ago. About my dog, Lacey." She smiled, the skin around her mouth creased in gentle wrinkles.

"Yes, of course, I remember," Carolyn answered. "How are you?"

"Oh, I'm fine, dear, just fine." Mrs. Arman's hand shook slightly as she fumbled in the pocket of her cardigan. "I wanted to come in and thank you for helping me find her." She pulled her hand out of her pocket and held it, fist wobbling, toward Carolyn. "The man who brought her back was very kind. He asked me to give you this."

It was something small balled up in a roll of Kleenex. Carolyn took it from her and then stood still a moment, not sure what to think. So Roy had returned Tóowish. Part of her was proud of him for having done the right thing, but another part of her suddenly felt sad. She knew how hard it must have been to give up this dog.

"Thank you," she finally said, placing the tissue in her pocket. "I'm glad she's back where she belongs."

"Well, it is nice to have her home again," Mrs Arman said. "Once you own an animal it becomes a part of you, don't you think?"

"Yes," Carolyn replied. "I think so."

They shook hands, Mrs. Arman's palm as fragile as a withered leaf in Carolyn's grip. With a goodbye nod, the tiny woman edged her way to the library exit and then stood outside fumbling with her umbrella, an Asian-style parasol. It took a minute, but she finally pushed it open, its white panels painted with what looked like the twelve signs of the Chinese zodiac. Carolyn watched the tiny images of dragon, rabbit, and rooster bobbing up and down in the rain, until they turned toward the parking lot and disappeared from sight.

At lunchtime, not feeling up to conversation with Mary and Sheryl, she decided to go outside. The rain had stopped momentarily, the sky still dark and angry-looking, a slight breeze blowing in from the north.

Carolyn walked slowly along the wet sidewalk until she reached the shopping mall across the street. She stopped inside Starbucks to order a coffee. Even though it was only November, the employees were playing holiday music. Bing Crosby crooned his white Christmas blues, making her feel suddenly nostalgic and sad. She ordered a tall mocha and considered drinking it there, but the site of the two tub chairs sitting empty by the window reminded her of that first conversation with Roy.

She ducked out of the coffee shop and headed back toward the library. The wind was beginning to whip again, and the first few drops of rain struck hard and wet against her forehead. She hurried to her car in the parking lot and, after fumbling in her purse for her keys, climbed inside. The rain started falling, its steady drops tapping against the windshield. She set her coffee in the cup holder and sat a moment, considering the surprise visit from Mrs. Arman. Suddenly, she remembered the ball of Kleenex in her pocket and reached for it. She unwrapped the tissue and sat up straight. There, nestled inside the white folds, lay a single round silver dog tag, the word "Toowish," and Roy's phone number engraved on one side. She picked it up and held it in her palm. At first cold and smooth, the metal warmed against her skin.

As she stared at the tiny tag, the memories she'd been trying to hold back came spilling forward, so vivid and real that she found herself clutching Roy's gift to her chest. She recalled the smooth dark skin on his hands, the heat of the sun on her neck in the canyon, the scent of cedar rising from his shirt. Instead of sitting alone in a cold car on a rainy afternoon, she was standing in a garden in the moonlight, feeling his arms around her, listening to the quiet chirp of the crickets in the grass.

The rain drummed hard on the car roof, bringing her back to the present. She studied the piece of metal in her hand, then reached up and undid the silver chain around her neck. After removing the single pearl she normally wore, she strung the tag on the chain and leaned back in the driver's seat. As the rain drummed against the windows, she let the hot tears spill over her cheeks. She sat there until the storm passed, fingering the tiny medal and reliving each sweet moment for the last time.

Chapter 14

Carolyn entered the Edelweiss Bakery, drinking in the smell of warm cinnamon rolls and cringing at the sound of a large cowbell as it banged against the doorframe. She greeted the owner, Hans, then set her purse on the counter and leaned against the glass display case. A dazzling assortment of cakes, pies, and cookies lay below. There were three large sheet cakes with white frosting, a pair of fluffy lemon meringue and coconut pies, and a large jelly roll, looking like a fat red porcupine with spiky coconut topping. In front, a pile of grim-faced gingerbread men with white trim and raisin noses stared up at her through the glass.

She finally pointed to a small chocolate cake at the back.

"I'll take that one."

"Would you like any wording on it?" Hans asked, as he slid the cake out of the case.

"Hmm. Let me think about that."

She paused a moment, then pulled a pen out of the cup by the cash register and scribbled some words on a piece of paper.

Hans raised his eyebrows.

"That's it?" he asked.

"Yeah. That's it."

He told her it would be a few minutes and suggested she have some coffee while she waited. She poured herself a cup from the pot on a small table tucked in the corner and found a booth by the window. Outside the day was raw and gray. The Styrofoam cup felt warm in her hand as she sipped her drink and reflected on how unseasonably cold this winter had been. She had on a sweatshirt and her thick down parka and still felt chilled and stiff.

Tomorrow, December third, would be Everett's fifty-fourth birthday. She'd driven the twenty miles north to this bakery in Escondido to order a cake for him, at this same shop where they ordered their wedding cake twenty-five years earlier. Usually, when she came in to pick out something special, she enjoyed the trip, lingering over the baked goods and listening to Hans and Frieda gossip about the other shopkeepers in the tiny strip mall. Today was different. Frieda was nowhere to be seen, and Hans must have sensed Carolyn's mood, saying nothing as he whisked the cake into the back room to finish it for her.

The past month had been difficult. She'd been tired and unfocused at work and useless at the counseling center. An overwhelming fatigue washed over her the moment she woke up and dragged her through each day in a dazed fog. One afternoon last week she'd picked up her cross-stitching and awakened two hours later, the needle and thread on the floor at her feet. When she reached for the car door this morning, she'd watched her hand move forward in slow motion, as if she were underwater.

Everett, on the other hand, alternated between bouts of overly solicitous kindness and sullen anger. Yesterday they bickered; as usual, it was over something trivial. This time, she'd gone outside and plucked a few oranges from one of their trees. As she carried them inside, thinking that she would juice them for breakfast, she found her husband waiting for her next to the kitchen window. When he saw the fruit in her hands, his cheeks turned a deep red.

"What are you doing?"

"What does it look like I'm doing?" She carried the oranges to the table and dumped them on the surface, catching them as they started to roll.

"You know those aren't ready yet. They won't be ripe until January or even February."

"How do you know? You haven't even tasted them."

"I take care of this yard; that's how I know."

She'd cradled one of the oranges in her hand like a softball, the fresh citrus smell on her fingers. She wanted to lob it at him. But in the end, she couldn't even get up the energy for that. Instead, she'd dropped the fruit on the table and watched it tumble forward, until it stopped near the edge, balancing precariously, as if the slightest breath would send it falling to the ground. They'd both stared at it in silence; then she'd walked out.

She'd driven around for an hour, following Highway 15 all the way to Temecula. She finally turned around and headed back to the counseling center, where she spent the entire afternoon. When she got home, the house was still. On the kitchen table was a small vase filled with pink geraniums from the yard and one of the oranges sliced on a plate. Beside it lay a small piece of paper, the words "I'm sorry" written in Everett's careful hand. She stared at the note and then picked up one of the orange slices, inhaling the tangy scent. When she tasted it, its sweetness surprised her. She'd not expected that much flavor from such early fruit.

The cowbell on the bakery door clanged suddenly as the frame shook from a quick gust of wind. The sudden noise startled her, and she noticed that her purse had fallen to the floor of the booth. She took another sip of coffee. This morning, Everett had acted sheepish and conciliatory. When she asked him what he wanted for his birthday, he'd shrugged.

"I want us to be happy," he said.

That would be a difficult order to fill.

She studied the cars in the lot outside the window and was about to reach for her purse when she saw a familiar white truck pull up in front of the travel agency next door. Roy's truck. Her heart began to bang in her chest, and she gripped the edge of the table as she saw Roy step out and slam the door. He had on the same rawhide jacket and jeans that he wore on the day they met. She watched him enter the agency and disappear inside.

"Miss Carolyn, your cake is ready."

She reluctantly turned toward Hans at the counter, wondering why he was speaking to her. Then she remembered her order. She got her wallet and paid him, then returned to her spot at the booth by the window. Roy's truck was still there. She hesitated. Should she try to talk to him? What would she say?

While she struggled with these questions, the travel agency door swung open and Roy reappeared, an airline ticket envelope in his hand. He stopped a moment and dug in his pocket and, without even thinking, she reached up and tapped hard on the window. He looked at her, his face serious and blank. He must have recognized her, for he seemed to square his shoulders, his jaw appearing set and firm. She motioned to him to come inside. He stood still a moment, then he put his keys back in his pocket and walked in through the bakery door, the clunking bell sounding a warning.

"Can I help you?" Hans wiped his hands on his smock and smiled expectantly at Roy.

"No, I'm all right."

Carolyn could feel her pulse jump and her face flush. She noticed how thin Roy seemed, his jacket hanging on him, his cheekbones high and sharp on his face. There were new lines etched around his eyes and mouth and a touch of gray at his temples, making him look tired and, for the first time, old. She wondered if she should be the first to speak, but didn't know what to say. He stood there, as if he was studying her, his expression somber. Finally, she broke the silence.

"How are you?"

"Fine." He paused a moment. "You?"

"I'm good," she answered. "I'm really good." The repetition of the phrase caused her to inwardly cringe. What was she trying to prove? It was time to be straight with him

"You look good," he said. "I like your haircut."

Carolyn raised her hand to her hair, which she'd recently had cropped into shorter layers.

"Thanks. It feels better this way." She paused a moment. "Do you have a minute to join me for some coffee? Or tea? I'm sure they have that here."

"No," he said. "I should get going." He gestured with the envelope in his hand, as if she should know what was inside. When he moved toward the door, she stood up.

"No, wait. Please. I—I have something I want to say."

She suddenly became aware of Hans standing behind the counter, leaning on the register as he watched them. She fished her purse out of the booth and waved her hand toward the door. "I'll walk you out."

They went to his truck and stopped beside it. Roy placed his hand on the door handle and turned toward her.

"Are you going somewhere?" she asked, pointing to the envelope he carried.

"Nowhere important. Just a local trip." He wrapped his arms around his chest. "What did you want to tell me?"

"I'm sorry about Luke." She stood still in front of him, facing him squarely. "I know how much he meant to you." Roy said nothing.

Carolyn stared out at the cars. It seemed to be their destiny to meet in parking lots.

"I don't think you ever knew this, but I had a son once, too. He died right after he was born." She started to push her hair behind her ear and then stopped herself. "I know what you must be going through. It makes you ache so much that you think you can't bear it. It makes you feel like you don't deserve to live." She gazed into his eyes as she spoke. "I don't think I've ever told anyone this, but there was a time when I thought that losing Jesse was everything. That nothing else mattered after that. But I was wrong. All the rest matters, too. It has to; otherwise, there'd be no reason for his having been born." She stopped and gazed up at the sky, but it was gray and unforgiving. "There'd be no reason for any of us being here." She looked at him. "Do you understand what I mean?"

He said nothing, but she thought she saw his shoulders relax a little, as if the air was slowly seeping out of him.

"I also want you to know that I'm sorry about how I left your house that last day. I didn't want to hurt you." She held his gaze with her own, forcing him to look at her. "What we had together meant a lot to me. I want you to know that."

Roy lowered his head at these words. Then he glanced up and gave her the first hint of his old smile.

"I know," he said.

She smiled back at him, uncertain what to say next. He pulled open the car door and set the envelope inside the seat. Then he looked back at her.

"Do you remember that first time we met, when we took Tóowish to the vet?"

She nodded, the events of that day etched clearly in her memory.

"Well, I remember you that day." He stopped, his eyes taking on a faraway look. "You were so quiet and sad." He smiled again. "I commented that you seemed nervous." He glanced down at his hand on the door handle, then back up at her. "You don't seem nervous to me anymore."

He stepped up into the truck and shut the door. The engine coughed and sputtered into life. Carolyn started to move aside, then shouted "Wait!" and ran over to the window. He rolled it down as she reached up under the neck of her sweatshirt and pulled out a silver chain. She unhooked the clasp and handed it to him.

"I think you should have this," she said. "She was always more yours than anyone else's."

He studied the tag at the end of the necklace.

"Are you sure?" he asked.

"I'm sure."

He reached up and draped the chain over the rearview mirror, then nodded to her before putting the truck into gear.

Her reflection suddenly appeared before her as the window rolled up between them. She wrapped her arms around herself as he waved to her before backing out of the lot. The truck moved through the intersection and disappeared from view. She wouldn't see Roy again, she was certain. But instead of feeling shaken by this chance meeting, she felt forgiven, as if she'd been released from a place where she no longer wanted to be.

A gust of cold wind blew over the lot, causing her hair to flutter against her face. She pushed back the strands and, as she pulled her parka close, saw that a feather lay on her sleeve, blown there by the wind. She removed it and held it in her hand, marveling at its lightness. When the breeze picked up again, she opened her palm to the sky and let the feather lift into the air. It floated toward the end of the lot and disappeared.

With a surge of energy, she turned toward her car. The bakery door swung open and Hans called out to her.

"Miss Carolyn, you forgot your cake."

She ran back, taking the pink box from him.

"I hope it goes well, whatever you are celebrating," he said.

"Thanks. Give my best to Frieda."

She set the box on the passenger seat and then started the car, stopping a moment to turn on the heater. As she put the car in reverse, she noticed that the box lid had sprung open. Inside, on the shiny chocolate surface, Hans had written the words "Me, too," in yellow icing. Below the inscription he'd drawn a tiny heart in red frosting.

As Carolyn drove out into the noonday traffic, she held onto the box to keep it from sliding off the seat. She expected that the cake would give off the aroma of chocolate but, somehow, when she sniffed the air the only smell she could catch was the scent of homegrown oranges.

BY THE TIME CAROLYN PULLED INTO THE DRIVEWAY, STORM CLOUDS had gathered overhead, turning the sky a sullen gray. She parked her car in the garage next to Everett's van and quietly pushed open the door to the house, tiptoeing inside, the cake box in her hands. She ducked into the kitchen hoping he wouldn't see her, then hid the box at the back of the lower shelf in the refrigerator. The air inside the house was cold and still. After hanging up her coat, she went into the living room, expecting to find him there, but the room was empty. She noticed that tiny particles of mist were beginning to form on the windows outside. It would rain soon.

"Everett?"

She knew he wouldn't be upstairs; it was too chilly and damp to be out in the yard. She finally opened the door to his bedroom and found him lying on his bed, his head turned to the side. He lay with his hands tucked into the front pocket of his sweatshirt, a navy blue blanket over his legs. Thinking he was sleeping, she went to close the door, but he stirred and looked at her.

"What time is it?" he asked.

"Five thirty. I didn't know you were awake."

"I was just laying here, trying to get warm." He pulled the blanket aside to show her the thick sweatpants he was wearing.

"I know. I'm freezing."

"Come join me," he said, patting the spot next to him. "It's warm under this blanket."

She hesitated, the angry words from yesterday still echoing in her head, then sat at the edge of the bed.

"Here." He lifted the blanket and wrapped it around her shoulders.

"No, you'll get cold." She pulled it off of her, then laid down beside him, dragging the covers up over both of them. She nestled closer to him, then looked up at the warplanes hanging from the ceiling. Through the dusky light she could see that there were many of them now, their wings spread out like frozen birds.

"There's a new one," she said, pointing to a green helicopter in the corner above the desk.

"It's a Huey," he answered. "I had a hard time getting the pieces to fit together."

"You made these planes for Jesse, didn't you?"

"Not at first." He was quiet a moment. "But after awhile it seemed right to share them with him."

Carolyn turned her head to gaze at her husband. Up close, she could see the lines around the corners of his mouth, a hint of gray in the tips of his eye lashes. She felt his breath on her cheek, hot and quick.

"He would have loved them," she said.

His eyes welled with tears and he turned his head away from her. She reached up and wiped a drop that rolled down the side of his face, then slid her hand toward his neck where the skin felt soft and warm. She could feel the gentle rhythm of his pulse against the palm of her hand. He turned and reached for her and pulled her close. They pressed their bodies together, and when he kissed her, it felt to Carolyn wonderfully familiar and strangely new at the same time.

They laid there long after the downpour started, listening to the soft drum of the rain against the roof until it lulled them to sleep.

Chapter 15

Carolyn stretched a length of clear plastic tape across the top of a cardboard box and sealed it shut. She scribbled the words "family room --mementos" across the sides with a black marker and then wiped at her brow with the back of her hand. Although it was early June, the sun blazed high and hot and the dimly lit garage was thick with humidity. She reached for another box and began stacking books inside, placing the larger ones at the bottom and the paperbacks on top. As she reached for the tape, she heard Everett calling her to come to breakfast.

"In a minute," she called back.

As she pulled a long piece of tape off the roll and pressed it across the box top, she marveled at the changes that had taken place in the past six months. Now that he was able to walk, Everett had discovered a passion for cooking. He spent time pouring through the myriad gourmet cookbooks he had recently purchased and shopped at Asian markets and specialty food stores for strange-smelling bags of dark-colored spices and exotic fruits and vegetables.

There had been a few flops. Carolyn smiled as she recalled one particularly pungent chicken curry. The seasoning had been so fiery that they'd been unable to eat it and had tried to wash away the burning sensation with three beers each. They'd spent the rest of the evening giggling and mildly drunk and had awoken the next morning with slight hangovers. But, he had a sensitive nose and a flair for presentation, and after a while their meals had become consistently savory and laid out on each plate like gastronomic works of art.

After sealing the box and marking it "books," she brushed the dust off her hands. Inside the house, she found Everett balancing against his leg brace with one hand and with the other prying a pair of Belgian waffles from the electric iron she'd bought him for their anniversary. The house smelled of cinnamon and vanilla, and she saw that there was freshly squeezed orange juice on the table.

The homey smells belied the starkness of the room. The kitchen and family room were stripped of all wall hangings and cardboard boxes towered in the corners. After twenty-five years, they'd decided to sell this house and had bought a one-story ranch-style home in Temecula. It had taken a while to choose the place. They'd scoured the county from the south to the north and found a house was on a half-acre lot backing a planted vineyard with a view of the Riverside mountains.

It had been strange driving past the Pala off ramp on Highway 76. Each time they went by the freeway exit to visit their new home, Carolyn felt as if a shadow passed over her heart. The fires in August had stripped the area lining the freeway, leaving the remaining landscape black and scarred. She'd read that they were started by someone burning a campfire in the painted caves. She wondered if Roy's home had escaped the devastation.

A few months ago, she'd seen his name mentioned in an article in *The Corridor News*. The reporter, Nancy Meza, described him as a spokesperson for the Pala tribe on legislative issues. In a feature story last week, Carolyn read that Roy was in Sacramento, working with an environmental group on a new ballot measure to fight the landfill development. The news surprised her; he must have left his teaching job to take on this new position. She'd wondered if he ever thought about getting in touch with her. Now, as she set plates and silverware on the table, she realized that after he returned from his trip to Sacramento, she would be gone. If he ever did want to reach her, he wouldn't find her at this address or at the library, which she'd left a month ago.

The realization that their relationship had truly ended suddenly made her stomach twist. She fought a wave of nausea, then took a few deep breaths. When her stomach had calmed down, she decided to help get breakfast ready and rooted through the cupboards until she found the maple syrup. She set it out, along with butter and marmalade, having to push aside the stack of paper covering part of the table. This was her application to Cal State San Marcos. She'd decided to go back to school next fall and finish her English degree.

After stacking the forms, she sat down and studied her husband as he stirred the last of the batter and poured it in the waffle iron. His t-shirt hung on him a bit. Since regaining the ability to walk, he'd lost some weight, which was surprising given his recent interest in cooking. He'd been working out with hand weights and his upper body looked firm and toned. His leg muscles had also filled out now that he was using them. Carolyn noticed that he seemed more settled in his body and that the lines on his face had smoothed out.

She, on the other hand, was gaining weight. She'd noticed the other day that the waistbands on her shorts and jeans were getting tight around the middle and ascribed it to eating too much of the rich dishes that Everett prepared. Deciding that maybe a piece of fruit would be healthier than a plate of Belgian waffles, she plucked an orange out of the bowl on the table and was about to peel it when Everett called her over to the kitchen window.

"Quick, come here," he said.

She joined him at the sink and squinted in the direction where his finger pointed. There, at the edge of the yard just inside the palm trees, was a coyote. It looked like the same one that had visited before, but there was something different about it. As it nosed around the bushes, Carolyn saw what it was. The fur was fuller and there were teats hanging from its underbelly. She could make out the tips of them as the animal moved closer into the yard.

"Look," Everett said. "In the corner."

At the edge of the grass, just below the fence line leading into the canyon was another coyote. This one was smaller, its fur a lighter shade of yellowish gray. It stepped tentatively into the yard, then froze, its nose pointed towards them.

"It's a pup," Carolyn said. "I think it sees us."

As soon as she'd uttered those words, both animals raised their heads toward the window. Carolyn thought that the mother coyote locked eyes with her for just a moment before spinning around and leading her young under the fence. Carolyn felt her skin crawl and her face flush. She fought down another wave of nausea.

"I'm going to miss seeing them in the yard," Everett said. "Oh, man, what's that smell?"

The caramel scent of burnt sugar filled the room as they both turned toward the kitchen counter. From the edges of the waffle iron drifted spirals of gray steam. Everett pried back the lid and covered his nose as dark smoke billowed forth, carrying with it the strong odor of burning waffles.

"Shit." Everett swung his one brace toward the cabinets and dug through the drawers until he located a potholder. Carolyn listened to him mumble as she turned back toward the view out the kitchen window. The yard was calm. Nothing stirred in the late morning heat.

Everett rattled plates behind her.

"Are you ready to eat?" he asked.

At first, she didn't answer. Seeing the coyote this time had shaken her, but she no longer feared it. Somehow, she felt she knew it, knew the hillsides and the scrub brush, knew the running streams, and the dug out burrows. She knew the scent of the rabbits stirring at the onset of dusk and the sight of the moon rising over the canyon, the howl of the pack as it prepared for the hunt, and the flap of an owl's wings against a black sky studded with stars.

She knew, as sure as if she'd seen it, that the night would come and that a heart that was wild and true would not only survive it, but own it and live to see another.

Turning back toward her husband, she took a deep breath and found her seat at the table.

"Yes," she answered. "I'm ready."

Luiseño Pronunciation Guide

Luiseño letters are pronounced pretty much as in English, with following exceptions:

- Vowels are pronounced almost as in Spanish or French, not as in English.

- The apostrophe is used for the 'glottal stop', the catch in your voice that you hear in between *uh* and *oh* as in *Uh oh, you're in trouble now.*

- The hooked s, ş, is for a sound similar to English sh.

- The letter x sounds like the raspy sound you make when clearing your throat, like the Scottish pronunciation of *loch*, as in *Loch Ness*, or like the German pronunciation of the composer's name *Bach.*

- The combination *ng* always sounds like *ng* in *singer*, never like *ng* in finger, even at the beginning of a word.

- The letter q is close to English k.

- The letter r is trilled, as in Spanish or Italian.

www.ingramcontent.com/pod-product-compliance
Lightning Source LLC
Chambersburg PA
CBHW070451260626
47161CB00004B/1272